muscat 'apedis'

PENGUIN BOOKS

ALMOST NIGHT

Ann Prospero is an acclaimed poet who lives in North Carolina. This is her first novel.

ANN PROSPERO

ALMOST NIGHT

PENGUIN BOOKS

PENGUIN BOOKS

Published by the Penguin Group
Penguin Books Ltd, 27 Wrights Lane, London w8 5TZ, England
Penguin Putnam Inc., 375 Hudson Street, New York, New York 10014, USA
Penguin Books Australia Ltd, Ringwood, Victoria, Australia
Penguin Books Canada Ltd, 10 Alcorn Avenue, Toronto, Ontario, Canada M4V 3B2
Penguin Books (NZ) Ltd, Private Bag 102902, NSMC, Auckland, New Zealand

Penguin Books Ltd, Registered Offices: Harmondsworth, Middlesex, England

First published in the United States by Dutton 2000
Published in Great Britain by Penguin Books 2000

3

Set in Janson
Printed in England by Clays Ltd, St Ives plc

To Anita, Jose, and Gregory
Loved and loving taskmasters

ACKNOWLEDGMENTS

Any expertise in this book comes from generous information given to the me by the City of Miami Police Department, especially Detective Delrish L. Moss and Sergeant Eunice Cooper; and the officers in patrol; and homicide detectives who patiently instructed me; and by the Miami-Dade County Medical Examiner Department, especially Dr. Emma Lew; and the doctors, assistants, and technicians in autopsy. The book is entirely fictional and in no way based on any living or dead person or on any actual incident. Any errors in portraying the procedures, or departures from regular procedure, of the Miami Police Department or the Miami-Dade County Medical Examiner are my responsibility alone.

My writing groups in Miami and Durham never let me become complacent. Thank you for your rigorous critiques. Thanks especially go to Jean Bradfisch, Charlotte Caffrey, John Dufresne, Nora Esthimer, Joyce Allen, Hakon Heimer, Fred

Welden, and especially Anita Smith. I thank librarians everywhere. They helped me, unknowingly and unselfishly, in my research. Most of my Cuban Spanish and Spanglish, so important to the book, comes from Willy Ramos's translations. He also added to my understanding of the Cuban American culture.

If the book is successful in depicting a loved and feared Miami and south Florida, it is because my knowledgeable, attentive agent, Esmond Harmsworth, and my brilliant editor, Ellen Edwards, knew I could write it. They gave me invaluable guidance. However, the most important acknowledgment must go to Miami and its environs—places of which I have intimate knowledge and to which I give deep devotion.

ALMOST
NIGHT

CHAPTER I

THE half moon still shone.

I walked to the kitchen. I stood at the window above the sink. I saw the moonlight white on creases in the palm fronds outside, and it shone on the faucet and an empty glass in the sink. It bounced from these inanimate things to shine on my hand.

And when I saw my moonlit hand, I yearned for the place I'd known since I was a child. Without thought I strode back to the bedroom, pulled on jeans, T-shirt, sneakers, picked up my ring of keys from the bowl beside the front door, and patted my golden retriever, Gilda, on the head.

"Come on, girl. Let's run away from here." I drove to my sacred place—the Everglades—away from Miami. Away from startling nightmares. And away from images of a murdered child and the man and woman we'd booked for that child's murder earlier that day.

Yet.

Miami sparkles. Green leaves spill over the streets from extravagant neotropical plants, and flowers bloom in colors as bright and clear as if they were new crayons in a freshly opened box. The sun glitters—on water, in windows, off the streets and houses and plants—and all night the neon signs and street-lights and headlights blare their gaudy colors.

Biscayne Bay borders downtown Miami, and its waters slap softly, urgently against a sea wall a mere block away from the city's towering new buildings. The nearby shipping port on a small man-made island connects to the mainland via a high, short bridge. Passenger ships and cargo ships leave Miami heading toward foreign ports. They glide away from downtown and past the MacArthur Causeway, where cars speed between Miami and Miami Beach. From the causeway, the ships look like moving, massive apartment buildings on their way out to sea.

At downtown's southern edge, a river runs into the bay. Seminole Indians and early settlers once traveled that river, the Miami River. Water pours out from its mouth into the bay—as if the craziness in the city were overflowing.

And there is a madness buried underneath Miami's beauty, a madness that resides below the surface layers of tourism and glamour. The putrid Miami is the one I most often see as a homicide detective in the Miami Police Department.

I'd been to a cocktail party at Bill and Fran's house. Bill and Fran are my parents. I was born around the time Miami began to grow up—not too long after Castro exultantly drove out Batista and his cronies. The lives of my parents didn't change whether Castro or Batista or Eisenhower or Kennedy were in power. They had always held cocktail parties for visiting dignitaries and the governor and people with old and new money.

Bill, an attorney and lobbyist in Washington, was in his mid-sixties. His black hair showed only a few strands of white and his tall frame bore no flab.

Fran, about the same age, looked more like a frumpy fifty. Her blond hair turned ashen and frizzy and showed remnants of her beauty. Every day she dug her hands into clay and built sculptures more sophisticated and complex than her critics dreamed her capable of. Her hands had turned red and raw after so many years of use, and beneath her cotton pants and tops she hid her thickened waist. For the party that night, she wore her hair pulled back and a dark top and skirt of a sumptuous fabric, but no makeup.

Peter had come. He wouldn't have missed an opportunity to mingle with the powerful. We stayed on opposite sides of the room. I'd demanded too much of him, he said the last time we spoke. I waved. He didn't see me.

Bill, his blue eyes glittering, did see me. He motioned me over to him with his raised glass.

"Honey," he said. "I want you to say hello to our new governor. You remember him?"

"Of course I do," I said. "Your kids came over to break the branches on our avocado tree."

"And you came to our house to break our windows," he said.

"Only once. We were playing softball in the field next door."

"You hit a home run?"

"Exactly."

A man stood behind Bill and smiled as he listened to us. Bill turned toward him as if he'd spoken.

"Come over here," Bill said to him. He put his hand on the young man's arm. "I want you to meet my daughter. You've already met the governor." Bill looked at me with the smirk I knew so well. The governor slipped away and began talking to the next gaggle of admirers. "This young man has been telling me how he appreciates our work for the Everglades."

"You've raised a lot tonight?" I asked Bill. Then I turned to the man, whose eyes were like deep water with the sun shining on it. "My grandfather owned large parcels of land out near the Glades. He left most of it to the national park system. Maybe you've heard of him? Andrew Cannon?"

"Sure, I have," he said. "He was one of the important pioneers in the area. By the way, my name is Martin Benson." He held out his hand. My father most likely had forgotten Martin's name and therefore hadn't introduced us.

"I'm Susannah Cannon," I said. "What's your interest in the Glades?"

"I'm a ranger in the national park system. I just transferred down here about six months ago."

"Has my father shown you around the city?"

"No, I heard about this fund-raiser and called him up about it day before yesterday. He invited me, and here I am."

Sounded like something Bill would do. Invite a stranger to the house. Martin was taller than I, and stocky without being overweight. Many more muscles showed than fat. Sun shone through his skin, browned and warm, and it shone on his hair, lightened and windblown even in my parents' house. He wore a jacket over an open-necked shirt, and no socks with his loafers. He could easily have belonged in the group.

"If you want to see Miami," I said, "I can show you some of it. And you can meet people interested in the Everglades through my parents."

4

"I can see that," he said, as he looked around the room. His gaze stopped on Peter, who looked back at him.

One of my father's friends came over to us.

"Suze," he said, as if he were surprised, "you look gorgeous tonight. You always look gorgeous." My father's friends like to drink, too. I checked Peter again to see if he thought I was gorgeous. He was talking to a woman. No, I think she was a girl dressed up to look like a woman. Maybe eighteen. I turned back to Bill's friend.

"You say that to all the girls."

Martin joined the older man's drunken praises. "I think you'd pass for beautiful—long blond hair, green eyes, great dress."

I shrugged and turned away from the two men, who began talking to each other about the watershed. I tried to find my mother. I needed to talk to someone about the dead child we'd found earlier. Peter wouldn't even acknowledge my existence. Bill smiled and smirked and joked with his friends. When I found her, she was in the kitchen, leaning against the red tile counter, wineglass at her lips, her eyes fixed on the man standing in front of her.

I left the party then. I wanted to sleep, even though it was just after six. I drove home, exhausted. I walked to my bedroom, Gilda following me, and dropped my clothes on the floor and fell into my bed naked.

Each time I fell asleep, I woke from nightmares. I finally gave up the effort and left the house. In the middle of the night, I drove to the Everglades.

I came home calmed. In a cool shower, I rinsed off the heat and I ran my hands down the sides of my body before I dried myself. I verified that my waist was small and my body firm. I

5

remembered the two men who praised my appearance. I combed back my wet hair to lie slick on my head—Peter loved my blond hair. I wore my usual that day—slacks, blouse, and light jacket. The jacket would cover the Glock. And earrings. Gold earrings. Small loops and balls.

I made sure Gilda had enough water for the day and was about to go out the front door when the bell rang. I looked through the peephole. Peter.

"Oh," he said. "You're leaving."

"Actually," I said, "I'm late for work. I have to leave right this minute."

"Can we talk?"

"Not right now," I said. "I'm sorry. Call and we'll get together. Soon." I reached backward for the doorknob and closed the door behind me, then locked it.

"Don't think I'm going to call you," he said, as I hurried toward my car. "You can forget it. If you want to talk, you call me."

"Peter, for God's sake. You could have talked to me instead of the homecoming queen last night," I said to him from the open car window. I backed out.

Traffic had begun to slow, and I raced the car forward a few feet to prevent another car from slipping in front of me. As I neared downtown, I pulled the car into a strip shopping center, where I went into a *cafetería* for take-out *café con leche*. I'd drink my morning coffee with one of my partners, Homicide Detective Rafael Hernández.

"Give me all you've got." I pointed to the small glass case perched on top of the larger case. When I first began driving at age sixteen, I'd stopped at the same shop on Eighth Street to take a box full of doughnuts back to school. Through the years, the street became better know as Calle Ocho, and the shop catered to a Cuban taste. Not only did it sell doughnuts and coffee, but also *pastelítos de guayaba* and *café con leche y una colada*.

"And two *café con leche*—to go," I said after she'd filled the box. "Not too sweet." I nodded hello to two patrol cops sitting at the back booth in the otherwise empty shop, each with a Styrofoam cup of steaming coffee and a doughnut on waxed paper in front of him.

I bypassed the expressway and crossed the Miami River bridge, my favorite way to get to the station. I like to see the river and bay view. The day hadn't turned bright yet, and the sunlight was still tinted copper, and the bay water, not yet choppy, was a moving image of the sky. Downtown, in contrast, looked gray and quiet. Its tall glassed buildings cast shadows but at the same time mirrored the morning light.

Street people already moved under the expressway and on the streets. Some pushed their grocery-store shopping carts. And pages from newspapers and red candy wrappers and empty paper cones on North Miami Avenue blew in and out of the gutter into the street. Morning traffic hadn't yet turned downtown Miami into a live animal.

I placed my packages on my desk. Rafael had already arrived for the day. His dark eyes had black lashes and his mouth was expressive. About eight years younger than I, he'd been in homicide four years. I liked his eagerness and willingness to take on whatever the job required. His enthusiasm had lasted, and I wondered how much longer he could maintain it.

Rafael and I drank the sweet, rich, strong coffee, and I described a great blue heron, feathers wet like just-washed hair, I'd seen out by West Lake in the Everglades that morning.

Then as soon as we heard Commander's end of a telephone conversation, we stopped to listen. The day had started and we were about to meet Carla Reeves.

"Secure the scene," she said into the receiver. "I'll send backups. Cannon'll be there in five minutes. Yes. Detective Cannon." Commander Bea Williams looked over at me. She was African American, a brown silk woman with rhinoceros hide, her head covered in tight white tendrils. Nobody knew her age. Nobody dared ask. She walked to the door of her glassed-in office, leaned out, and said. "You're lead, Suze. A woman found murdered in her bed at the Bay's Edge Apartments. Sounds like the killer did a job on her." She stepped back inside her office. "Hurry up," she snapped.

Rafael smoothed back his thick black hair with a free hand and stood to put on a finely tailored suit jacket. He wore a gun in the leather holster crossed over his back. I glanced at his back before he covered it and could see his lean muscles move under the handkerchief-thin cotton of his shirt. His tawny skin and hard lean body attracted the women at the station. We teased him about it.

I waited for him to drain the last of his *café con leche*, and he followed me into Commander's office.

"The officer on the scene called Homicide as soon as he arrived. He doesn't know what had been touched before he got there. I ordered backup."

"Are they there yet?" I asked.

"Not as of two minutes ago," she answered, her sarcasm crisp that morning, "but they'll be there before you will. The victim's female, cut, left on her bed—the manager verified it's her apartment. Here's her name." She handed me her notes. "It's a sadistic one. You know what the mayor'll do. And the press." She sighed and looked down at her papers. Not only was she the first female commander in Homicide, she was the first African American, and she made sure everyone knew she didn't give a damn what the unit thought of her.

Rafael and I drove toward an apartment building located on the bay in Coconut Grove, one of Miami's older, higher-priced sections. The Grove was shaded by mature oaks and mahoganies and flame-flowered poincianas, though by September the abundance of the poinciana blossoms had fallen and returned to the earth. From the Bay's Edge balconies, you could see sailboats and motorboats crisscrossing the water by day. In some lights the bay's water was aqua, but most of the time you saw the gray-hued water as heavy and polluted. By night the city across the bay from the apartment building lighted up the sky like a permanent fireworks display.

I had already phoned Elton Hall and Craig Burns, my two other team members, by the time we pulled into the apartment building's circular drive. My turn for lead. I'd coordinate, notify next of kin, attend the autopsy, and order tests and investigations.

Rafael and I entered a lobby lined in pink-hued faux marble, gray rugs, and rose-colored deep-cushioned sofas and chairs. The columns scattered throughout the lobby were mirrored from floor to ceiling.

"Miami Homicide," I said, holding up my badge. The doorman raised his hand, snapped his fingers to get the attention of a young man, and pointed toward us when the boy looked up.

"*La policía*," he said. "*Llévalos al piso doce.*"

On the twelfth floor we saw two uniformed officers posted at a doorway halfway down a long, red-carpeted hall. Ends of yellow tape hung down on each side of the door. Only two other people stood outside: one a small woman with her face buried in a cloth, one a big red-faced man.

I headed toward the taped door and nodded at the uniforms.

"Who called the police?" I asked.

"I called. I live down the hall. I heard a woman wailing and looked out my door to see what was the matter. Turned out to be the maid." He stopped, then said, "My God."

"What'd you do?"

"I went inside. Someone carved her up. Literally. Blood all over the bed. My God."

"Wait here," I told him, then pointed at the small woman. "Who's this?"

A cop stepped up and said, "Carmenza Rodríguez. Works—worked for the deceased. Found the body."

"*Sí, sí,*" she answered.

"You wait here, too."

Rafael and I bent down to pass under the yellow tape and entered the apartment.

Ahead of us was a small foyer, then the living area, and a hallway extended to our left. The walls were painted an ivory color, the carpet matched. There was a sofa and chair covered in a moss green fabric, the wood a warm, dark shade, and bookshelves of the same kind of wood lined one wall. The bookshelves were like the shelves in my mother's studio, though Fran's were dusted with dried clay. She would place her clay sculptures on the shelves before she fired them.

I turned to see a patrol officer standing at the end of the hall to our left.

"Down here, Detective." He motioned us in his direction with his arm. I swear he looked as if he was directing traffic.

His pumped, hardened muscles bulged below his uniform's short sleeves, and his gun fit snugly in its holster.

As Rafael and I walked down the hall toward the cop, I whispered, "I bet he works out, has a pretty wife, and three kids at home."

"She's in there," said the cop. "The maid pulled off the sheet. That's when she found her. And," he looked at his notes for the name, "Albert Simonton says he used the phone there to call." He pointed into the bedroom. "She was just like that when I arrived." And his mouth tightened, lips closed.

Standing at the foot of the bed, I understood. Her eyes were blue, green. I couldn't tell. Red stippled the whites. They were open. Her mouth was open.

Strands of her auburn hair strayed over her face and curled around brass earrings. She was nude and the paleness of her skin could have been due to death. Maybe not. I moved to the side of the bed that was close to her head. A slice barely the width of an artery had marked her neck. Underneath each breast a gash glistened red, like red crescent moons. A thin film of dried blood covered the top surface of her torso. The blood flowed from the cut to pool down around her body and then soak into a black sheet. Some of the blood, but not all, had congealed.

She was awkward and vulnerable looking as she lay there with her bent knees spread open, exposing her genitals. Her palms faced up, eerily still, as if they were about to grasp the air beside her shoulders. The top sheet hung down to the floor where the maid had dropped it.

Both the uniform at the doorway and Rafael at the foot of the bed were watching me. Both men were of the younger generation, and I wouldn't have to prove to them I was man enough to do the job. Only to myself.

"No wonder Commander bitched this morning. Wait'll the press gets news of this," I said. "You'd think the killer'd at least wait for tourist season to come and go. You know, out of deference to the Convention Bureau."

They laughed. I laughed. And I felt very alone.

CHAPTER 2

DR. Lal Raja, who'd completed her pathology residency at San Francisco, entered the room, and I saw her check the expression on my face, then look away. Raja, as we called her, pulled her black hair back at the nape of her neck. One time she told me she remembered the women in India wearing silk saris and black kohl. She wore, instead, red sneakers, black jeans, and ornate silver earrings. And black kohl.

"What do we have here?" Raja asked.

"Commander wants results yesterday. I want preliminaries."

"So, what's new?" Too many times Raja had dealt with a sense of urgency while in residency and later on the job. She wouldn't allow herself to be rushed. "Looks like she was alive when her breasts were cut. See the blood? Her heart was still pumping it," she said. "But the neck. The blood didn't spurt and that means she was fading fast when he—and I assume the perp's a he—punctured the jugular. Her heart was barely beating. Not dead yet, but almost."

Raja wouldn't need me, wouldn't want me around. She'd know what to do all by herself. "I'll be out in the hall," I said to Raja and Rafael.

I left the room, which was packed tight with the odors of sweat and blood, and walked down the apartment's hall. And the image of my morning drive surfaced. For moments—the length of time it took me to leave Carla Reeves's bedroom and reenter the twelfth-floor hall—I let the images of the fast drive down the road through the Everglades flood through me—the soft salt smell of the Gulf as I stood at Flamingo inlet, the swift sunrise and the way it touched the clouds, changing them from dove to silver to coral to flamingo and to brilliant white, and the water below that layered in colors from pale green to aqua and black as the depth increased. Those brief moments in the Everglades, even just in memory, lifted me away from the horror waiting in the room behind me.

Then, in the hallway outside the apartment, I turned to the man I first spoke with. "I'll talk to you in a minute. Stay here." In the background I saw doors open, people peer out briefly, then step back inside their apartments. The number of people waiting for their glimpse had begun to grow larger. "Keep these people back," I said to the uniforms.

I motioned for Carmenza Rodríguez to follow me down the hall, away from the others.

"Ms. Rodríguez?" I said to the woman. Her skin revealed she had an Indian or Negroid bloodline and the gray streaks in her black hair indicated an age of more than thirty. Her small stature and frame showed she was probably from Central America. She wore a simple white blouse and a pleated red-cotton skirt, faded and unpleated by many washings and ironings.

"*Sí. Me llamo Carmenza.*"

"You speak English?"

"*Sí.*" She raised a dish towel to her eyes.

"It's very important that I find out exactly what you did this morning. Can you tell me?"

"Yes. I tell you." She removed the dish towel from her face. "I come at seven thirty. In the back door." She spoke with a marked accent. "Sometime Miss Reeves here. Sometime no here. When she no here, she leave note in kitchen. I look. No note. No money. I say she come later with money. She do that sometime." She dried her eyes with the dish towel. "Miss Reeves go work early, early. Like me."

"Did everything look normal, the same as always, then?" I asked.

"*Sí.* I go get laundry. I do that *primero. Y* go to next job. I go to bathroom for towels. All clean. Towel folded. No like Miss Reeves."

"How was that different?" I asked.

"Like someone clean before me. Miss Reeves no fold towel. No clean sink. No clean floor. I afraid she no want me no more."

"So you didn't do much in the bathroom except take the towel." Thank God for small favors.

"*Sí, nada. Pero* I take dirty clothes. She keep basket in closet. In bedroom. I take it out." She demonstrated with her hands at each step—as if she lifted the basket, set it down, and picked up the clothes off the floor. I imagined her attention focused only on the clothes basket in the darkened room, where the shades were drawn and the morning's bright light had yet not entered.

"And I put in towel and pick up clothes on floor—she tell me no wash her clothes—and go to bed to get sheets." She raised the dish towel to her face. She was silent a moment before she continued.

"The sheet look funny, *pero* I take—and then I see." She pulled a phantom sheet toward her. "Blood. *Horrible*." Then she said, "I run away. I cry. I scream. I say 'Miss Reeves. Miss Reeves. She hurt.' "

"Do you have any idea who would do this to Ms. Reeves?" I asked.

"No." She appeared genuinely surprised I'd asked. "She nice lady. *Muy fina*."

"Did you ever see any strange men around? Did she bring men home?"

"Ay. No. She had boyfriend. Long time." She motioned backward with her hand. "No now."

"Do you know his name?"

"No. No know." Not much out of her. Clean bathroom. Dead before maid arrives at seven thirty.

I walked her out to the hall and saw Craig and Elton coming toward me. "One of these men will take you to the station where you can tell him again what happened."

"I go work for *Señora* Gutiérrez *ahora*," Carmenza said. "No go."

"This won't take long," I said. "And Detective Hall will drive you to where you want to go when he has taken your statement." Then I looked directly into her eyes and spoke, probably louder than I needed to. "This is very important, *muy importante*."

I nodded toward Elton. "Take this lady down to the station and get her story. She's in a hurry. You can drive her back to wherever she needs to go." He stared at me silently, an athletic man, tanned skin, graying hair. He'd joined the police force at a time when there were no women police, and even fewer female detectives. He'd staked out his maleness for almost twenty years before I joined the force. He was among those who called me cunt when I was going through police academy, almost fifteen years earlier. I couldn't forget it. I would say this for him: He didn't quit the force as some of them did. And approaching sixty, he was one of the best.

Even though I'd been in Homicide with him for about ten years, he hated taking orders from me—a woman. You can imagine how he felt about Commander.

I turned to the waiting man and led him away from the uniforms and onlookers. I wondered if he drank too much or ate too much salt. He wasn't overweight exactly, but he hulked over me and his face was red. He didn't compare well to Elton, though I supposed he was about the same age.

"You are Albert Simonton?" He nodded. "Tell me your story. Exactly. Step by step."

He repeated the part he'd already told me and added, "I was getting ready to go to work. I have my own company, you know. Medical equipment supply." He waited for me to write down that fact.

"How old are you?"

"Forty-five." He was lying.

I watched his face as he continued. "The little woman kept yapping in Spanish, and I couldn't understand her. My neighbor—she's lived here longer than me—was standing next to the maid and she called me to come down to them." His face became redder as he talked. Did it become redder when he lied? Or just when he talked? I wondered.

———

He gestured toward the murdered woman's door. "The door was cracked open. I didn't break in or anything." I nodded. "I go in and don't see anything wrong. I don't hear any moaning." He paused, took a deep breath, and blew it out between pursed lips.

"Then I walk back toward the bedroom, calling, 'Hello. Anyone here?' No answer. I go on back, still calling, and when I get to the bedroom door I knock on the frame. I don't want to walk in on a woman unannounced," he said. I'll bet, I thought. "That's when I see her on the bed."

He looked away from me toward the taped door and breathed in deeply again.

"She was still, very still, and I go closer and see the blood." He stopped in the telling for a bare second, then continued. "Oh, my God. What I saw. I dialed 911 right there and then. I told the woman who answered, 'This woman—she's dead.' "

"Did you touch anything other than the phone beside her bed?"

"I don't think so. I got out of there as fast as I could and said, 'Don't go in there. For God's sake, don't go.' The cops were here in a couple of minutes. Sirens and all."

"We'll interview the neighbors, the doormen, find out if anybody saw or heard anything unusual," I told him. "How about you? Did you see or hear anything out of the ordinary last night?"

"No. I stayed inside all night. Cooked. Watched TV. Didn't hear or see anything unusual."

"Do you have any witnesses who will corroborate your story?"

"You think I'm lying?" He looked down at me, his red face

on his out-of-shape body. He could have been an ex–football player.

"Who knows? We follow all leads. I repeat: Any witnesses to your activities last night?"

"I'll have to think about it."

"A detective will interview you." Then I said to one of the uniforms. "Take his name, address, and phone number. And get his prints." I turned back to Simonton to say, "Just for comparisons."

"Raja," I said as I entered the bedroom again, "found anything yet?" She remained bent close to the woman's crotch as she answered.

"I'm combing her hair now," she said.

Raja combed through the woman's pubic hair and saved each removed hair in a plastic bag. Any hair that didn't belong to the deceased belonged to the killer. Bottles and vials filled with liquid from the vaginal wash were on the floor beside her case.

"I haven't done the mouth and anus yet. There are no wounds on her back, but both wrists apparently are broken. X rays will confirm." She looked up at me, finished with the combing. "Or not."

Dr. Lal Raja's hands never shook when she cut into a torso and opened it to remove the organs. Raja disconnected as if she studied amoebae under a microscope and had not dug into death with latex-gloved hands. She never turned away from that which made Elton vomit. When I caught him retching, I smiled at him and thought—That's man enough?

Raja continued.

"The air passage was compressed and she has a crushed larynx—See the red in the whites of the eyes? But probably she bled to death. Look at her skin color. Though either could have brought about her death. We'll do the whole routine, and you know how long it takes." Then she looked down at the body again. "That's blood coating her torso. It's from the cuts under her breasts. I'll try to determine how the blood was spread around. There are no obvious finger or palm prints, which we would have seen if he spread it with his hands. I did find a couple of hairs on the torso. Possibly body hairs or pubic hairs. Let me think about it some more. We'll talk at autopsy."

Raja gestured toward the body. "Also look at this. There's trauma around her mouth." She carefully lifted Reeves's upper lip to show me cuts on the insides of her lips. "It appears the killer pressed something—his hands, a pillow, something that didn't damage her face—over her mouth." I looked over the surface of the dead woman's face.

"Do you think it's possible she didn't scream during all this?" I asked.

Raja pressed her latex-gloved fingers on the dead woman's neck and collarbone.

"She couldn't scream. Something definitely traumatized her neck. Red marks from here to here. He probably damaged her vocal cords," she said.

She finished her preliminary and began photographing the body and scene, even though crime techs were waiting, with their cameras ready, for her to finish.

Raja stacked her vials in her case. She wrapped the body in the black sheet on which it lay and, in doing so, covered Carla Reeves's face. Evidence might be found on the sheets. When she did that, there was merely another body soon to be placed in a body bag. The books stacked on shelves and beside the bed, the baskets on the dresser, scarves and underwear tumbled inside them, the dirty-clothes basket left beside the bed by Carmenza Rodríguez, clothes the maid had picked up off the floor, folded, and placed on a chair for Miss Reeves to put away when she got home. These were Carla Reeves now, whoever she had been.

Two attendants rolled in the morgue stretcher with a body bag folded on top. They opened the thick vinyl bag, unzipped it, picked up the sheet enclosing Carla, and slipped her inside. They zipped the bag closed. Less than two minutes.

The attendants wheeled the body out of the room where we stood, and I spoke to Rafael. "Look around for personal info: where she worked, family names, friends." I'd have to tell someone Carla Reeves was dead, murdered, and, when asked, tell him or her how.

"Craig," I said, "ask the techs to examine every inch of this place, especially the bathroom. Maid said it looked different this morning."

Craig leaned his head into the bathroom. He had a hard, compact body, that of a former college wrestler. His mud-brown hair flopped over his forehead, and he jerked his head to keep it out of his eyes. Before tournaments he shaved it off.

"Looks clean," he said, "very clean. Spotless."

"That's what's different."

I put on shoe coverings and a new pair of latex gloves and walked into the bathroom. The bathroom's white tiles and fixtures could have been in a magazine ad. Someone had wiped to a shine the mirror covering the wall above her sink, etched-glass shower door, tile floor and walls, even the toilet. I opened the cabinet under the sink. Toilet paper, tissues, sanitary napkins, and tampons. Carmenza had already taken the folded green towel and placed it in the clothes basket. There were no other towels or washcloths. The wastebasket was empty. And no soap. Probably it had been flushed down the toilet.

"Have the techs bag the towel in the clothes basket separately," I called out.

In the living room the drapes were closed, as they had been in the bedroom, casting a subdued light through the ivory satin. One clear, simple wineglass sat on the table in front of the moss green sofa, with its pillows neatly placed against its back. The books and CDs lay jumbled on the shelves I'd noticed earlier, and magazines were scattered about on the table beside the wineglass. A *New Yorker* was open to a movie review. I saw black high-heeled sandals under the glass-topped coffee table.

The heavy drapes rustled. I turned to face the windows and saw nothing. The air conditioner recycled on at the same time.

In the kitchen a second wineglass sat clean and sparkling and dried beside the sink. I found damp paper towels in the trash can. The dishwasher had been partially loaded, and the washer door was still warm from a recent washing. I wondered if Carmenza had started the machine. Or had the killer? The refrigerator contained only a recorked white wine bottle and a half-full bottle of apple juice. I walked over to a tall cabinet and opened it. At the sound of the cabinet clicking open, the drapes rustled again, and a black-and-white cat ran from under the drapes to me, where it twirled slowly around my legs.

In the cabinet, a bag of cat food sat with its top curled closed. I picked up the bag and poured the pellets into the cat's bowl. The cat purred and promptly began chewing on the dried food. Carla Reeves must have done this countless times.

"What did you see last night?" I asked the animal, taking off my gloves. "Where were you?" It ate without stopping, all the time purring.

I bent down to pet the cat and thought of how my dog's fur

felt on my fingers when I petted her. The previous night, in the dark and quiet of three in the morning, my golden retriever had watched me go into the kitchen and pick her leash off its hook. By the time I reached her, she pranced, and her strawberry blond fur rippled with her twisting movements. I recalled the way her fur moved and the memory reminded me again of the Everglades wind wafting over the saw grass. And I recalled why I'd driven in the night down to the Glades—the images of a child lying beaten and starved in the darkened room, a cat lying curled, its head on its paws, asleep on the same bed. And then, at the same moment, the memory brushed past me of an infant in my arms.

I'd been rubbing my fingers through the cat's fur, my eyes focused above her, and I didn't notice right away that Rafael stood at the kitchen door watching me. When I looked up, when I turned my head abruptly toward him, I saw a flicker of recognition, of something seen. Just a flicker, then it was hidden. He showed me the wallet.

"A driver's license indicates she was forty-one, she has blue eyes and red hair, her height is five feet eight. There is also a business card from Miami Publishing Company on Brickell. It identifies her as advertising director."

"Next of kin?" I asked, taking notes as he talked.

"There is a card behind the driver's license. It says, 'In case of emergency, notify Patricia Reeves,' and there is a phone number. 'Relation: mother.' That is all I have found." I wrote the name and number in my notebook. The telephone exchange was Coral Gables, the same as that of my parents.

"I'm going back to the station," I said. Craig stood behind Rafael. "We'll all meet around lunchtime. I'll try to notify her mother by then."

On the drive back to the station, I felt as if my mind and will had clicked. We worked like a team of basketball players—minus two—or a single body in peak condition. As I drove, my mind churned. Motive, opportunity, means. Thousands of tiny pieces. Like solving a puzzle. The game was to find the pieces and place them in the right order to make a picture. I was determined to find the pieces and put them together. By logic and intuition—and eventually by sheer force of will. My intuition told me we'd also have to find out why. Why so brutal? Why Carla Reeves? How did she end up like this? Was murder this man's finely honed craft? A hobby? It sure looked like he got a kick out of torturing her.

In this line of work we saw pure evil and most of us believed in its existence. And at times we glimpsed an evil that was larger than a mere human invention. That was scary. The peace I'd attained during my visit to the Everglades had vanished. Just as well. I had work to do, and work was one of my means to peace.

Only ten o'clock in the morning. The sun heated the air until it felt thick inside the white city-issue car, and I wished I were in my own car. I rolled down all the windows to let the wind blow in, touching me, almost bruising my skin, tangling my hair. I wanted to press the pedal to the floor, zoom north up I-95 right out of Miami. Sometimes I got that urge.

Instead I pulled into the police parking garage and went to the unit to file reports. Back to routine. I listened to my messages. Harry, my ex-husband, had left a message. I hadn't heard from Harry in many months. I liked it that way.

There were no other messages.

I dialed Carla Reeves's mother, told her I needed to speak to her about her daughter, and arranged to go to her dress shop on Miracle Mile in Coral Gables. I'd walked by it many times in my life but hadn't gone in. Once I bought a black dress from the shop next door to wear to a reception with Peter. He didn't like it much. I never wore it again. It was a beautiful dress.

Peter. He wasn't going to call me. If I wanted to make up with him, I had to phone him.

CHAPTER 3

C ORAL Gables is one of Miami's cities within a city. It was a planned community first envisioned by founder George Merrick before his moneymaking and artistic fantasy was destroyed by the 1926 hurricane—a time before forecasts and before the civilized gesture of naming these seasonal beasts.

My grandfather, Andy, had made a fortune by living according to the rules he'd learned as a boy in Mississippi. When he first came to Miami, before the hurricane, he bought as much land as his deputy sheriff's wages would allow. And, unlike Merrick and other investors in this untamed land, he never borrowed a cent. After the hurricane, land was cheap, and he bought more, some on the east coast, some further west near the Everglades, some the same land Merrick lost.

When I reached the age of six or seven, my mother and father shipped me down to Andy's as often as they could—most weekends, most summers. I was lucky. Andy gave me freedom to roam and enough love to grow into a moderately healthy adult. After his wife died, he moved down to one of his parcels in the east Everglades. There, he and his foreman built a house out of limestone they'd cut out from the ground and of mahogany and pine they'd sawed down and shipped out to a mill to finish.

My first memories of Andy—and the only Andy I ever knew—were of him in his weathered stone house, cooled inside by ceiling fans. Electricity had come to the Glades by the sixties, and Andy made use of it by having low-level lights installed. An open space surrounded the house and fruit trees grew there. Loquat, grapefruit, kumquat, avocado, and mango. I've never since had mango as good as Andy's.

He and I sat on his back porch, a porch that extended the width of the house underneath the wide, cooling overhangs.

"Them lizards are my pets," he'd say when green anoles scampered up the sides of the house. And he'd reach over from his rocking chair to cup his hand over one on the wall, gently carrying it over to me as he held it under his thumb.

Andy taught me to know the Everglades, to identify both plants and animals. He told me that the seeds for those trees and shrubs had blown across water from Cuba or the Bahamas or the Yucatán. Or from North America's Gulf coast. Or they were deposited by birds flying over or by passing animals—raccoons, possums, armadillo, deer, mice. Even alligators.

At the very back of Andy's homestead clearing, I could see the edge of a dense and dark hammock looming in front of a bright and sunny pineland. In my imagination, the shrubs and small trees in the hammock, a tropical hardwood forest, grew wildly. They were menacing in the shaded forest, as were the massive oak and mahogany and royal palms they grew around. The hammock in its silence and stillness and deep shade froze my loneliness and made it insignificant.

For a least a year I walked through that hammock, willing myself forward, hyper-aware of sounds and smells and movement. I willed myself to survive even though I saw a strangler fig wrap itself around a mahogany's trunk. The strangler fig would slowly, insidiously squeeze the life out of the mahogany. My grandfather showed me the poisonwood and warned me to stay clear of its poison ivy–like leaves. And I knew the leaves leaned purposefully toward me. Andy told me the name of the dahoon, a small tree with glossy leaves. I had heard strange names from the kids at school, names of evil spirits, and I was sure dahoon was one of those names. There was another tree I later learned to treasure because of its copper red thin, peeling bark—the gumbo limbo tree. To me it looked like skin. Sunburned and peeling skin. Up on the long, low branches of the oak and mahogany trees, air plants grew, and I knew they waited for me to pass beneath before they fell.

The hammock was not a cool haven it would later become. Instead, leaves brushed against me. Nets of mosquitoes swarmed in the windless space. I was sure dark things lurked hidden in the shade and underneath rotting logs. I heard ripe berries plop as they hit the ground, and the air swirled with their sweet, rotten smell. I knew much later it was the smell of death. Mockingbirds and scrub jays and falcons squawked warnings, and lizards brushed by me, all eager for a bite of young girl, all loud in the silence.

I walked through that hammock in order to reach the other side. I could do that, even then. And on the other side was sunlight and breeze and the pineland.

Stepping over into the pineland where the sun heated my skin and the breeze cooled my sweat, I felt as though I had entered a landscape planted by God. I picked up pinecones for my collection on my grandfather's back porch. I watched a male green lizard, a fragile anole about the size of my little finger, strut on the slash pine's bark, nod his head threateningly, and extend his crimson throat. I sat under a canopy made by low-growing palmetto leaves, careful not to scrape my bare arms on their sawtooth edges. When I stumbled on the rough limestone, barely covered in a white dust, and scraped my knees and the palms of my hands, I could always run to Andy's house. And my grandfather would chew a piece off his cigar and rub the wet stub on my scrapes and cuts and scratches.

As a woman, I loved every bit of the hammocks and pinelands as much as I believed my grandfather loved them. He died shortly before I graduated from the police academy, and now when I went to the Glades we were close again.

These were my thoughts as I drove toward Mrs. Reeves's shop where the uniform agreed to meet me. Decades ago, a developer convinced the Coral Gables city commission to rename a mile-long promenade lined with small, expensive shops Miracle Mile. And the shop owned by Carla Reeves's mother was near the end of Miracle Mile, where there were working fountains and the courthouse. Both had been designed during the Merrick era.

When the uniform and I entered the store, a young woman behind the checkout counter looked over at an older woman standing near the dressing rooms. There she stood, a pale, aging replica of Carla. She came toward us—red hair with strands of white and gold throughout, her face a web of fine lines, pallid skin, light blue eyes, the same slim build as her daughter, taller, frailer.

"I'd like to speak with you privately," I said. I handed her my card. She did not even glance at it.

She quietly stared at my face, looking for what I would tell her. My guess is that she already knew, but she said, "We can talk in the storeroom." She walked away from me, sounding irritated. "There's no one else here right now. Only Betsy and I."

In the storeroom crammed with boxes and hanging clothes, Mrs. Reeves asked, "Was Carla in an accident? Is that what you want to tell me?" Then she added, "I'm prepared," and I knew she wasn't.

I began. After all these years I still dreaded telling the news, but through terrible mistakes I had learned to be clear. Otherwise they didn't get the message I'd brought them—someone they knew, and possibly loved, was dead. Violently dead.

She waited for me to go on, straining to see in my face what I had to say.

"We found your daughter this morning."

"Should I go to her?" she interrupted.

"She's dead. Someone murdered her last night." That's the way I do it. Direct. No pretending.

The sound was keening, like a small animal caught by a hawk. I had heard it in the Everglades and sometimes late at night.

"No. Oh, God. No."

Betsy appeared among the shelves and looked on, not moving, not speaking. She looked like a farm girl, plump and fresh and young, though she probably lived out in West Miami and went to the junior college near her home.

I said to her, "Does Mrs. Reeves have any close relatives or friends you can call? A husband?" I disobeyed police procedure and put my arms around the shaking older woman. Don't get personally involved. Usually I got away with it.

"I'll call her daughter," Betsy said, as she ran down the narrow isle made by the shelves.

"You don't mean Carla, do you?" I called after her.

"The other one," she said. "Roberta. She lives real close."

It seemed like hours, but it was minutes, and a buzzer sounded.

I heard Betsy say, "Back here, Roberta. Everybody's here." Then whispers as the two women approached us.

Betsy came back with a woman who wore jeans shorts and a T-shirt. She could have been thirty-five. She had short brown hair and the Reeves blue eyes. The woman walked directly up to Mrs. Reeves and enclosed her in her arms.

When the younger woman spoke, she said, "Oh, Mom, I'm so sorry."

I waited while the two women grieved together, though the woman I assumed was Roberta did not cry. I steeled myself for the business to be conducted and hoped the next step would be completed with little or no emotion.

"We'd like a relative or friend to come to the medical examiner's to positively identify the body," I said. "You can ask someone who'd know Carla by sight to do this for you." I offered them an out.

Patricia Reeves raised her head from her daughter's shoulder.

"I want to see her," she said. "I'm going to see her." She looked angry, fierce. "I want to see Carla, my beautiful little girl."

"Mom, I don't think that's a good idea. I'll call Howard," said Roberta.

"No," Patricia Reeves said. "I'm going." And she stood up straight again, tucking her blouse into her skirt. She'd stopped crying.

I drove us to the morgue.

From the fifth-floor window in our unit at the station, all along one wall, I could see the medical center, in the middle of which was the Miami-Dade County Medical Examiner's Office. The morgue. Driving up to the building a visitor felt as though he or she were about to enter a modern, brick, low-rise office building. The lobby, though, looked like that of an exclusive hotel decorated in subdued elegance. Tropical greenery grew luxuriantly outside windows the length of the front wall. A wide oak staircase ambled down underneath a broad skylight that allowed in a bronze-filtered Miami sun. However, most visitors didn't like the sleeping arrangements in the adjoining building.

"This is Carla Reeves's mother." I spoke to a pleasant and polite receptionist.

"Yes, we're expecting you," she said. "Go ahead into viewing room A."

We entered a room about half the size of my bedroom, with chairs and sofas on three sides and a television set at one end and no windows. I turned on the television, and Mrs. Reeves and I waited without speaking while the static cleared to show a Miami-Dade logo.

"We'll see a picture of Carla in just a moment," I explained to her. I picked up the telephone and said to Raja's assistant, "We're ready."

On the screen a face appeared. By this time, someone had

closed Carla's eyes and mouth and had tucked a plastic sheet under her chin. The TV lights shone on her earrings.

"That's not what I came here to see," said Patricia Reeves. "I want to be with her. I want to see her, not a picture. I have pictures."

"It's not necessary for you to go through that, Mrs. Reeves. We don't usually allow family members downstairs."

"Carla is my daughter, my baby. I want to see her. Now." She stared at me, this time not searching for what I had to say but with her face set and closed. She was a woman who knew how to get her way. I decided not to fight her will and called Raja to ask her to prepare Carla Reeves for a personal viewing. I heard Raja's loud, irritated sigh.

Mrs. Reeves and I walked down the wide stairway to the ground floor and through a small opening to the next building. We entered the room where students observed autopsies from behind railings, and we stood in the same place to wait for the body to be wheeled in.

Mrs. Reeves watched the attendant push in a wheeled gurney, on which Carla Reeves lay entirely covered from view by a plastic sheet. Raja followed close behind. I heard Patricia Reeves suck in her breath and saw her pull her shoulders back. She stood as tall as her slender frame would allow.

"You can stand here and make the identification," I told her.

"Please," she almost whined. "Let me be with her one last time." I felt a great reluctance. I didn't want her to go near the body. But I guided her toward the gurney. Raja pulled the sheet down as far as Carla's chin, revealing her face. The same view as the one on the television monitor.

"Oh, Carla, Carla," Mrs. Reeves said, as she bent low over

Carla's face and stroked her hair back. "I'm so sorry. What happened, baby?" she asked her dead daughter.

"Don't disturb evidence," I said immediately.

Without warning, Patricia Reeves jerked the sheet back, exposing the nude, unwashed body. Blood smeared over Carla's torso and dried on her neck and the edges of her body where it had pooled under her when she lay on her bed. The cuts under her breasts gaped. The keening again. The mourning of a hawk. Frankly, I wasn't prepared.

I yanked her away from the body, and Raja grabbed the sheet where Patricia Reeves had dropped it. She motioned to the attendant to wheel the gurney back into the examining room.

"What animal did this?" screamed the mother. "An animal!"

I led Patricia Reeves out the door into the hall where the sweet and dusky smell of death became less prominent.

I told her over and over again until her cries slowed, "We will catch her killer." I emphasized each word. I knew, however, we might not catch the killer. Probably not if he'd selected Carla at random.

"What good is it going to do?" she said. "Even if you find him, she won't come back." Patricia Reeves tried to pull her arms from my grip. She repeated the words, "My baby, my baby, my baby."

"Carla was brutally, savagely murdered. And she was raped." I didn't go into details. "You saw her—the cuts under the breasts, the dried blood. You might not have noticed her neck and her wrists. You'll get the full report and then you'll know it all." I hammered at her, trying to reach a woman who was drifting further and further from me.

"Whoever killed her will probably do the same thing to another woman. He'll do it again." I held onto her arms. "Are you listening?" She nodded. She was silent. I waited a moment before continuing.

"Help us."

"Yes."

"I'll drive you back now and talk to you tonight or tomorrow."

"Yes," she said. "Take me home." Calmness—no, passivity—enveloped her.

"I'll call your daughter to be sure she meets you there."

Roberta opened Patricia Reeves's front door, led her inside, and closed the door. I would've said, at that point, Carla Reeves had a loving family.

I stood on the porch for a moment before I drove away from Patricia Reeves's house, through the neighborhood intertwined in my life like a web of nerve fibers. And in my family's life. Coral Gables. My car turned automatically toward my parents' home, an old habit. Six blocks farther away, a lifetime away, from the morgue.

Years ago I had wanted to go to Cuba to get an abortion. Not likely. When my parents were teens, it was not uncommon for girls to disappear for three or four months when they first began to show. They'd give birth to their illegitimate babies and return empty-handed to resume their lives. No one spoke of the matter.

The place in Georgia where I went was a home for unwed mothers and Fran knew about it from the old days. I hadn't admitted I was pregnant, neither to myself nor to my parents, until the sixth month when I began to show. I remember feeling relieved I wouldn't have to quit high school to take care of a child. I never told Fran and Bill who the father was. Nor did I tell the father. I'm sure he worried about it.

Don't think about it. Don't think about it, I repeated to myself.

After the baby was born, immediately given up for adoption, and I had graduated from high school, Bill sent me to his alma mater, University of Florida. Grateful for their swift solution to my problem, I followed Bill's direction, though I had dreamed of a college in New York. The morning I left for Florida, he gave me a list of people he expected to be important in the state and said I should be sure to contact them during my four years. However, as soon as I got to my dorm, I flushed the list down the toilet and opened my bottle of vodka. My roommate picked up her plastic glass and filled hers with vodka, too.

Even for a party school, our drunkenness in class crossed boundaries. During probation periods, I refused to go home and supported myself waitressing at bars. There was a young man whose eyes glittered like my father's. I loved him, and I thought he loved me. We lived together for a few months. One night, a woman with red hair and big breasts sat next to him at the bar, and he leaned over to kiss those breasts.

I don't know where I got the courage—or the rage—but I didn't hesitate that night. I picked up his beer, poured it over his head, and watched it roll down into the laughing woman's dress. But it was rage that helped me. I walked out of the bar, stopped drinking to the point I got drunk, stopped smoking, graduated, and made my decision. The police academy.

When I told Fran and Bill I'd been accepted at the Miami Police Academy, Bill raised his glass for another Scotch and Fran said please excuse her, she had work to do in her studio.

That night I refilled my glass with wine, raised it to Bill, and said, "Not a bad wine. Where'd you get it?"

Don't think about it. I clamped my jaw tight and drove past my parents' house—used to be mine, too—and the thoughts came anyway.

I had no feelings when I handed the baby, a little boy, to the nurse. None. But now they came.

When Homicide answered a child-abuse call, we knew the abuse had gone all the way to murder. Choked or burned or beaten or shot to death. The methods were infinite, the results the same. When I saw those dead children, I always thought of my boy and prayed his adopted parents treated him well. Silly prayers. My baby was a grown man. I reminded myself I had abused my baby when I abandoned him. I had those feelings on the case in Overtown the previous day.

Nothing worked in the apartments—water backed up in sinks and toilets, walls crumbled, roofs rotted and leaked, rats and roaches scampered amid strewn garbage. A neighbor had called the police and reported screams and loud bangs in the rat hole next door. She was tired of it all, she said, and "I told them 'Ya'll stop, or I'm going to call the cops.'" On the tape of her call she slurred her words. Patrol answered the call. When they saw the child, they had the sense to detain the two adults who were inside the apartment. A woman and a man. The cops stretched yellow tape across the entrance to preserve the scene for the crime techs.

By the time we arrived, one uniform stood outside the door, guarding the entrance. Rafael and I entered to see a woman seated on a sagging and broken red couch. Her eyes bloodshot and puffed. A tissue up against her nose, the right cheek of her dark skin further darkened and swollen, her lips cracked open and bleeding. Her wounds were fresh, a signal she'd been beaten just before our arrival, and older sores and bruises revealed there had been earlier beatings. A man in a white T-shirt, his sweaty, muscular arms glistening in the light from the doorway, leaned sullenly on the wall near the couch. The other uniform stood near the two adults, his hand on his holstered Glock.

The woman and man didn't move or turn their heads when we entered.

"I'll meet you back there in a minute. Go on and check it out," Rafael told me.

Before I entered the back room, I passed through the kitchen in the three-room apartment. The surface of a refrigerator showed rusted scratches through yellowed white paint. Garbage filled the sink and spread to the floor in front of it. Papers and beer bottles littered a corner of the room, and dark stains dripped down the wall. These sights were not unusual. I entered the bedroom.

The room was like a still life, an oil painting. Early afternoon light from the shaded window cast a yellow hue to the dark room and highlighted the still figure on the bed. She was small and naked. Black and purple bruises colored her arms and legs and torso and face. Her lower lip was split. Blood, now dried, had trickled from her hair onto her ear.

Her hair wiry and wild. Her eyes closed. No sign of breath. The cat sleeping at her feet woke as I neared the bed and jumped to the floor. I put my fingers on her throat and felt no pulse.

"Which one of you did it?" I asked as I stomped out of the bedroom.

The woman pointed, fear in her fingers, her eyes mute.

"What you mean, woman? I didn't do it. No way. Not me," said the man, still leaning on one shoulder against the wall. I saw no bruises on his arms or on his face.

"Let me see your hands," I said. He wasn't quick enough. "Now," I shouted. His knuckles were scraped, his fingernails torn.

"Go on," I said. "Out the door. You're going downtown."

He'd try to get away. That would be my excuse. I took my Glock out of its holster under my jacket.

"You son of a bitch! Go ahead. Run," I dared him. The uniform watched, smiling. But my partner, Rafael, saw that I was out of control. He moved quickly. He held my arm and whispered close to my face, a ragged, fierce whisper. "Wait for me in the car. I'll take this creep downstairs. I promise you, he's not going anywhere."

I jerked my arm away from Rafael. I walked out of the apartment to our car. Rafael called after me, "Detective Cannon, call for backups, a medic, and the medical examiner."

We booked the man and woman in the county jail. Rafael didn't speak for a while once we were back in the unit, but instead he studied the white cards where he wrote his observations while at a scene. I watched him place them one by one in a neat stack on his desk. My hands shook.

"Look, Suze. We're all stressed. Believe me. You're not unique," he said finally.

"Stress," I sneered. "That's too nice a word. It's more like hate. I should've taken the guy out. Saved us all a lot of trouble." Rafael smiled.

"And you'd be the one in trouble, Suze. Let's go work out tonight. Get a drink."

"My parents are having a party for the new governor," I said in answer to his invitation. I didn't want to be involved with any part of Homicide. I needed a party. The irony is that, there, I didn't evade my feelings and memories for a few hours. I found myself immersed in them. Peter was at the house and I wanted him to hold me again and listen to me this time. He and I did not even speak.

CHAPTER 4

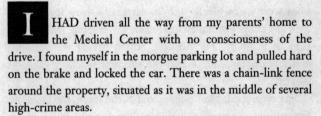

I HAD driven all the way from my parents' home to the Medical Center with no consciousness of the drive. I found myself in the morgue parking lot and pulled hard on the brake and locked the car. There was a chain-link fence around the property, situated as it was in the middle of several high-crime areas.

I entered the morgue's examination room, glad to be working. In there, death meant no more than a puzzle to be solved. In there, death had no more meaning than that of a possum lying squashed on the side of the road. Tomorrow and yesterday didn't matter in the morgue. Only the present moment mattered.

During autopsy, we examined the most intimate parts of a person, what few people in that person's life had seen or would see. At the moment of Carla's autopsy, she, Raja, and I were like lovers, two of us performing intimate rituals on a third.

Carla Reeves's washed body lay on the examination table.

Vials of blood to be used for drug testing and DNA analysis rested in their holders on the other side of the room. Her abdominal cavity was spread open where Raja had made the crosscut. At the same time, her assistant was peeling the flesh away from the skull and forehead, ready to cut into the head with a rotary saw, open it, and remove the brain.

"No more hysterical relatives," Raja said to me.

"Who'd have guessed she'd pull that one," I responded.

"You didn't," Raja said, then continued as if nothing had happened earlier that day, "Her organs appear healthy and normal. The marks on her throat are from compression. Occlusion of the airway and crushed larynx. She was definitely alive when he made the incisions."

Raja showed me Polaroids. "See all the blood? Also, the incisions were made neatly with an extremely sharp instrument, such as a scalpel, and they were made by someone with knowledge of anatomy. For example, when making the incisions under her breasts, he cleared the ribs, not touching them." I looked.

She continued. "As I pointed out at the scene, the blood on her torso was smeared to a thin film, and there were pubic or chest hairs dried on this film of blood. I conjecture he was on top of her sliding in her blood. At the end, when her heart had almost stopped, he precisely pierced both the interior and external jugulars on the left side of her neck."

"Made sure she was dead," I said. "Confirmed intercourse?"

"Yes. And no sign of oral or anal intercourse."

She lifted internal organs to the work area behind her and weighed them, talking the entire time she worked.

"You want to know at what point she died. The victim died

from loss of blood, though strangulation was clearly a contributing factor."

The internal organs had been replaced in the body cavity, bagged in red plastic, and the opening closed with black stitches. Raja examined again the slices under Carla's breasts, carefully pulling the skin back from the wound. Raja's silver earrings shimmered and jangled when she moved her head as she bent to probe the body.

She stood to face me, and she asked, "You've seen this MO before?"

"Not this one. I've seen enough sadistic murders to know one when I see it."

"Sadistic. Yes, I'd say that. He needs to inflict pain for sexual gratification and he took his time. He didn't kill her quickly. Now, look at her body."

I looked.

"He was neat, elaborate, knowledgeable in how to place the cutting instrument." She pointed to the slices under the breasts and the puncture on her neck. "This was not a spontaneous murder. He planned it with meticulous attention to detail. I know we don't usually get into the psychology of these murders, but while I was at San Francisco in residency, we autopsied eight bodies, all murdered by one man. They came in over the entire period I was there. Apparently this killer got his kicks in prolonging death. Suffocated his victim to unconsciousness, let her revive, and raped her, then repeated the suffocation and rape several times until the victim finally died." She put her hand on Carla before continuing. "One of the victims escaped and told the police the story."

"Are you saying the perp suffocated Carla Reeves till she was unconscious, then let her revive?"

"From what I can see at autopsy, I think the pattern is similar. However our killer had a great deal of medical knowledge. He revived her, cut her, and broke her wrists when she struggled. And raped her several times. And his goal was to kill her in the end. Her death was purposeful, not a side effect of his activities."

"The anticipation of the victim's death, and the pain she experiences before her death, excite this perp. He'll kill again," I said.

"You're right about that. Now you're going to have to figure out what kind of woman the perp needs to fulfill his sexual fantasy."

We finished the autopsy on Carla Reeves. On my way out, I stopped at a morgue assistant's desk to dial Rafael's number at the unit.

"I'm still at the morgue," I told him when he answered, "headed back to the unit. Had lunch yet?" It was after two, I was late for our prearranged lunch, and I was starving. I needed food and ten minutes to recoup.

"I'll order," Rafael said. "Craig and Elton left a message that they ate lunch on the way in. The usual?"

That meant Rafael's favorite—*medianoche*, a grilled sandwich with ham and cheese on Cuban bread.

"Sure," I said. I didn't care. "Get me some Cuban coffee." That I needed.

Commander liked to talk over our findings, help plan strategy. I would be ready for her only after eating. I had parked my car in the morgue's lot under full sun, and when I opened its doors it was hot enough to cook scrambled eggs. At the station, I splashed my face with cold water and wet my neck, chest, and arms in the women's bathroom off the lobby before heading upstairs.

Rafael had already taken a bite from his sandwich. He'd put two apple bananas, the tiny ones that taste like apples, on top of my box. I liked fresh fruit.

"Thanks," I said.

"Got them from a cart behind the courthouse on the way back from the *cafetería*," he said. "I saw pineapple, but they weren't the peeled ones."

"I'll take anything I can get. Thanks. Your kindness overwhelms me," I said.

"Do not take it personally," he said. "I do the same for Commander. Even for Elton."

I ate two bites of the sandwich and drank the Cuban coffee, then leaned back in my chair, a little more sure I'd get through the day.

"Raja's found chest hairs, pubic hairs, skin samples under the victim's fingernails. If he used his hands to strangle her, we'll have fingerprints. How about in the apartment?"

"The techs dusted everything," he said, sweeping his hand as if he included the entire apartment. "You should see the place. Covered in black dust. In the bathroom they found a couple of prints even though the entire room had been wiped clean. All of it. We are printing Carmenza Rodríguez, the man who called 911, and the victim."

"The question is, why was he so careful of his prints? And then left hairs and skin samples behind. As well as semen."

"He is arrogant. He is cocksure we will never catch him," said Rafael. "Maybe his prints are on file somewhere. Who knows how that kind of mind works?"

"Make sure the residue in her glass is tested. I'd be interested in whether he drugged her. One way or another we need to know how he got her into bed without a major struggle."

"The techs are looking for blood traces throughout the apartment now," Rafael said. "Maybe he cleaned up the bathroom because they had a fight in there."

I took another bite of the sandwich and glanced over at the Commander's cubicle. She hadn't come back from lunch yet. Who was hassling her this time? The chief? Mayor? Commissioners?

"Hey, here come the boys," said Rafael. Craig and Elton strolled toward us from the other direction.

"Let's hear what you've got," I said to them.

"Carmenza what's-her-name told her story, how she found the body, how nobody understood her—I could hardly understand her—how the police came. The whole bit," said Elton. In many subtle and not-so-subtle ways Elton showed he wasn't happy that Miami's power base had shifted from good-old-boy to Cuban. I was sure his father hadn't told him it would happen that way. And I was sure he hadn't realized Carmenza wasn't Cuban.

He continued in the same tone. "She told me several times she was going to be late for her next job. I got it all on tape. Probably the same story she told you."

Then, on cue, Rafael reacted. It was his assertion that he had a right to be a policeman. He didn't like Elton's anti-Hispanic attitude. He straightened his posture in his chair as Elton spoke and then interrupted Elton's story with his own.

Rafael enunciated each word. He knew his command of English irritated some native-English speakers. English was not his language, it was theirs. Elton was beginning to learn

Spanish. Craig had learned Spanish in college and spoke haltingly. As did I. I promised myself I'd take a Spanish-language course.

"So far," Rafael said, "I've talked to the residents who live right above, below, and beside Carla Reeves's apartment. Nobody heard a thing, they say."

"Typical," someone said.

"The next-door neighbors, the ones to the left of the Reeves apartment, weren't home. I'll go by tonight," he continued. "The apartment below hers is empty, and an elderly man who lives above her goes to sleep at seven every night. At least this is what he told me. Across the hall and on the other side, they do not hear nothing. Not a sound all night." Every now and then the Spanish double negative creeps into his impeccable English.

"How about the doormen? Albert Simonton? That woman who was with the maid?" I asked.

"Lucinda Matterly? She said she heard nothing until the maid came out in the hall screeching," Rafael said. "That is the word she used."

"Take her prints. Tell her we need them to compare with any found in there. Although I'm sure she didn't rape Carla," I said.

"Who knows? Maybe it's Louis Matterly in drag." That was Elton.

"Simonton gave us his prints."

"Simonton's a suspect. Carla was cut by someone with medical training, and Simonton admitted to me that he owns a company that sells medical equipment. Craig, find out how close Raja and the techs can come to identifying the instrument used to cut Reeves."

Rafael looked down at his notes. "I called the doormen on duty last night and told them I'd interview them. And there is a security camera at the back door."

"God. We found her just this morning," I said. It seemed long ago. "What else have the techs found?" I asked Craig.

"You know all those books she had? In the bedroom, on the floor, in the living room?" he asked. "They went through every single one and found a couple with someone's handwriting, like notebooks or diaries."

"We'll check them out. If they are Carla's, she might have named her killer," I said.

"From what little I read, I'd say the writer was very depressed." Craig continued with his new information. "Carla's guest last night, Thursday at eight, was Roy Jamison. That's the name the doormen wrote in the guest book. The doormen don't remember what the man looked like. We haven't found any names like it locally."

We continued analyzing the information we knew at that point.

Commander walked toward us, and I scooted my chair over to give her room. As I did so, I bumped into Rafael's arm. He glanced at me and then handed me two slips of paper with telephone messages.

"I forgot to give these to you," he said in a low voice, almost a whisper. Peter had called me after all. He'd bypassed my voice mail and left messages with a live receptionist. The other was from Martin, the man I'd met at Bill and Fran's party last night. My reaction was to think, "How the hell did he get my number at the station? I'll kill my father if he gave it out." I folded both messages and stuffed them in my pants pocket. Rafael watched my every move.

Commander began, "I've seen the MO on this guy. Or at least what we've got so far."

"You should have seen the body," said Elton.

"I did. I opened the computer file and looked at the photos," Commander told him. "You all know, don't you, he was killing more than Carla Reeves?"

"She's the one who's dead," said Elton. He was the tallest of the four of us, even seated. He sat with his legs spread apart as if he were still on his motorcycle. The chair could hardly contain him. When he sat like that I couldn't stop myself from peeking at his crotch to see if I could tell whether he was as big there as he was elsewhere.

"Elton," she said, "don't act as stupid as you are. I'll explain it to you, nice and simple." She turned slowly in his direction, aware that her mere presence in the room irritated him, a boss woman and an African American. And I knew she would remind him, if she chose to do so, of the night sticks that pounded her father's head to a pulp as she watched, her white school blouse and navy skirt and brown-and-white oxfords flecked with her father's blood.

"The killer is not after a person, but a type." Commander glared at Elton and asked, "Do you know what I mean now?"

Elton never admitted to not understanding her. If he did understand, he wouldn't admit to that either. He looked over her head at the chalkboard behind her, at the list of murders, solved and unsolved and consecutively numbered. Carla Reeves was the latest entry.

"He gets his kicks from power, and snuffing a person is the ultimate power. This murder, sadistic as it was, will satisfy him only for a while—like he was falling to sleep right after sex. You do that, Elton?"

She was goading him. She continued. "He'll begin his search for the next victim, and kill again. But he's looking for a type. You know what I mean? Long black hair, red hair, tall, short, fat, petite, smart, stupid. That's what we have to figure out. What turns him on? What type was Carla Reeves?"

"That is one weird perp," was all Elton said.

"You're so right, Elton," said Commander. "They all are. Think about the times you're called when a man beats up a woman, or a woman burns her child. Think about the kids dead from a drive-by shooting. The rapes. Deliberate starvation. Think about them and the crimes like them. Because they all have to do with power." She was on a roll. "Power. Not sex. The perp feels power. He or she is superhuman for a while, in control. And the victims are unhuman, types—dumb bitch, stupid blacks, spoiled kids, stingy Jews—you name it. You know about that, Elton?"

I interrupted her. "We'll check files for similar crimes."

"Well, then," she said, "I don't know what you're waiting for. Start digging. Let's catch the son of a bitch sooner rather than later. Don't look only in the murder files. Look in domestic abuse, random killings, hate crimes, rapes. I think you all know the story real well."

"Carla's murder was sexual," Elton said. I wanted to kick him. Elton didn't think straight when he was goaded. Or possibly *he* was goading *her*.

"I already told you, Elton. And I thought it was nice and simple enough for you." Commander needs her victims, too. "Carla's killer gets his kicks out of power. He needs to control his victim, to create pain, to give life and take it away. Otherwise he can't get a rise. He needs to dominate. You know what I mean?"

All of us sat there for a second, saying nothing. I thought of how similar Commander and Elton had become.

I brought Commander up to date on our investigation that day. "I told PR to release only the information that a woman named Carla Reeves had been found murdered in her apartment and that she was advertising director at Miami Publishing Company."

Together we reviewed the preliminary autopsy and crime tech reports.

"Someone must have seen them together," said Commander. "Cannon, do a reenactment. Trace Reeves's last steps."

Then she got up and said over her back, "The perp is looking for another victim as we speak. Stop him." She walked back to her glassed-in office. Creakily. Her arthritis hurt.

For a full minute we didn't speak. Craig wrote notes. Elton ambled over to the coffee machine with his empty mug. Rafael pulled the dictionary from his shelf and opened it. I drummed my fingers and then finished my _medianoche_.

"Assignments," I said when we'd settled. "Craig. Go through evidence collected by the techs—even if they're not ready to send up a report. Send them back to the apartment for more prints. The perp was in the kitchen. He and Carla sat on the couch. Check the bed headboard."

"There're the journals," he said. He wore plastic tortoise-shell glasses at work. He jerked his head back to clear his forehead of the hair hanging down.

"We'll read them as soon as one of us has a moment," I said.

I looked at Elton. Commander had dragged him through the mud face first. He acted as if nothing had happened. In his early days on the force, before women became police, before African Americans and Hispanics refused to grovel, Elton and his buddies strutted the streets like bullies who owned them. More recently the police department and city had begun to reward crime-solving abilities. Elton had collected enough medals to prove he solved crimes and to prove that he had reason to strut.

I gave him a job I knew he'd do well. "Talk to the manager, workers, people who hang around. See what you can sniff out. That building operates on gossip."

Rafael waited for me to give him an assignment. "Check the people who live next door to Carla, the doormen, and Simonton. And call Raja. See if she's come up with any new information." I sipped my black coffee, felt no caffeine surge, then continued. "You and I will do the reenactment. We've got to work out a timeline." Elton raised his eyebrows but didn't look up from his notes.

"What is that supposed to mean?" Rafael snapped at Elton.

"What are you talking about? I'm sitting here keeping out of everyone's business," replied Elton.

"This," said Rafael, raising and lowering his eyebrows several times. "I saw it. Craig saw it." Craig raised his hands, as if he were blocking a body blow, and walked away. "Suze saw it."

"Leave him alone," I told Rafael. I slammed down my legal pad onto my desk. "Direct all your snide remarks and innuendoes and general hate for each other somewhere else," I said to all of them. "Direct them to where they belong. Shut up and stop the son of a bitch."

Elton stood up, stared at Rafael for a second, and stalked toward the exit after Craig.

Rafael and I sat at our desks. If Elton and Craig had been with us, they would have been on the other side of a partition seated at their contiguous desks. We'd have stared at each other through burlap and particle board, no longer standing and shouting. The unit's general noise hummed—phones rang and conversations continued and papers rattled. Nothing had changed. Blowups happened too often for the unit to care. Or notice.

We were on edge. The testosterone and adrenaline geared us for the grueling battle we each knew lay ahead. When the rhythm of solving the case settled over us, we'd let logic and intuition guide us again, though I expected flare-ups all along the way.

"You don't want to do the reenactment with me, do you?" I said quietly.

"Why not? We are professionals. Come on. Let us take a break," said Rafael, standing and stretching his arms over his head. "And go to the *cafetería* to get some Cuban coffee. Sound good?"

We walked the two blocks from the police station to Flagler Street. The traffic had begun to pick up on the portion of I-95 that ran downtown, and the drone of cars and tires accompanied the sound of our steps on the sidewalk. The September afternoon sun bounced off the pale concrete of the Metro Dade Commission building, the Center for Fine Arts, the Dade County Courthouse, and the newer, glassed office towers beside the MetroRail elevated tracks.

We crossed Flagler and entered the *cafetería*, the air conditioning turned up till I felt chilled. One guava pastry lay in the two-foot-square glass case near a window that opened to the sidewalk. Passersby stopped all day long at the window to order a tiny paper cup filled with strong, sweet Cuban *cafecito*, then chase it with water from a bright yellow cooler.

"We'll split it," I said to Rafael when we saw the one pastry.

To the woman behind the counter, I said, *"Café con leche, para dos, por favor. Y el pastelito de guayaba."* Neither of us said a word to the other. We sat at one of the little Formica tables in the small café and watched the woman prepare our coffee, an act she repeated at least a hundred times a day. She screwed the metal container packed with dark, finely ground coffee into the coffee machine. While it bubbled out into a stainless steel pitcher, she poured milk into another pitcher, sweetened it with two to three heaping teaspoons of sugar, and held it under the steam spout until it frothed. She poured a small amount of brewed, thick *cafecito* into two cups on the counter. She pushed them and the pitcher of steamed milk toward us. She took the pastry out of the case with tongs and set it on a white plate. Rafael went to the counter and brought it all to our table.

"You are troubled," he said. I supposed he was referring to my edginess, a mood left over from the previous night.

"I don't discuss my personal life with my coworkers," I said. "It's safer this way."

"Safer? What do you mean?" he asked.

"Nobody gets hurt," I said.

"Hurt? Suze, I won't get hurt. Me macho man," he said, and pounded his chest with his fists. I laughed. "I think you need a friend, someone you can trust. I will never hurt you. My partner."

"I don't trust anybody," I said. "I don't trust my lovers, my friends, my parents, my partners. I only trust myself."

"I am sorry for you then," he said. "Because you are very, very alone."

I said nothing. We both drank our coffee.

Then he said, "Ah. I think I know." He put his hand over

mine and said, "You will never have to worry about me, you know, loving and leaving you. I only want to be your friend. That is all."

I withdrew my hand. I thought to myself, while at the same time smiling at him, "You are too sincere. I don't believe you."

"Back to work," I said, and stood, pushing my chair under the table so its legs scraped the linoleum floor.

We walked back to the station, talking of the weather, the Dolphins, the quality of Cuban pastry, but nothing of what was on my mind. Standing at his desk, Rafael brushed out the creases and folds of his jacket and walked away.

I was due at Miami Publishing Company to find out more about Carla Reeves. But before I left the unit I wanted to call Bill to complain and then to return Peter's call. I put off calling Peter and dialed Bill's number first.

"Suze, my dear sweet Suze," he said, happier than necessary. "What can I do for you? Anything you want."

"I can't come for dinner tonight," I told him. The happier he got, the more I shrank away. "We've got a big case right now. It started this morning."

"Oh, God. Not again," he said in his disappointed voice. "What's Miami coming to?"

"There've always been lots of murders here," I said. "Don't you remember?"

"No. I don't remember them," he said. I chose not to argue the point with him.

"Did you give my telephone number to that ranger who was at your party?" I asked. "You know I don't want you to give out my numbers."

"He's a nice young man. We get along well," he said, not answering me.

"I'm glad you do," I said. "Make sure he calls you, not me."

"Come for dinner tomorrow then," Bill said.

"Not tomorrow. Sunday," I told him.

CHAPTER 5

P ETER'S secretary answered.

"Are you happy?" he asked when he answered.

"I'm surprised. I believe you promised, or was it threatened, not to call me first."

"I broke my promise," he said. "It's not the first time, is it?"

"No," I said. I laughed. I felt as though red and coral and white poinciana flower petals were falling at my feet.

"I want to see you," he said. "Tonight."

"I'm lead on a new case and I don't know how late I'll be."

"Call me when you are free. I'll come over." He didn't ask about the case. "Anytime."

"Sounds serious," I said, trying to be nonchalant. "If I'm not too tired, I'll call."

"Come on, Suze. I'm making up with you. Just call, and don't give me the pretense that you might not."

"We'll see," I answered. He knew I'd call him and I'd welcome him and I'd love him.

Peter Bledcoe and I had met a year earlier at a party for the governor. At the time, Peter was a prosecutor for the state's white-collar crime division. In the midst of the Miami celebration I noticed a man standing next to the bar. His beard was neatly cropped. He watched me as I joked with the governor and placed my hand on the arm of my old family friend.

"Do you know the governor?" Peter asked me later when we stood together by the celery and carrot sticks. Close up I could see his beard had a few streaks of gray blending in with his sideburns. My lips came up to his chin.

"He and my parents have known each other for a long time," I explained. "When I was a little girl, our families got together pretty often. They'd come to our house. We'd go to theirs. We kids played together. Until we grew up to be teenagers. Then we went our separate ways."

"Good contact," he said. I made no answer.

I didn't like Peter at first. I refused to flirt with him. For a while, that is. It was his persistent and patient attentions that I first responded to. Peter began our affair with a campaign of calls to me at least once a day.

"Suze, have dinner with me tonight. I'll pick you up," he'd offer.

"If you'll come with me, I'll get tickets to the New World Symphony tonight," he'd say. I went. I saw that his eyes were hazel—sometimes green, sometimes gold.

"Can I come over tonight?" he'd ask. "I'll bring a bottle of good wine." And he did.

He kissed me and kissed me until it was I who seduced him and led him to my bed. His lips were soft and knowledgeable.

And, somehow, at an unidentifiable point, the tables turned. At first, he wanted me and, I believed, needed me. Then I needed him. Oh, how I needed him.

Recently, in a workshop held for cops on abuse, I listened while a male social worker told his audience that to a woman sex meant love. To most men it was a physical act. That difference in perception caused many fights. The male cop seated on one side of me nodded his head in agreement. But I don't believe that's true for all men. Is it?

By the time we became a couple, Peter no longer worked for the state. "Whately and Smotters offered me a job. It's an offer I can't refuse," he told me one night after we'd made love. He didn't ask my opinion about his moving from a state job to the private sector. I thought of my lawyer father who'd turned his back on a state job to make lots of money in a private firm, eventually setting up his own partnership. And I thought of my refusal to follow in his footsteps.

"Next step," I told him, "is forming your own firm." He thought I said that admiringly.

"I intend to," he said. "But not quite yet."

From the wide windows of his office at Whately and Smotters on the twenty-first floor you could see the bay below dotted with sailboats and ocean liners steaming out into the Atlantic. At night the city's lights streamed northward far up the coast, and to me they seemed to stream into infinity. Peter worked late and when I was involved in a case, working late myself, I'd stop by his office on the way home. He'd turn out the lights and lock the door, and we'd make love in front of the windows and the night city.

In contrast, from the windows of Homicide at the Miami Police Department, I looked over the interstate toward all of

Miami-Dade that stretched westward. Miami was lit up at night, and its African American, Haitian, Cuban American, Nicaraguan, assorted Hispanic, Anglo, middle income, excessively rich, and underclass divisions became, in the distance, blurred and no longer split by the boundaries we knew were there. I've never made love in front of our windows with anyone.

I thought about our affair and looked out the unit's window and wondered what Peter would think of the view. When I finished my coffee, I looked back at the notes I'd taken in preparation to go to the company where Carla Reeves had worked. Her office was in the building next to the river and the bridge I'd crossed going to the station early that morning and would cross the following morning and the mornings after that.

I sensed a figure walking toward me. Commander.

"Are you up to this case?" she asked in her usual abrupt way, proceeding right to her bottom line. She wanted results and she wanted them fast. She was passing on to me the pressures she received.

"You doubt it?" I asked her.

"I'm warning you, Suze. Don't jeopardize this case with your bleeding-heart emotions." she said. Then after a moment, as if she were deciding whether to tell me, she said, "I told them if anyone can work the case, you can. But mess up and you're out." She turned away from me and walked back to her office. She was referring to my reaction the previous day to the Overtown murder of the child.

If nothing else, at least Commander got my adrenaline pumping. As soon as her back was turned to me, I phoned the magazine company where Carla worked.

———

"I want to speak to the person in charge," I told the sweet voice on the phone.

"That would be Mr. Bierman," she said. "Donald Bierman. Hold on."

After first going through his personal receptionist and secretary, I got to the man himself.

"This is Donald Bierman," said a man's voice, as if he'd been interrupted. He had a deep, throaty voice, almost gruff.

"I'm Detective Susannah Cannon, Homicide, Miami Police."

"Yeah," he said. I was taking too long. "You want a contribution?"

"This morning we found a murdered woman. A card in her wallet says she's an employee of your company," I said.

"Who's that?" he asked. I could hear papers rustling at his end of the line.

"Did Carla Reeves work at Miami Publishing Company?" I asked.

"Carla! My God," he said. "She didn't come in today. That's not like her. She's dead?" The rustling had stopped.

"Yes," I answered. "I want to talk to you and your employees."

"I can't believe it," he said. "Who'd want to murder her? What a great gal. Was she robbed?"

"I can't go into details now."

"You want to come here?" he asked.

"How about now?"

"Sure," he said. "Now's a good time."

It was still bright daylight. Though the police station and the offices of Miami Publishing Company were within walking distance of each other, I drove with my air conditioning blowing on my neck and chest. I wanted to be alert during the interviews at Carla's office, and walking through Miami's heat would not have permitted it.

Driving across the Miami River bridge, I heard a blast from a boat signaling the bridge tender to open. I sped up and ducked the car under the lowering barriers. Rain clouds filled the southwestern sky, and the still air was heavy. In the distance I could see where rain had already begun to fall—dark clouds touched the earth.

The building stood next to the Miami River and the bridge. The river formed downtown's eastern boundary. Casuarina trees and Brazilian pepper shrubs hid it from my view, but it flowed close to the building's parking lot, and I heard sailboat lines clattering against masts and smelled diesel fumes left behind by passing motorboats. Not a leaf stirred.

Up on the third floor I entered a door labeled OFFICES OF MIAMI PUBLISHING COMPANY. Even though it was late afternoon, a large open office space was filled. Men and women bent toward papers. They keyed in words that flowed onto computer screens. I walked down the side of this large room toward the receptionist, oddly at the back of the office. In doing so, I passed a room on my left that was separated from me by a glass partition. I looked through the glass to see pages in varying stages of layout spread on drafting tables and color screens twice as large as those on the desks.

At the back of the warehouse-like space I showed my badge, and the woman said, "We're expecting you. Go on in. Mr. Bierman will be right with you."

In a moment, he opened his door. He was a small man, with thin gray hair combed over his balding head, and he wore a white short-sleeved shirt, the collar open. I couldn't tell whether he was sixty-five or seventy or seventy-five. Most of the time I could pinpoint age. Sometimes it wasn't possible. Maybe he was fifty-five.

He said, "Come in, come in. Can I get you anything? How about some coffee?"

He looked me over as I came into his office and said, "You're about as big as I am. Which is not big. I thought you'd be a Brünnhilde."

We waited for the coffee, he talked, and I listened.

"Carla dead. I can't believe it. She was so alive. You should have seen how hard she worked. One of the best advertising directors I ever had. And I've had a lot. All the sales people reported to her. She came early, stayed late. Good girl."

The coffee came, mine black. It was good. He poured cream into his and stirred in a couple spoonfuls of sugar. His movements snapped like the lines on the masts outside his window. No wonder everyone was occupied by their tasks when I walked in.

"What do you publish here?" I asked.

"We put out three magazines. There's *Florida Water*. Gets lots of advertising, all geared to water sports and recreation, boats, yachts, that sort of stuff. *Florida Style*. Covers fashion, decorating, entertaining, arts. Good market. Then the new one, *Florida Nights*. That one's getting attention from advertisers. Mostly because of the readership—young, restless, anxious to spend money to keep up. Carla's idea. We're doing okay. Got the market covered," Bierman told me.

"And what exactly did Carla Reeves do?" I asked.

"She was the one with lots of style. She knew what the readers of each magazine wanted, and she made sure we gave it to them. The advertisers couldn't wait to buy ads. Hers was an impossible job—always insisting the magazines appeal to the advertisers. It's demographics, you know. I tell you, I don't know how I'll replace her. She was with me—almost eight years."

"Tell me about her."

"I knew her at the office. That's all. My wife and I, we keep to ourselves. Too many church activities to have time for office socializing. End-of-year party at a fancy place for the employees, but that's all. They do their thing, we do ours." Bierman placed his hands, fingers intertwined, on his desk.

"But at the office," he continued. "I can talk about that. Carla was smart. She could remember every detail of every magazine. And she was persistent. A successful person is always persistent. She knew I wanted the advertisers to buy space, you see. She knew they wanted quality and wanted readership with money to buy their goods. She acted like she was being judged on how the magazine looked." He turned away from me for a moment.

Then Bierman, turning back to me, said, "Knew what she was doing. Great energy. You know, it's that kind of determination made this place such a success. God, I'll miss her."

"You said she was persistent and determined. Describe that for me."

"She wouldn't give up. She worked like her determination took her over." He looked out his window at the bay. "Who knows. Maybe she wouldn't give up because she knew I admired that in her. If she wanted something for one of the magazines and she knew it would make advertisers come knocking at our door, she'd go for it. To keep me happy. Always tried to keep me happy. Lots of people do that."

"And you let her."

He gave a little laugh. "That's part of managing a profitable business. Sure, I let her try to please me. I think that's what made her successful here. She was willing to play that game."

"How would you describe the overall atmosphere here? Was there competition in that game to please you?"

"Well, sure. That's good, don't you think? Get a lot more done when there's competition among the staff. But Carla didn't let it get out of hand. She became sort of the go-between. She tried to make everybody happy. That included me, of course. Graphics. Editors. All of them. People would go to her, complain, and she'd try to accommodate. I didn't care as long as they produced."

"So employees here liked her."

"You could say that."

"If she had no enemies here, who were her friends?"

"Friends." He stopped talking a moment, then began again. "There's something you need to know about Carla. She was real quick. And on top of that she was a beautiful woman—taller than you or me, but not too tall, slim, long red hair, high cheek bones, turquoise eyes. What a combination." He looked off into the corner of the room and then said, "She didn't have many friends, certainly not here. She kept it professional. Outside work? I don't know. Truth is, she couldn't have had much time for friends outside work."

Bierman liked Carla. A lot. And he knew more about her than he admitted.

"Were you personally involved with Carla?" I asked.

"No way," he answered. "I never got personally involved with any employee. Not good business. Business first. That's my reputation."

"Can you think of anyone who might have resented her enough to kill her?" I asked.

"For God's sake, no. Who'd want to kill Carla?"

"Is there anyone here who knew her well enough to know about any grudge against her?"

"Miriam Morales, her assistant. You should talk to her," he said. "They'd go out for a drink or dinner when there was a late deadline. They had lunch together when Carla had time for lunch, which wasn't often."

"Who's going to take over her job?" I asked.

"Me, for now. Then I've got to go looking again. Need someone real good for this job. Like Carla."

"I want to talk to Miriam Morales," I said, "but right now I want to see Carla's office."

"You'll have to see Miriam at home. She left. Very upset when I told her about Carla. My secretary will give you her number and address. And I'll show you Carla's office myself."

He walked with me down the hall. "This is Miriam's. That's Carla's," he said, pointing to an office behind Miriam's. "Carla's window opens up to the bay, too. Like mine. Look around all you want. I've got work to do." He turned to walk out the door, then turned back. "You think she knew whoever killed her?"

"I don't know. Will Miriam Morales get Carla's office now?"

"No. She's not right for this job. This job requires a person who will give it all they've got. Miriam wouldn't do that. Not for this company."

He left me alone in the suite of two offices, his shoulders bent and his hand up to his face as he walked away from me. After he left, I couldn't hear any noise except the palm fronds twisted by the steady offshore wind and brushed against the window, scratching as if they wanted to be let in. I wondered how Carla had worked with that noise as background. Maybe she didn't hear it. Beyond the palms I saw a gunmetal-blue bay that seemed to fill the window frame with serenity and timelessness.

In the main room outside her office—phones ringing, keys tapping, yelling across the room, low private conversations, shoes stepping down the linoleum-covered hallway—there was noise. I hadn't heard the office noise when I was in the middle of it. Standing at Carla's window I heard it only in memory.

I looked over the room where Carla had studied magazine pages and talked into the phone, writing notes as she talked. Yesterday afternoon. I saw her sharpened pencils stacked, points upward, in a blue ceramic cup. I saw two notepads, blank, waiting to be written on and placed near the phone. I saw a black phone set with buttons and white numbers and letters and blinking red and green lights. I saw a dictionary placed at the front of her desk next to a phone book and a thesaurus.

Her office showed organization and planning. Her desk was an exquisitely crafted rosewood and had a broad work surface. Bierman had said it was rosewood. My mother would have approved. I remembered the warm dark wood in Carla's apartment and realized it too was rosewood. I wondered if there was a connection.

Three stacks of paper had been placed beside each other on the desk's surface. Tear sheets from each of the three magazines lay spread out beside them. On the right-hand top corner of some of the tear sheets were the initials *CR*. A calendar showing the entire week lay open. Two chairs situated for conversation angled toward each other and the desk.

I began opening drawers. Most held vertical files and when I flipped through three or four picked at random, I found them labeled MEETINGS, READERSHIP SURVEYS, and MARKET SHARE ESTIMATES.

In a bottom drawer, there was a woman's collection of makeup, slippers, a brush, tea bags, Advil, Tampax, and a small prescription container half filled with a generic tranquilizer. I pictured Carla holding the container in her hand, flipping the top off, shaking out a pill, and swallowing it with water.

I closed the drawers and made a note for the crime techs to take all the desk contents. We'd have to get Bierman's permission.

I flipped through her calendar. There were several appointments penciled in for Friday. One appointment was lunch with Miriam. She had missed them all. On the previous day, Thursday, Carla had appointments scheduled with various departments at the office—graphics, editorial, design, Bierman with advertising in parentheses. At six thirty she'd written "Leave!!" and at eight, "Dinner with Roy." The night she was murdered.

I turned back the pages for the previous week and saw the same kinds of appointments with graphics, design, editorial, and advertising clients. Then again, on Thursday, at eight, "Dinner with Roy." Lunch on Friday with Miriam. The week before that was the same, except this time she'd written on Thursday, "Meet Roy, Biltmore, 8 p.m." Either Roy or Carla was obsessively consistent.

I leafed through the calendar back to January first, and throughout the past eight months there was no notation of Roy again. In fact the only man's name noted for social engagements after office hours was an Edward. That name appeared from January first, the start of the calendar year, till the middle of March.

A Rolodex sat next to the phone on her desk. I'd ask Bierman for permission to take it and the calendar with me. Then, from the phone on Carla's desk, I dialed Miriam Morales's number.

"Oigo," answered a woman.

"Miriam Morales, please," I said, hoping the person who answered spoke English.

"I am Miriam Morales," she said.

"City of Miami Police. I'm Detective Cannon, investigating Carla Reeves's death. I'd like to talk to you."

"Yes, yes," she said. "She was my good friend. I can't believe she's dead. We were laughing just yesterday." Then she added, "I'm so sad. How could I have stopped it? I keep thinking."

"I'll stop by tonight. Will you be there?" I asked.

"Please. Not tonight. I cannot talk about it tonight. Come tomorrow."

I used the same phone to call Patricia Reeves and got the same answer: tomorrow, not tonight.

I returned to the station, frustrated. A handwritten note lay on my desk, and my phone blinked red. I read the note first and decided to listen to messages later.

"Call Raja." She'd been at the station.

"What's up?" I asked her, eager to get to my notes, to look behind the obvious.

"You wanted preliminary findings yesterday, I remember," she said. "There are several you may find interesting. First, the alcohol level in Carla Reeves's blood is going to register very high."

"We could smell that," I responded.

"It'll show she was severely impaired. I doubt she knew anything was wrong until the killer began to strangle her and cut her. And I doubt she could do much about it. In other words, she couldn't put up much of a fight."

"Her wrists were broken," I said. "That's a fight."

"True," admitted Raja. "Another factor you might consider is the probable noise made during the murder. Even though she couldn't pay much attention to what was going on or make any coherent plan to defend herself, there must have been some noise involved—even if she couldn't scream, she could moan, and the bed banged on the wall. Did you notice the scrapes the headboard made on the wall? I could see them clearly in the photos I took."

"No one has acknowledged hearing anything unusual," I said. She continued talking as if I hadn't spoken. That's how she was.

"I'm stepping over my bounds by discussing a psychological profile" she said, and I knew that wouldn't stop her, "but if you were to do one of this killer it'd show one of his requirements to be risk. In the Reeves murder it was risk of discovery. Remember, the apartment building is crowded, and he easily could have been heard."

"You mean, if anyone cared enough to risk being thought of as nosy," I said. "Go on." I was rushing her. I was annoyed. And I don't know at what.

"We found bits of undigested food in her stomach, indicating she ate just before she died. That'll give you some clues as to where she ate. I'll fax the list over to you first thing in the morning. When're you getting in?"

"First meeting scheduled at seven thirty."

"You've had a long day, haven't you?" she said.

"No doubt about it," I said. I wanted to finish up at the station. I wanted to call Peter and go home.

"Listen to me," Raja said. "Go home, get some rest. You'll do a much better job tomorrow if you do."

"Yes, Mom," I said, though I knew, unlike Raja, my mother wouldn't have noticed how I was feeling. I could picture my mother's hands stroking clay, her eyes focused on her sculpture. But I couldn't picture Fran noticing me sitting there watching her, needing her hands to stroke my face.

CHAPTER 6

I PLACED the phone in the cradle and saw Al Miranda walk toward me. From this distance he still looked fifteen years old. We were high school lovers. He was my first. He was of medium height, had the build of a runner, chestnut brown hair, and a brisk walk. He got close enough for me to see the smile on his face and his hard eyes. He'd grill me for the latest information.

"Al. Just the person I need to see."

"I have no doubt that's said ironically," he said. He patted me on the head as he had when he came over to mow our lawn long, long ago. Now I was past my mid-thirties, and I was almost as tall as he was. He plopped down in Rafael's chair and said, "Obviously you know why I'm here."

"Coffee? Black?"

"Anything to affect my central nervous system."

I filled an extra mug. He talked. "The messenger of death

sent me to you again. Your public information office is not telling us anything, and there's a big story here." Al worked for the local paper and covered the crime scene. If I knew him at all, I knew he'd already gone out to interview the apartment manager and doormen—and anyone else who'd talk. Damn him.

"Are you going with what you already know in tomorrow's paper?" I asked.

"What do you think?" he answered.

"Here's a deal. I'll tell you what we know, what we saw, if, and that's a big if, you promise not to release the information," I said.

"Give me a good reason not to. I already know what she looked like when she was found, who found her, who called the cops, who she is."

"Same reason as always," I told him. "We don't want the perp to know how much we know." I didn't tell Al that, at that point, we didn't know much.

"Yeah, but," he said, "witnesses have already told me this is a bizarre murder. There's a big story here. Prominent woman. Grisly murder."

"Sure, the perp did a job on the victim. What's unusual about that for Miami?"

"For one thing," he said, "though I have to do more digging, I've a fading memory that this type of murder occurred before. Somewhere in this region. Do you know anything about past murders with the same MO?"

"No," I answered. Then I remembered hearing about a similar murder months ago, but I couldn't place it. "That's a good tip, though. We'll do research here on it. Let me know what you find."

"Not on your life, honey. I'll let you read about it in the

papers." He'd been a senior. I'd been a freshman. We'd both been timid.

"Are you trying for another newspaper award?" I said, not asked. "Let's cooperate on this one. We'll keep you informed at all times, but you hold the initial story for at least a day. In tomorrow's edition, print only the essential facts—an apparent murder victim found in her bed at the Bay's Edge Apartments. You can use her name. Next of kin have been notified. Whatever the *Herald* does, the rest of the media will follow."

He leaned back in his chair, drinking his coffee, looking me in the eye, and deciding, I think, whether to wait.

"Okay," he said. "I'll hold the big story only for the next twenty-four hours. Then you and I'll review the policy again." Hard ass.

"That's all I ask," I said.

Al left me seated at my desk. The coffee jump-started my system, and I watched him walk away. I couldn't remember myself as the young innocent who fell in love with the dark and handsome and remote senior.

I checked my messages. Among them was a call from my father. Again.

"Call Bill Cannon," his voice said. I dialed my parents' home.

"Hi, Bill," I said when he answered. "What's up?"

"Sweetheart," he said with his alcoholic warmth. I could smell it as if he was standing next to me. "I miss you."

"We talked only a few hours ago," I said.

"Come over. Your mom says I can invite you for dinner."

"When?" He didn't remember our earlier conversation.

"Tonight."

"It's too late tonight," I said. "I'll try to come by Sunday,

day after tomorrow. I'm working late Saturday night. Everything okay?"

"Hunky-dory," he replied. "You were at the Everglades party last night. Right?"

"Yes," I said. "I was there."

"You come for dinner Sunday," he said. "I'll invite some interesting people. They like the Everglades, too."

"You do that," I said. "But there's always the possibility I won't make it."

I found what I was looking for in the dead case files and took the folder to Commander.

"What is it?" she asked, irritated.

I opened the folder on her desk.

"Four months ago Homestead police found a woman who'd decayed to the point where the details of her death were sketchy. She lived in a house in the middle of six acres. No close neighbors. A UPS man came to the door and smelled something bad."

"Lordy, if he was a typical UPS he didn't stay long," said Commander.

I laughed and continued. "He wrote in his delivery log that no one was home and there was a godawful smell. That was the third time he'd tried to deliver the package. When his supervisor saw the notes, he figured he'd better call the police. The police went out to check and immediately recognized the smell. Decomposing flesh. There were flecks of blood on the bedroom walls and laid out on the bed they found a female covered with a sheet. She'd been cut under her breasts. At autopsy the medical examiner determined the victim died from asphyxiation. There were broken bones and a crushed larynx."

———

Commander looked at me silently and waited.

"I knew there'd be others. I hadn't surmised we'd find other murders committed before the Carla Reeves murder, though." Commander waited. "Al Miranda knows there are others, too."

After she was sure I'd finished, she said, "Maybe the Homestead murder and the Carla Reeves murder were committed by the same perp. Maybe not. How do you propose to find out?"

"I'll start with Homestead PD, look at the autopsy report, talk to the detective on the case. And," I added, "if the Reeves and the Homestead murders have the same MO, I'll start on profiling the two victims."

"What's Al going to do with his information?" Commander asked.

"He hasn't uncovered it yet, but he will. And when he does, he'll connect it right away to the Reeves's murder," I told her, "whether we do or not. You know how he sticks his nose into every crack."

"And sometimes he comes out smelling. Tell him we're cooperating with him. At this point, play down any link. And play him out. You know what I mean?"

"Keep the mayor, the commissioners, the tourist board, off our backs."

Commander didn't smile, but looked down at her papers. "Right. We may have to hold a press briefing soon."

I called Homestead. The detective who worked on the case was retired, and I dug out his name and home telephone number from someone in their homicide unit. When Detective Dominoe answered, I identified myself and my quest.

"That was one strange case," he said. "Absolutely no leads, but the woman was definitely murdered and raped. Sadistically."

"The report I saw says there were flecks of blood on the walls."

"She must have put up one hell of a fight. Her jaw was broken and her skull cracked. But none of those things killed her, according to the ME."

"Suffocation?"

"Right. No prints though," Dominoe said. "If we find the perp, we've got lots of DNA. Blood, for one thing. Scrapings."

"I'd like to come down tomorrow to look at the scene," I said.

"I'll get someone to take you. But it's pretty much cleaned up. There's lots of photos, though."

I looked up to check out movement at the back of the room. I saw Al was back. He carried his yellow legal pad. Always ready.

Al stood beside my desk. "I've got a deadline. Walk to the elevator with me, Suze."

"What'd you come all the way back for?" I said.

"Something's going on," he said. "I've been watching the unit from over there. I saw you go through the dead files and into Commander's office. Off the record, what's happening?" We waited for the elevator to come up to the fifth floor.

"I can't tell you about it right now. Just that we're broadening the investigation. And don't forget, any of your stories will cause all hell to break loose. We'll get it from all over, up and down—they'll all be yelling for us to solve this crime. You know how the commander feels about that kind of pressure. Don't instigate hysteria."

"Look," he said, "the murder happened. And obviously more than one. That's news. I'll help you as much as I can, and I don't cause the alarm. That happens, too."

He stepped onto the elevator.

I'd arranged for interviews with Patricia Reeves, Miriam Morales, and the Homestead PD for the next day. Rafael and I would reenact Carla's last hours the next night.

The end of one hell of a long day. I needed—Rest? Peter? Night? Sweet night. I decided to forgo rest.

I called Peter. I justified my call by telling myself that he'd asked me to call him. I didn't remind myself that I'd done the same thing more than once before.

"Come for a late dinner," I told him.

On the drive home, I began to anticipate spending an evening with Peter. I stopped at a small Grove grocer located in a newly built white store in the style of old Florida homes with porches and narrow wood siding. I stood at their meat and fish counter and ordered a slab of salmon, feeling like a princess while the butchers smiled at me and wrapped my order in white paper and handed it to me over the high ledge. I felt generous and abundant as I picked out peaches and plums and lettuce and onions and still-warm French bread. Peter said he'd bring the wine, and I spent five minutes selecting yellow roses from the store's black bucket filled to overflowing with cut flowers.

The first thing I saw on entering my house, after I petted Gilda, sprawled on the cool terrazzo, was the red light blinking on my answering machine. I listened to the messages, holding the two plastic grocery bags by the handles with one hand. The roses stuck upright next to the lettuce. To my surprise, it was a wrong number. Peter hadn't called, neither to say he'd be late nor to cancel.

I'd just placed the tall yellow roses in a clear glass vase when Peter arrived. He wore sandals and a shirt, open at the collar. I reached up and pulled his head down to mine and breathed in his odor, as if I couldn't get enough of his clean aroma. I wanted to inhale him. He put his arms around my waist. For me, it was as if nothing had gone wrong between us.

"I'm glad to see you, too," he said, and pecked the side of my face. I pulled away before he did.

"I'll trade a glass of wine for help making the salad," I said. I poured the chilled white wine he'd brought and turned on the gas grill on the patio outside the kitchen. While the grill heated, I sliced French bread and set the glass dining table on the darkened patio with the blue and white china my mother had given me when I got married. The set belonged to her mother, a woman I never knew. My mother's mother lived in Denver and died before we could meet.

Going back and forth inside the kitchen, I kissed Peter on the neck every time I passed him. He cut cucumber and green onions and tore the tender lettuce leaves into the salad bowl. Once he turned toward me as I approached him and kissed me quickly on the lips. Gilda lay by the kitchen door, out of my way, her head resting on her paws, her eyes closed.

I lowered salmon filets into lemon and herb marinade. Peter shook the jar containing oil and vinegar salad dressing. "Got a red pepper?"

"Look in the refrigerator," I told him. I knew I didn't. What I bought at the store on the way home from the station was what I had in the refrigerator—coral-pink salmon, peaches, and plums.

Peter forgot about color in the salad and picked up a piece of bread and his wineglass. He followed me out to the patio where I placed the salmon on the grill and closed the cover.

"I want to swim after dinner," he said. "I want to feel you

naked against me in the water." He put his arms around me and spoke softly next to my ear.

After dinner, we took our wineglasses and the bottle over to the chairs beside the pool, and I turned off the pool lights. We stretched out our legs in the lounge chairs and placed the wine on a table between us. It was a desultory mood. Only the moon and the city's lights reflected on clouds illuminated us, but gradually we became accustomed to the dark and our skin appeared lit by a blue light.

After a few minutes sipping the wine, not speaking, listening to a cello concerto from the living room speakers, Peter placed his empty wineglass on the table, undressed, stood by the edge of the pool, and dived into the water. His legs were sinewy in the blue light. He was a natural athlete, but had chosen to go into law where he had no time to participate in sports. Other than sex.

"Come in," he said when he surfaced. The water still lapped the sides after his dive. I, too, undressed beside the pool, certain we were unseen in the dark and through the palm fronds surrounding the screen. I slipped into the water and reached over to his shoulders, pulling his body close to mine. He felt warm and alive in the cool water and he was hard and erect.

"I've missed you," I said to him, and put my hand down. "I've wanted to get close to you." He held me by the waist and leaned his back against the side of the pool. I twined my legs around his hips. He lifted me up only high enough out of the water to kiss my breasts and then placed his hands on my buttocks, pushing in hard. We stayed motionless for a moment. I'm not sure I wanted anything more than that. The utter closeness.

Then he twisted away from me, swimming the length of the

pool, and back to me. He pressed his entire body against mine. Underwater his bare body shimmered, and a dark seam marked where our bodies met. The phone rang.

"Let the machine get it," I whispered in his ear.

"You sure?" he asked in a tone just above a whisper. "Could be important." He held me close.

"Yes," I whispered, "I'm sure." The moment had ended, though. He began swimming back and forth down the length of the pool.

I called out, "I'll pour us another glass of wine."

I picked up the bottle, ready to pour when I heard Peter lift out of the water and turned to see him toweling himself beside the pool. With one hand he took the bottle, with the other he dabbed the towel over my drying body. He took one of my hands and said, "Bring the glasses." He led me into my bedroom through the sliding glass doors that opened to the pool.

We did not close the pool doors, and the sheets and our skin both turned pale and ghostly in moonlight reflected from the pool water and the clouds in the sky.

I poured us each another glass of wine, and we sipped it, Peter lying propped on my pillows and I seated on the edge of the bed. After a while he said, "Give me your glass," and he took it from me to set on the bedside table where I kept one of my guns in the drawer. He settled back and down, cushioned by the pillows, and I kissed him on the lips, the throat, his nipples, his navel, and down his thighs. And I kissed his hard velvet cock. I rubbed my lips against it, and I licked it. He placed his hands on either side of my head as if he were holding himself, and I tasted him. Was there some way you could get inside each other? Fall into each other? That was what I wanted. I raised myself up and straddled him and with my hand put him inside me and felt as if I were filled with him, with his slow surge, slow and powerful, and the craving washed over me, over my toes, over my breasts, over my womb, and for the moment I no longer craved. I lay quiet, my head on his shoulder, and we did not move, until my bent legs hurt and I rolled off him to lie beside him. I didn't want it to end. I thought, "This must be what Carla wanted. Is this what killed her?"

Neither of us slept. I turned on my side to face Peter and said, "We were so incredibly close. Did you feel it?" Peter said nothing. I waited. "I love you," I said.

He leaned over and kissed me on the cheek and said, "I can't stay tonight." He sat up, his back to me. Something inside my chest froze.

I sat up also, my back to him. "Why are you doing this?" Silence. Then I spoke and it didn't matter whether he was there or not. "No, wait. The question is, 'Why am I letting you do this to me?'"

He said nothing. I expected nothing.

"First you pull me close, then push me away." I stood up and continued, "God, this is dumb. It's dumb because I invite you over and we go through all that—dinner and roses and wine and swimming—and all you want is to fuck," I said.

"What is it you want, Susannah," he said as he zipped up his pants, his back still toward me.

"I know what I don't want," I said. "No more games, that's for sure. I'm tired of your games." I stood at the open hall door. "Leave. The sooner, the better." I don't know what I meant. I know I wanted him to come to me and say that he loved me and it was all a mistake and he wasn't leaving.

He picked up his shoes, socks, and tie and walked out. The

front door closed firmly, and the engine of his car roared before he put it into drive. I lay down and tears welled up in my eyes. But I didn't cry.

"Damn Peter," I said aloud.

Then I heard a woman's voice in the backyard.

"Tina. Tina." From the bed where I lay, I saw Tina's mother's face pressed against the patio screen. Gilda barked lazily from the kitchen. She knew Tina's mother. She just wasn't used to her standing outside the patio screen.

"Wait there, Mrs. Hathaway," I called out. And then to Gilda, "It's okay. Everything's all right." I grabbed a robe and ran out the side screen door.

"It's pretty late for you to be out, isn't it?" I took Mrs. Hathaway by the arm, and we headed back to her house. I didn't want her to wander off alone. She had done that once and was missing for an entire morning until an attendant at a nearby gas station noticed her.

"Tina's lost," she said. "I can't find her."

"Maybe she's in this house behind us. Let's go see." We walked through the undergrowth, the leaves and weeds scratching at my legs in the dark, until we reached her back door. I knocked. I could hear the television and then steps heading toward us.

"Who is it?" Tina called out.

"Susannah," I answered. "And I've got a friend with me. I think you know her." Mrs. Hathaway smiled. Tina opened the door and stared at her mother.

"How'd you get out?" she asked.

"I had to find Tina," Mrs. Hathaway said. "She's lost."

"I'm Tina," she told the confused woman. "You've found

me. I thought you were asleep." Tina looked over at me and said, "Thanks, Susannah. I hope she didn't bother you."

"Not at all," I said. "I wasn't doing anything important."

Back in my house, I saw the red light on the answering machine blinking from the call that came while Peter and I were in the pool. I cleared the dishes off the table, stacked them in the dishwasher, put leftover food in the refrigerator for dinner some other night—if I got home—and wiped the counters. I made instant decaffeinated *café con leche* by heating milk, instant coffee, and two spoonfuls of sugar in the microwave. A poor imitation of the real thing. I took my coffee mug into the bathroom and showered. I wanted to wash all of Peter off me. Only then, dressed in T-shirt and shorts, did I play back my messages.

"I found a mango," said Bill's voice. "Remind me to give it to you when we have dinner Sunday night." There was a space of about four seconds with no sound but his breathing, then he said, "Maybe it'll fatten you up. You look like you could use a few extra pounds."

Damn Bill.

CHAPTER 7

BLACK clouds billowed overhead as I drove toward Miriam Morales's house the next morning. Drops fell at first as if splashed out of a cup of water from a high building, then suddenly the rain came in torrents. A tropical squall in Miami's rainy season. It'd be over in fifteen minutes. I could barely see beyond the front of the car. I turned on my lights and continued driving by watching the path of the rear red lights on the car in front of me.

Miriam Morales lived in an older area of Miami, Shenandoah, built up in the forties and fifties. I drove on back streets. The squall passed. I began to see new houses squeezed in between older homes. Shenandoah used to be the area where Miami's Jewish population lived. In the 1960s the first wave of Cubans moved in. Shenandoah gradually became part of an area known as Little Havana, an area primarily centered on Calle Ocho. The early settlers named that street the Trail. One could drive all the way on this street—the Trail, Eighth Street, Calle Ocho, whatever you wanted to call it—from Biscayne Bay on the east coast of Florida to the Gulf of Mexico on the west coast in three or four hours.

Most of the older houses in the Shenandoah section of Little Havana were cement block and stucco, two bedrooms and one bath with an attached carport, and mature fruit trees—grapefruit or orange in the front yard and mango or avocado in the back. Fifty-by-hundred-foot lots. The Morales house was no different.

I walked through wet grass to the open front door. Mosquitoes attacked my legs. Miriam Morales stood inside.

"Come in, come in."

Her dark brown hair hung down past her shoulders, thick and straight. Her large eyes were brown and matched a fine linen suit she could have worn to the office, her legs long below her short skirt.

I felt inadequate as I noted her European elegance. An Anglo who needed a restful night's sleep. I automatically put my hand on my head and smoothed my hair, sprinkled with rain. I pulled it off my shoulders and wished I'd put it in a ponytail.

"Please. Tell me what happened to my Carla." Then she added, "Now I know why she did not come." She dabbed her eyes, taking care not to smudge her black mascara.

I told her minimally about Carla's murder. Then I said, "You can help us. Start by telling me what you remember about Thursday."

"Day before yesterday," she said. "Can you believe that? We were supposed to meet for lunch Friday."

Then she told me about Carla and their last conversation.

She remembered it clearly. "Carla," she said, "acted like a girl, a kid. You know, like in high school? She and Roy were going out again last night. The first time he called her it was because he wanted to place a full-page color ad in *Florida Nights*. It was an automobile ad, he told her. He saw her name and picture in the magazine. He asked her to meet him for a drink to discuss it. She told me he couldn't meet her during the day at the office." Miriam wiped her eyes carefully. "Do you think he was the one?"

"I don't know," I answered. "We'll follow up on all leads. Go on."

"Afterward she said she was going to meet him again."

"Did she?"

"Yes, but she didn't talk too much about it." She wiped her eyes again. "I didn't pry. I only heard what she wanted to tell me. Like when she broke up with her last boyfriend. She told me about that. She was very, very hurt."

"I don't get the connection."

"Carla did not believe any man would ever love her. She said that to me after she and Edward broke up. I think that is why she did not talk about Roy too much." Miriam dabbed her eyes again. "She did not want to get her hopes high."

I asked, "Could you identify this man in a lineup?"

"No. I never met him," she said. "Maybe if I had met him, I could have warned her. Maybe I could have saved her."

"There wasn't much you could have done," I told her. "It happened. That's all that's left to know. All we can do now is catch the killer and convict him. That's our retribution." I asked, "What about other men in her life?"

"I met a few of the men, but she had not many boyfriends.

Most were acquaintances. Edward Daniels came to the pool sometimes."

"Tell me about him."

"They broke up, about six months ago." Miriam waved her hand as if she were brushing back time. Carmenza Rodríguez's hand movement. "Maybe March, April. Sometime in the spring."

"Do you know why?"

"Not really. But she said she tried and tried to make him happy. She wanted him to love her." Miriam then said, "Carla attracted men the way she knew best." I looked at Miriam and thought they must have been quite a pair out at the apartment's pool.

"In what way?"

Miriam laughed for the first time that afternoon.

"Sex. She thought if a man wanted her sexually he also loved her. The men she attracted did not want love. They wanted what she offered. The sad thing is that love is the only thing Carla wanted—a man to love her."

Then she said, "She was a good person. She did not deserve the kind of treatment she got. She was no fool. But she was lonely."

Miriam was quiet, her arms resting loosely on her crossed legs. "She told me Roy kissed her in a really sexy way."

"Go on."

"He kissed her hard and her lips were puffy afterwards. I saw them." She wiped her eyes again. "But she was happy. Tell me. Do you think he did it?"

"I don't know," I said.

I left Miriam Morales and drove to Patricia Reeves's home. I thought about the portrait we were gathering of the murdered woman. Carla had taken a man into her bed, even prepared the bed for him with black sheets. A simple enough decision.

She was a highly competent professional, a friend and advocate of her coworkers, and insecure about her appearance. But she used her appearance to attract men, and she used sex to satisfy her need for love. Like many women I knew.

Good Lord, I'd taken men into my bed.

At what point, I wondered, did Carla choose wrong? At what point did she make the mistake? How could a woman tell whether the men in her life were capable of murder? Were my partners? Was Peter? Oh, God, no. Don't think that way, I told myself.

In Patricia Reeves's Coral Gables neighborhood, mature live oak and black olive trees shaded sidewalks and cooled the air. Even though this was the rainy season in south Florida—about nine inches of rain for each of four or five months, and rain fell daily—sprinklers ticked their sweep across lawns thick with rich, green, closely mown grass. At the Reeves house, coral pink impatiens on either side of the walk bloomed, their color matching the paint on the house's walls. I thought of standing beside Carla at the autopsy where the morgue paint was as cheerful as the impatiens.

Patricia Reeves and Roberta Reeves Steiner invited me into the house. Roberta left the room to make tea while Patricia Reeves showed me photos. The collection covered an entire wall on one side of the living room and ranged through the period of the girls' childhood to young adulthood. In most of the photos the girls faced the camera, smiled, posed, pointed their toes, lifted their chins, and as they grew older in the photos, their high cheekbones, long limbs, and flowing hair dominated.

"As you can see, my girls were the beauties of the whole state," said Patricia Reeves. "Here's the newspaper photo taken the year Carla was chosen as Orange Bowl Queen. And this is Roberta. She was a princess that year. Sisters. Everybody was so excited about that."

Orange Bowl Queen. I remembered my silly effort to be the Orange Bowl Queen. When I was sixteen I took Bill's car—a Jaguar, he always drove Jaguars—and tried to find the address downtown. I wanted to become the adored and beautiful Orange Bowl Queen. My mother was busy in her studio and certainly never thought of me as a candidate. I went into the offices I'd finally located and climbed up dark wooden stairs. When I opened the clouded-glass door to the Orange Bowl offices, I saw two young women and their mothers waiting to be interviewed, their hair and makeup and breasts and clothes all in place—both mothers and daughters. I backed out, said, "Excuse me," and on the way back to the car saw my reflection in a storefront window. I cried. I'd never look as good as Bill's girlfriends. The following week I got my ears pierced. A few months later, I was sent to Georgia to have an illegitimate baby.

"Mom, you're not taking Detective Cannon on a tour of your gallery, are you?" said Roberta, when she brought in a tray with white china cups and saucers rimmed in gold and a matching teapot.

The Carla I'd seen on the black sheet had kept her hair long and flowing, her body trim, as if she were an aging Orange Bowl Queen. Roberta, on the other hand, had sun-dried skin, lined and drawn.

Both women saw my glance. Mrs. Reeves said, "Carla kept herself beautiful."

Roberta placed the tray on a table in front of a white sofa. She ran her fingers through her short hair. She wore no makeup and no jewelry. Today she again wore a T-shirt, this time with full-length jeans and sneakers. She was about ten pounds over an ideal Orange Bowl Princess's weight.

"Carla was my splendid child," said Patricia, reaching into her pocket for a tissue, wadded and torn. "Where are the tissues?" she asked, and left the room. Roberta and I waited without speaking. Patricia Reeves immediately returned and stood in the hallway door for a moment before she rejoined us.

"Sugar? Cream?" Patricia Reeves asked me as she poured a cupful of tea. "I gave Carla so much," Patricia said to me, not looking at Roberta as she talked. "She was such an exquisite girl. You saw those pictures. I can't even think of what that animal did to her body." She raised a fresh tissue to her eyes.

"We're doing everything we can to catch the man who did this to your daughter," I said. "The areas I'll cover today can help us in our search for the perpetrator. Did she go out with many men?"

Patricia gave her answer. "Men couldn't help falling in love with her," she said. "She was splendid in every way. Beauty. Intelligence. Personality."

Roberta erupted. "Are you kidding? She went out with many men and fucked any guy who even thought about it. And if he didn't think about it, she made sure he did." She abruptly walked out of the room into the kitchen.

"I'm sorry," Patricia said to me. "We're all upset. Very upset." She kept her eyes trained on the white porcelain china rimmed in gold.

We drank tepid tea and pretended it was still good. Roberta came back into the room.

"I know this is difficult right now," I said. "Do you think any of her male friends was capable of killing her?"

"Some were jealous," said Patricia. She raised her eyes to meet mine. "But I know of none who would have done such evil to her."

"She had a boyfriend named Edward," I said.

"Yes. Edward Daniels." She turned to Roberta. "Carla and Edward loved each other." Roberta stared at her mother. No communication between them. None.

"Edward is a computer programmer. He works at home. When they broke up, Carla came to me. I told her, 'Don't worry, honey. Men fall in love with you all the time.' She was heartsick, though. She told me she was getting old and ugly and no man would want her. And she said she wanted a baby."

"What about someone named Roy?"

"I haven't heard that name," said Patricia. "I talked to Carla the night she—you know—a little while before she went out. She sounded rushed, and she said she bought new sheets and wanted to make up the bed with them before she went out. She didn't have time to talk to me then. But I didn't worry. I knew she'd look her best. I gave her lots of clothes from the shop." She dabbed her eyes with a new tissue. "I remember one of the last things I said to her was that I was glad she was dating again and to make sure she dressed to show off all of her beauty."

Roberta remained quiet, seated on the couch across from her mother, still staring at Patricia. I wanted to talk to Roberta, without her mother present. I passed around a small notepad.

"I'm taking the phone numbers of anyone associated with Carla. Roberta, would you write yours down in my pad?" I handed the notebook to her, a blank page opened for her to write her number.

When I got back to the car, I opened the notebook and read, "Carla was a very sick woman. Call me."

The manila envelope lay on my desk. I removed Carla's journals from it. There were two, and my thumb ruffled through the journals' pages. Both contained mostly blank pages. I saw the entries were dated. The time period was scattered over days and months and years. The entries were written with pencil and pen, in red, blue, black, and green.

I pictured Carla picking up a journal, her hair falling over her face, opening it to a blank page, and dating an entry with any pen or pencil she happened to have nearby. The journals were more akin to the baskets on her dresser than her desk at the office.

I began to read the first entry of more than twenty years ago.

August 21, 1979   I open this book with Ward. He knows the joy and pain I have so deep inside. It is the same with him. It is as if I had known him before we met.

September 15   Talked to Roberta but I can't seem to touch her. She talks and I'm thinking about Ward.

Oct. 20   No matter how I look or think or the color of my eyes or the brilliance of my conversation or what I create or what I accomplish. Nothing makes a difference. I am alone. Ward has left me.

Dec. 23   Dreamed of Dad again. He walked away from me, and though I ran and ran and caught up with him and touched his shoulder, he didn't stop. I woke up crying.

Nothing for two years. Then a repeat. Over and over she felt a passionate, frantic need for a particular man. And when he eventually pulled away after a few days or weeks or sometimes months, she wrote about a deep and barren gloom.

I flipped through the pages, hoping to find a key to one particular man, the one who killed her. My phone rang.

"This is Roberta Steiner," said the voice. "Carla's sister."

"I'm glad you called," I said to her, sounding like I really meant it. "I was going to call you in a few minutes."

"We couldn't talk with my mother around," she said. "I'm sorry Carla's dead, but I'm not surprised she was murdered—while having sex. I warned her. She had absolutely no sense about men. None. She thought if she fucked a man, he'd love her. She thought love was all the external stuff—how she looked, what she wore, how good she was in bed, in the kitchen, on the job. She was wrong."

What is love? I thought. But I asked, "You and Carla were close?"

"Not in the past few years. We used to be real close and alike—man after man after man. Always picking out men who'd leave. That way we could try to charm them into staying. With whatever it took to keep them around. Of course, we never did. I hit bottom, attempted suicide when another man left me, and he sent me to a psychiatrist. That experience changed my life. Carla and I went our separate ways afterward."

"And Carla didn't change," I said. "She was murdered instead."

"I truly believe it was only a matter of time before she brought the wrong man home. Dad left when Carla was seven and I was six. Mom showed us the only way she knew how to be loved. She taught us to concentrate on appearance, to not be a person, to be a woman who is easy to use up and discard. Cartoons. You saw the gallery."

"Cartoons?"

"Yeah. Cartoons of women. According to Mom, a man

wants beauty and compliance and neediness. And that's what Carla gave them. Poor Carla. She was good at spotting men who wanted all three of those attributes. Abusive men."

"Can you give me names?" I asked.

"Sure, I can. Her boss, a couple of waiters who were extravagant in their admiration of her, a photographer—the list goes on and on."

"Did you say her boss?" I asked her.

"I never saw him with her, but when we were over at Mom's, she'd mention her recent conquests. Lord knows if she was telling the truth."

"Did she say when she had an affair with her boss?" I asked.

"As far as I know, it was ongoing."

"Have you seen her journals?"

"Journals? No," Roberta replied. "I didn't know she kept any. But I understand her sickness. I played the same fantasy many times. No more." Roberta stopped.

"Make a list of as many of Carla's male friends as you can remember," I said. "Let's talk about Edward Daniels."

"Ed fit Carla's requirements. He was abusive—psychologically—and for sure unable to love. That meant she had to win him over. By the time those two came to Mom's, he was ready for the leaving part and Carla wasn't aware that it had begun. That's part of the dream. You've got to get hurt. In other words, you get a Daddy to love you for a while, a kind of love, and then he walks out again."

"What kind of person was Edward?"

"Like I said," continued Roberta, "he wasn't a guy I'd like these days, but the right kind for Carla. Angry, skittish, passionate, elusive."

"Do you think he was capable of killing her?"

"I think any and every man she went to bed with was fully capable of murder. Each one was abusive one way or another—physically or psychologically. She's lucky she lived as long as she did. I feel very sorry for her."

A moment passed. We were both silent. Finally, Roberta said, "I loved her and I know that if it weren't for lots and lots of very expensive therapy, I might have been the one on that bed."

Roberta finished. I again paged rapidly through the years in the journals. I was looking for men's names. And I sought an answer to my own conundrum—sex and love, love and sex. But I didn't know I asked a question. I didn't know I wanted an answer.

There were names, and I wrote them in a list. There were very few last names. I paid particular attention to Edward and Roy entries, though I noted one that lasted longer than others.

Sept. 8, 92   DonDon wants me all the time. I'm glad. He likes my work, too. It'll be fun. For a change.

5/17/93   DonDon took me shopping. Nice stuff. He's not a bad lover.

Dec. 26, 94   The usual party, then time alone at my place. DonDon gave me gorgeous earrings. And, of course, a little loving. I bought special wine for him. Will he leave Betty?

October 15   Edward, Edward, Edward. I think of little else. I want you to love me. Please love me. Please. I'm so ashamed. I wish I were free of this craving.

Nov. 2   Edward can't stay away from me and I don't want him to. I cook for him. I take him to the pool—and he struts around my chair as if he owns me. We go up to bed—and he puts on music and lights a candle and pulls me close to him. Sometimes he stays all night. Please let this last.

12/26   DonDon doesn't mind that I talk about Edward.

January 17   I asked Edward to stay all night again. He said no.

Jan. 21   Called Edward to tell him about launching the new magazine. He answered his phone and said, 'Judy! You called early tonight.' Oh God.

1/22   Edward. He's inside me. I'm so hurt, in so much pain. Call me, Edward, call me. Please.

Then this entry:

March 22   I'm bleeding inside, from my heart. Edward's gone.

She didn't write about Edward again. She wrote sporadically as she had throughout the journals. Between March and August, she described men without her typical passion. She boasted about men she met at parties, especially high-placed political figures. Then on August 25, three weeks before her death, she described two things—her depression and meeting a man.

8/25   It seems to take me hours to wake my brain up. I go to sleep after 2. I'm weepy. And all the while, I go to the office, flirt with DonDon, gossip with Miriam, manage advertising. The day is full of Miami's sun and rain and heat and sultry air. And tears are at the back of my eyes.

DonDon was Donald Bierman. She sounded like she wanted to die.

Sept. 8   Roy loves me. I know it. He lets me make him happy.

9/14   Tomorrow Roy and I will merge. I need him so much. I'll help him. I'll love him, not hurt him.

There were no more entries. Carla was murdered in her bed the night of September 15. I closed the book and sat there with my hand on the cover. Roberta had said she might have been the one on Carla's bed. And I realized I might have been the one.

My team had arrived for the two o'clock meeting. I must have had lunch, though I couldn't remember. I wasn't hungry.

All three men looked more relaxed than they had late yesterday. Compared to them, I felt as though my face was drawn from lack of rest and the skin under my eyes was puffy and dark. I wanted to check my appearance in a mirror but wouldn't let them see me do that. Here I was, a woman pretending to be a man. They all went along with the game, even Elton. Sometimes I wondered if he still saw me as a cunt and what that meant to him. Elton calling me a cunt. That's one of the things that piqued Harry's interest in me when we were in the police academy together. I guess Harry wanted to check it out. Peter liked me to use that word. It excited him. No more for him, I thought.

I pushed the envelope with the journals toward the back of my desk and focused on my team's reports.

"I talked to the next-door neighbors," said Rafael. "I believe we can pinpoint the time of the killing. The man told me he stays up to watch the news every night. In the living room— right next to Carla's bedroom. If there were no wall, his sofa would back up to Carla's bed.

"He heard a loud bang and figured she had knocked her bed against the wall. Actually, he said he wondered if she was moving furniture because he heard what he thought of as grunts."

"What time did he hear the bang?" I asked.

"He said he was watching the eleven o'clock news and at that point they were showing pictures of the Dolphins game on Channel Seven. He remembered because he was annoyed to be interrupted. I called the station and found out they showed the game clips at eleven twenty-six."

"And?" I asked. I wasn't listening to reports anymore. I heard a detective across the room talk to his partner about the latest drive-by shooting. He leaned against the partition next to the other detective's desk. They could have been two guys standing in their backyards, beers in their hands, talking about the game that afternoon.

The other woman in Homicide, besides me and Commander, opened her metal desk file drawer and cleaned papers off her desk by placing them in appropriate files. She worked quickly, preparing to leave for the day. Early shift. By the time she had left, only her books—crime law and MPD procedure—and photos of her two children, her husband, and her mother remained on view. She was young.

I turned toward Rafael. He was saying, "The information I have uncovered means he was killing her a little before and after eleven thirty."

"Any other reports of noise?" They all shook their heads. "What else have you got?" I asked.

Rafael continued. "I talked to the two doormen on duty Thursday night. The head night doorman, Enrique Quintana, seems to have been watching Reeves for a while. He talked about her short skirts, her red hair, and her long legs. I am bringing him in for questioning."

"Is he a suspect?" I asked.

"Could be. And he might have seen something, noticed

something. We should question him," said Rafael. "You never know."

"I've read some journal entries," I told them. "Carla Reeves was a very unhappy woman." I flipped open my notepad. "I doubt Edward and Roy are the same person," I said, "but we've got a problem with Donald Bierman."

"Her boss, right?" asked Elton.

"Yes, and yesterday when I interviewed him, he denied knowing Carla personally. She wrote about him in her journal. They had a sexual affair the entire time she worked there.

"He went to great lengths to tell me about his church activities and his life away from the office with his wife. I think he's worried. Maybe she asked too much of him." I thought to myself, Peter accused me of that.

"If Bierman killed her," said Craig, "he was extremely careful about leaving prints. There are no prints on the back of the bed. None. Wiped clean."

Elton sat resting his chin on his hand, eyes closed.

"Your report," I said to him. "What'd you get from the manager?"

"Gossip." Elton stood to pace around our desks as he spoke. "According to the manager, Carla Reeves left early most mornings, even before he came in. The doormen told him that bit of information. The manager said she came home late, and brought various men home with her. She wore skimpy bathing suits to the pool."

"Sounds like Rafael is right. They watched Carla Reeves rather closely. Were you able to verify any of that?" I asked.

"I went down to the pool," Elton said. "One of the men talked about her little bathing suits. When I asked about who she had with her, the people who talked to me each remembered someone different—a good-looking woman with long black hair, men, a man about her height with a ponytail, an older woman, and more men."

"What do you think?" I asked Elton. He'd spent the last forty-two years on the force, twelve of them in Homicide. He could retire anytime he wanted, but whenever anyone asked, he said he wasn't ready. I found his experience and cunning useful, if not exactly lovable.

"People noticed her more than who she was with. And she had a lot of different men at her place. That's something everybody mentioned. She brought the wrong man home this time."

"Rafael," I said, "check the fax. Raja said she'd send us a list of the contents of Carla's stomach."

"Craig, go through Carla's Rolodex. Bierman let me take it. List all the men she's got in the file. You and Elton can call them and check their alibis for Thursday night."

"I'm going down to Homestead to look at the photos and files on a murder there. Unsolved and with an MO very much like Carla's killer," I told them.

I pulled the strap of my purse over my shoulder, ready to go. Elton called me back to answer the phone. It was Detective Dominoe, the Homestead detective.

"Detective Cannon," said Dominoe. "We have to re-schedule our meeting."

"I can't put our meeting off," I said. "I must find out whether we're dealing with the same killer. Whether the Miami killer has been murdering women before he hit here."

"We can't meet today," he said. "We're tied up with a migrant strike. These dead women aren't going anywhere. This case down here in Homestead will be the same when we meet as it is today." Homestead's priorities were not the same as Miami's.

"My meeting down in Homestead has been canceled for the time being," I told my team. Then I called Fran and Bill. Fran answered.

"How'd you like a dinner guest tonight?" I asked.

"You mean how about tonight instead of Sunday," she said. No fooling her.

"I'm available tonight," I said. "I need company. I don't want to think. Bill always provides an entertaining evening."

"I understand," she said. "I'll call your father and tell him. He wanted to invite some other people over when you come."

"Let's get some Cuban coffee," I said to Rafael. The walk to Flagler felt good and he and I brought back *una colada*, a pineapple fruit cup, and packages of banana chips.

"Pass around the Rolodex," I said. "We'll all make calls."

The names were Carla's business associates. We had no success in finding her killer through these calls. We were all frustrated. When I walked out of the unit this time, I did so hurriedly, before the phone had a chance to ring.

CHAPTER 8

MY parents lived in the same house I grew up in, a two-story historical landmark on Coral Way, west of Miracle Mile in Coral Gables. In that section of town, the same section where Carla Reeves's mother lived, Coral Way was a two-lane street lined with tall sculptural oaks and pink side-walks. Weathered limestone blocks formed an arched front portal to my parents' house, and the new white, cottage-casement windows, the mildewed red-barrel-tile roof, and fuchsia-flowered bougainvillea climbing up the front walls completed the hacienda style envisioned by Merrick.

My parents had had a wall placed around the house, and now I drove through a wrought iron gate, designed by my mother and made by a Cuban-refugee artisan.

"Susannah. You're still driving that old car," Bill said, looking through the screen door out into the circular driveway. The car's tires had crunched on the Chattahoochee gravel as I drove up to the front. When I opened the screen door, he leaned down and kissed my cheek. I had turned my head so he'd miss my lips. After the kiss, Bill raised his drink to his mouth.

Standing at the screen door, I saw again that his tall frame retained its lean youthful lines. I hoped I'd inherited that part of his genes. And I could see his eyes. His eyes—so full of bravado and swagger when he drank—reminded me of why I'd run from them as a teenager. He was never overtly sexual with me, but he brought me along on some of his trysts and encouraged my adoration of him. An almost sexual adoration, as if I were worshipping a rock star. I didn't begin to love him, really love my father, until after I got over the adoration—and then the hate.

"It's the same car I've visited you in during the past eight years," I responded. "And how are you? Any other guests?"

"I'm not doing well, Susannah," he said. "Your mother's mad at me. No one's here yet. You're early."

"What'd you do now?" I asked. I almost laughed, but their games were sad. At least I was no longer caught in the middle.

"I was late last night," he said. "I couldn't help it." He almost whined. "Thanks for coming over tonight. You'll save my ass." He grinned the secret grin, the one I had thought was mine alone when I was a little girl.

"I didn't come over to save you," I said. "How about a drink for me? I'd like some of your good Scotch tonight." I led him toward the kitchen where he kept the liquor.

Gravel crunched outside, a car engine shut off, and the doorbell rang.

"Come in," said Bill, loud enough for me to hear in the kitchen. "Suze is in the back with Fran." I heard footsteps as

Bill and his guests approached. "You know Jimmy. And Carol."
Jimmy was a city commissioner.

Three more times the gravel crunched and the bell rang.
Apparently, Bill still had enough power that he could invite
people over for dinner at the last minute. And they'd come. Bill
had even invited a dinner partner for me—the ranger whom I'd
met at the Everglades fund-raiser.

When I opened the door, I saw he'd had his hair cut and the
clothes he wore looked new. Again he wore an ironed shirt
open at the collar, along with creased khaki pants and brown
leather loafers without socks. He fit in—Old Miami casual.

"I'm afraid I don't remember your name," I said. "I know
you called me."

"You're Susannah Cannon," he said. "Homicide Detective.
And I'm Martin Benson. Your father asked me to come over.
He said you'd be here."

"Come on in and join us in the madhouse," I said to him.
"Can I get you a drink?"

"I don't usually drink," he said.

"Come meet my mother, then I'll take you out back with
everybody else."

Martin followed me into the kitchen. Fran was not the same
beauty who'd stood alone with the man in the kitchen the other
night. At the small dinner party that night, her age was more
evident—her figure had grown softer and her face filled out
enough to hide the lines. She had let her ashen blond hair flow
loosely that night.

When I entered the kitchen, she stood beside the stove with
her glass of white wine in hand. I put my arm around her waist
and pulled her close to kiss her cheek. I had come to understand that in her time, a woman had to sacrifice many dear

things in her life to pursue her art. For Fran, I was one of those sacrifices. Bill was another.

"Smells good," I told her, pouring Scotch into my glass and Bill's. "What can I get you?" I asked after the introductions. I gave Martin the Coke he asked for.

When I came back to the kitchen after taking Martin to join the other guests, I said to Fran, "How do you stand Bill's constant childish behavior?"

She smiled just at the corners of her mouth and in her eyes.

"He leaves me alone," she said. "I leave him alone. It's worked out fine."

"He said you're mad at him," I said. "How come?"

"Annoyed. Not mad. He can't stand any hint of criticism. But he kept me waiting after he'd told me he'd be home for dinner. And he'd been drinking. I smelled it when he came in the front door. Frankly, I don't see how he can continue to lobby successfully in Washington, but they all drink like that."

I stood there watching her face, a habit I'd gotten as a homicide detective.

She laughed and turned to open the oven to check the roasting chicken. "I completed another sculpture while he was gone. That'll be ten new ones for the show." Then she said, "I haven't seen Peter for a while."

"He was here at the cocktail party," I said. "Didn't you see him?" I doubted she did. She might not have left the kitchen.

"No."

"I saw him. I wish I hadn't. He was furious with me that night. He was mad enough to kill me if he thought he could've gotten away with it."

Fran laughed, now facing me with her wineglass raised to chest level.

"Couples get mad at each other all the time. And then get over it. One of you will call the other soon." She loved Bill. I understood that now.

"If it depends on me, Peter will wait a long time for me to call him." I didn't tell her about our latest fight.

Fran turned to stir the cream of mushroom soup she'd made with fresh mushrooms, the aroma lifting into the room when she raised the lid.

"I'm going outside. Socialize. Let me know if I can help you with dinner."

"Nothing to do right now," she said, and turned her back on me again to tend the chicken roasting in the oven. "Go take care of Bill and the guests."

"Susannah," exclaimed Bill, sounding happy and excited to see me. Martin, who was in the small group talking with Bill, looked over at me and smiled as if he too were glad to see me.

Fran called us in to dinner and when we arrived at the table we saw bowls filled with cream of mushroom soup and a platter with roast chicken, browned and crisp and surrounded by roasted potatoes and carrots. A large wooden bowl contained a salad of torn lettuce and red peppers. The tablecloth she'd chosen for that night was the color of persimmons. Candles had been lit and low light came from sconces on the walls. She had invited us into a painting.

Jimmy sat on one side of me and Martin on the other. My mother had arranged to sit between commissioners. And there was a partner in Bill's firm who had come with his current girlfriend.

At one point in the evening, Martin and I turned to each other, since Jimmy seemed entranced by Fran and the partner's girlfriend was interested in Bill to the exclusion of all others.

"Your father is a generous man," Martin said to me. "I like him a lot."

I laughed. "Are you saying you like him because he's generous?"

"I don't want you to get that impression," he replied. "I'm glad he's generous. And I also think he's a terrific guy."

"You're not the only one to think that," I said, glancing at Bill soaking up the girlfriend's attentions. Martin turned to look at Bill and the young woman, and he grinned.

"Everybody, not just me, thinks he terrific," he said. "I can tell you love him a lot and want to make sure he's happy."

"True." Martin was perceptive. I thought of how Peter would have behaved in such a setting. He'd have had the total attention of the commissioners.

"And he does what he can to support the Everglades. You have a deep attachment to the Everglades, don't you."

"I do," I said, relieved to get off the subject of my father.

"What do you like about the Glades?"

"I told you my grandfather owned land out there and donated most of it to the national park. My history with the place goes a long way back, and my family has been connected to the Everglades since my grandfather first came here."

"I know about your family's connection, what about you specifically?" he asked.

"Me?" I was hardly prepared to talk about me. "I love the space, the solitude, the birds, the heat, the sun, the clouds—I love it all. I've got some great photos of the place, especially of birds."

"Photography's your hobby, right?"

"You guessed right," I said.

Martin said he had to leave early. I walked him out to his car.

"I'm glad you and Bill get along," I said.

"I told you," he said, "I like the man and I like his interests. He invited a group tonight that believes in preserving the Glades from development."

"He knows I love the Glades. He tries to make me happy. I try to make him happy," I told him.

"I've noticed that," he said. "Would it make him happy if you and I went canoeing in the Everglades?"

"Whether it does or not," I said, "let's do it."

"Your father was kind enough to give me your telephone numbers. I'll call. Again."

I entered the house and went directly to the patio. I heard water running in the kitchen and dishes clattering and the refrigerator opening and closing. Fran would take care of the kitchen while I took care of the guests.

I arrived home late after the dinner party, and Gilda seemed particularly nervous. I let her out the back, figuring she had to go to the bathroom—quick. But she nosed through the underbrush, pushing aside leaves and pine debris I'd let build up on the ground. She was running after a lizard, I thought, and I waited lazily for her to return. She did, carrying something in her mouth, and she dropped it at my feet. I leaned backward to reach the back porch light and saw what she'd brought me. A cigar box tied tightly with package string and a single bud of a hibicus blossom tucked securely beneath. I untied the string, opened the box, and saw its contents. I dropped it and stepped back, away from it. Nothing moved in it. Gilda began to smell the contents, but I pushed her away and looked more closely at a tiny newborn kitten, its eyes never opened, its neck punctured and blood matting the fur down one side of its body.

"What in the hell is this?" I said out loud. Gilda cocked her head. I stroked her back and said, "Good girl." My heart felt like a ringing alarm. I scanned the backyard, out into the dark. I saw nothing. Gilda had not returned to bark or search out more gifts. I grabbed her collar and pulled her inside the house. I locked the door.

My heart slowed once we were inside. I put the cigar box and flower and string in a plastic bag. I twisted a metal tie to close it tight and placed it in my refrigerator. A teen prank, I thought. The gang unit would see this. I locked all my doors and windows and set the alarm. I usually didn't set it, but that night I did. Nevertheless, I didn't sleep well.

The next morning, Sunday, the radio turned on at six, and I lay awake listening to a Berlioz symphony and watching the daylight increase. In my shower the water ran cold over my body. I dried myself, pulled on jeans, a T-shirt, and sneakers, and started coffee. Gourmet coffee on Sundays. I wrapped a bagel in a paper towel and filled the thermos.

I drove to Matheson Hammock Marina, a little south of the Grove. The marina was surrounded by dark mangrove. I sat on a park bench, poured coffee, and ate bits of bagel. Gilda watched and anticipated my throwing bits to the gulls. In the past she'd reached the bagel twice before the gulls did.

An offshore breeze came in cool that early in the day. The sounds were simple. The water pattered against the sides of moored boats. Men banged on their boat down the dock and prepared to launch it. Their voices drifted to me on wisps of wind. When they started their boat's powerful engine, they inched it out of its mooring into the waterway, and the noise went out with them. Then silence again. I watched sails of an incoming boat float, as if belonging to a ghost ship, behind an offshore island's casuarina trees. Gilda chased first the gulls, then the bagel.

If I'd had my baby boy with me, he could have enjoyed the morning. Or would he have been one of the teenagers who killed kittens for kicks? I would have raised him right, I thought. The kitten and Peter and Bill were stirring up old feelings. Don't think, I told myself. Get up and get busy.

My beeper vibrated, and I thanked God. Commander's code.

"Come on, Gilda. Breakfast's over." I snapped the leash onto the dog and walked back to the car where I dialed Commander from my cellular phone.

"Cannon here," I said when she answered. "You beeped?"

"Another one, Suze. The Reeves MO. Go there now. I've called backups to secure the scene. Make the other calls from your car on the way over." She added, "Phone me from the scene."

The backup cops taped off the entire lot of the two-story duplex on a south Grove street. I opened the windows of the car for Gilda and tossed the keys to one of the uniforms as I walked into the building.

"Watch her for me."

I looked down at the bed and saw a human form covered by a pink-flowered sheet. Blood soaked through the sheet from under the breast areas, creating other types of flowers, and blood formed an outline of the body's left side. I pulled back the sheet slowly.

Blood smeared like a wash over the dead woman's torso. The cuts under her breasts had leaked blood, now dried, down her ribs to the sheets. There it blended in with the blood from her jugulars that had seeped down from her neck to soak the bed and cradle her body. This one had bled more. I looked across the room and down onto the rug to see if it had spurted. Some blood had leaped out to the gold-colored rug, but the amount seemed pitifully little to me. Red stipples dotted the whites of the eyes, and I expected to see signs of strangulation. I looked down from her eyes and saw her lips, bitten and dark with blood and bruises, not lipstick. Her neck looked distorted, reddened, abraded.

There was a difference in this one. More rage, more passion, loss of control. I wondered if the killer was the same and what had provoked his rage or passion. Possibly an insider privy to the information had leaked it or had used it in this murder. Who knew the details? Quite a few.

One cut-crystal wineglass sat on the bedside table. A rose-colored dress with a satin sheen on the collar, flesh-colored lace panties, but no bra, were draped across a chair. High heeled shoes, pumps, stood under the bed—tucked as if an orderly woman had slipped them off while standing beside the bed.

Angels and fruit floated above the pillows on the carved-wood headboard. The dresser was bare except for a polished silver bowl, severe in its simplicity, filled with lavender pot-pourri. The dead woman was very different from Carla.

I turned away from the body and the contents of the bedroom to check into the adjoining bathroom. Rafael arrived then, also in jeans and a T-shirt.

"I was on the bike when you beeped," he explained, looking down at his jeans. He motioned his head toward the body. "Another Carla?"

"Maybe," I said.

"Who found her?"

"A friend. She came to pick her up for their Sunday morning walk. The door was ajar and she walked in to find her friend still in bed, covered with a sheet."

The uniform standing in the doorway handed me a slip of paper. "Here's her friend's name and number. She's waiting in the kitchen."

I went to the bed again. Were there similarities between Carla and this victim? What triggered the perp? Slender. Not a young woman. Pretty. Her hair color was different. This one was a honey blond and cut short. And her eye color wasn't the same. Carla's were a blue. This one's were pale brown, with yellow flecks. I looked closer at her face.

"I've seen this woman," I told Rafael. "Can't remember where. What's her name?"

Craig entered the duplex at the same time as Raja.

"The rape kit," I said.

Raja leaned over the body and examined the face. "Teeth marks," she said to no one. Raja checked the dead woman's hands and wrists. "Nails broken. Looks like fragments of skin underneath some of the nails." She raised the woman's half-closed eyelids.

"Have an artist sketch this victim while she's at the morgue," I told Raja. "Before you examine the brain. And have her draw Carla, too. She'll have to use a photo. Carla's mother has many, many photos," I said.

Elton arrived after the crime techs. Rafael emptied a purse he'd found on a table beside the front door and picked up a small leather business-card case. He called out the name on the business card, and I remembered. I'd met the woman at a Red

Cross fund-raisers' meeting. Fran asked me to attend the meeting when she couldn't go.

Janice Cantwell made abundant floral arrangements, a profusion of blooms patterned after Dutch Renaissance paintings. These designs were her trademark at her flower shop in the Biltmore Hotel.

"I know who this woman is," I said. "The victim had a flower shop in the Biltmore, coincidentally the place Carla had her first meeting with Roy Jamison. Remember? Meet Roy at Biltmore, eight p.m."

No one in the room bothered to respond to me. I asked Rafael, "Did you find names of next of kin in that purse?"

"Nothing so far," Rafael answered.

I handed him the paper the uniform had given me. "The friend who found her," I said. "Find out what she knows about her walking buddy."

The usual gawkers were outside the yellow tape, and Gilda waited for me, panting and drooling. I'd forgotten about the dog and drove by my house first to let her inside before I went to the station. Beside the front door, my answering machine blinked and I ignored it. On the way to the station, I called Al. I'd promised to keep him up to date on information related to the Reeves case.

"Let's talk," I said to him. "There's another victim with the same MO as Carla Reeves. Can you meet me at the station?"

"I'm on the way," he said, sleep still in his voice.

When I got to the unit, I headed straight toward Commander's office. She'd missed church that day.

"I've called Al. He's on the way over," I reported. She leaned back in her chair, listening intently. "I don't think we should wait for a profile before we talk to the media." I watched for her reaction. She gave it to me.

"I'm sure as hell bothered," said Commander. "As of right now we've got two murders, maybe three, related somehow."

"I'll get a profile right away."

"That's not soon enough. We've got to stop him. Now," she almost shouted. And she stared at me as if she were daring me to cross her. I wasn't about to do it. No way.

Then she said, "You're reporting to the entire unit tomorrow afternoon. I want Raja here, too." She gazed at me, hard. "At the moment you're still lead."

Al sat at my desk, lounging back in my chair, and I saw him before he saw me. He had married a couple of years out of graduate school and had a son. His boy was younger than mine. I don't think he knew about my son. He and his young family lived in a house they'd bought in north Coconut Grove while houses there were still affordable. Not far from me.

"What's your son doing these days?" I asked.

"He's on the school's soccer team, junior varsity," he said.

"I bet you go to all his games."

"Beth does," he said. "I go when I'm free. Stop the chitchat. What's going on with the Reeves case?"

"Let's get coffee first," I said to him. "Sunday morning coffee." I told him about our new victim and the possibility that her murder was related to the Reeves murder.

"Al, it's important you release only certain facts. I saw the story in this morning's paper. Are you going to run one every day? Even when there's no new information?"

"It's a sensational case," he said. "And it looks like we've got two. Not only two murders that may be linked, but two in three days. Now that's creepy."

"Don't stir up trouble," I said to him.

Al left, almost at a jog, to go to his paper and write the story. I went into Commander's office and talked about the information we needed to get out. Then I asked the public information officer on duty to come upstairs to write the release. As soon as it went out, the PIO phones would be jammed.

The PIO officer left to write the story, and I saw sitting on the stained, mustard-colored sofa a woman with white hair. She was tanned and young, and she wore a tennis hat, white golfing shirt, new tight jeans, and clean white sneakers.

"Hello," I said to the woman. "I'm Detective Cannon. And you are?"

"I'm Marge Talbot, Jan Cantwell's friend."

"I'm investigating the murder of your friend. You found her, didn't you?"

"Your other detective talked to me at her house," she said.

"I want to talk to you now," I said. "Tell me about how you found her."

"I just stepped into the bedroom and saw the bloody sheet. I didn't go in any further. How did this happen?" She had surprised blue eyes.

"Maybe you can help us find out how it happened," I said. "First of all, tell me who was Janice Cantwell."

"She was well liked, a fun person. We enjoyed our Sunday morning walks, and we'd talk and talk about all kinds of things. I guess we didn't walk fast enough to get out of breath." Talbot spoke rapidly with a Florida Cracker accent, the accent of someone whose family had been in Florida for a long, long time. I could imagine her on the dance floor at the Riviera

Country Club, a country club in Coral Gables notorious for its exclusiveness and its unwillingness to admit certain ethnic groups, though there were token abridgments to the rules. "We talked about men a lot. She dated every now and then, but nothing regular. Men loved to be seen with her. You know the kind?" She paused long enough to wipe her eyes.

"Jan complained about her life—all the parties and dinners and openings. Although I can't imagine what she was complaining about. She went to a lot of that sort of thing. Business, mostly. She actually said to me, 'Every now and then I want to stop, but then I start right back in.' " Marge Talbot paused and looked at me and continued, since I hadn't stopped her.

"Jan was an artist. She made beautiful paintings. Watercolors of flowers. She used to sell her paintings before she opened her flower shop. But that was years ago, before I knew her. We do such silly things when we're young, don't we?" I didn't answer but could agree. "Then she opened the flower shop at the Biltmore and made a fabulous success of it. Just fabulous. There were always rumors around her, but she was my friend and I knew her as a simple, kind woman."

"Rumors?"

"You know. Like who she was dating. Those were big names and I don't want to repeat them, but I can tell you they were right at the top of the political world—city, state, and nation."

"I'll need a list of those names," I told her.

"Oh, Lord. Now I've put my foot in it. But if you insist, it'll take me a day or two to remember them all. Can you wait that long?"

"Get the list to me as soon as possible." Roberta had said Carla mixed with political figures. "Detective Hernández said you'd bring in Jan Cantwell's brother's name and number. I understand there are no other living relatives." Cantwell's parents had died one after the other about five years earlier. She had been divorced since 1990. She had no children, and her brother was her only immediate family.

"I dated her brother before he left Miami. He'll be broken-hearted when he hears how horribly she died. I couldn't call him and tell him. I just couldn't. Here's his number. You do it. He lives in Philadelphia now." She reached into her back pocket and pulled out a folded piece of note paper on which she'd printed his name and telephone number.

She turned to leave, her head bent low, her hair swinging forward. I heard a *swish-swish* as she walked out—the tight denim brushing against itself. She left behind an odor of soap.

"I'm calling from the Miami Police Department," I said to Janice Cantwell's brother. "I'd like to talk to you about your sister."

"What about her?" said Philip Cantwell.

"I'm sorry to have to tell you about this, but her body was found this morning. She's dead."

"It can't be Jan. You must be wrong. I just talked with her yesterday. She's coming up for a visit."

"Janice was found in her bed in her apartment. Marge Talbot confirmed the identification," I said.

"What happened to her?" he asked. I explained as well as I could over the phone, and as I talked I heard him crying and saying over and over again, "Oh, God."

"Mr. Cantwell," I said after a moment, "this is difficult news to hear over the telephone." I think he heard me. "I'd like to talk to you about your sister's conversation with you yesterday."

"Not now. Tomorrow," he managed to say. "I'll come to

Miami. I'll have to make arrangements. She was my little sister. We shared a lot."

"Let me know your plans. It's important we talk about your last conversation with her."

"Maybe I'll come tonight," he said. "I'm not sure. I need to call Marge." He started to cry again. "I can't talk now." He hung up.

My next call was to Fran. She must have known Janice Cantwell, I thought. They were both active in the Red Cross.

Bill answered.

"Fran's in the studio," he told me.

"I need to talk to her," I said. "She may know a murder victim we found this morning, and I'd like to get the inside scoop."

"Who's that?"

"I don't think you know her," I said. "Janice Cantwell."

There was silence. I thought we'd been disconnected. "Bill?"

"I'm here," he said. "Not Jan. Please. Not Jan."

"You knew her," I said, not asked. I remembered her well then. A young Jan. I was sixteen, and she didn't look older than eighteen or twenty. She was my father's mistress, lover, paramour— any of those names would do. I heard my father crying. "I'll call later, Bill. If you see Fran, ask her to call me. It's important."

In about five minutes Fran called. That meant Bill had gone to her studio.

"Bill is tormented," she said. "What did you say to him?"

"You knew a woman named Janice Cantwell, didn't you?"

"Sure," she said. "We were on the Red Cross fund-raising committee together, for one thing. She has a florist shop in the Biltmore. Does beautiful arrangements."

"We found her murdered this morning," I said. "I recognized her as a woman I'd met at the Red Cross meeting you asked me to attend."

"Murdered?" she exclaimed. "Jan? Oh, no. What happened?"

"We think it was someone she knew well enough to take to bed with her. That's where he murdered her. And her clothes were beside the bed as if she'd taken them off and placed them there. We found no rips, no signs of force."

"I'm so sorry," she said. "It's truly horrible. Is this what you told Bill?"

"Yes," I said. "I told him."

"She was one of Bill's women for a while."

"And you knew about it?" I asked.

"Sure," she said. "You were about sixteen."

"You had your first big show the following year," I said. She had been focused solely on her sculpting during that time. I remembered how, at the show, she touched a young man's face as if it were one of her sculptures and reached up to kiss him. How I'd watched as he'd responded, then backed away, turning to see where I was. That man was Al.

"Do you know anything about Janice Cantwell's personal life?" I amended that question: "I mean in the past year or so."

"We talked a little during the Red Cross campaign," Fran answered. "She looked great. She wasn't much older than you. Early forties. She said she'd been divorced a while, and her business had been really good."

"Was she going with anyone in particular?" I asked.

"I don't know that much about her," my mother answered. "I've always believed she's one of those women who loves to be loved. She needed someone." The unspoken words were there—Fran didn't need anyone but Bill and I did.

"Come over tonight. Please," she said. "You are the only one who can comfort him. Bill needs you. He needs you very much."

CHAPTER 9

TWO men were seated on the same sofa where Marge Talbot had waited. They examined the unit from their seats, neither speaking to the other. I watched them while I talked with my mother on the phone. When I finished the conversation, I walked over to the two men.

"Edward Daniels. Enrique Quintana. Right?" I asked. "Mr. Quintana, come with me. You wait here, Mr. Daniels."

The interrogation room was painted in a color that matched the sofa. There were no windows. Years of pounding and writing and setting coffee cups and Coke cans on the surface of the wood table had left it looking like a piece of public school-room furniture. I seated Quintana and asked if he'd like some coffee.

"*Sí*, sure," he said. "With sugar and cream."

"I'll be right back," I said, smiling, closed the door, and left him alone.

"Rafael," I said. "He wants coffee with cream and sugar. Will you take it to him? I've got work to do."

"Right." He smiled at the setup.

I read over all the papers on my desk and finished my cup of coffee. Eventually, after I thought Quintana had waited about the right amount of time, I wrapped a day-old pastry in a napkin and took it to him. Rafael came with me.

Quintana wore a starched white shirt, overshined black leather loafers, and black jeans. I watched his eyes. They were deep brown and hinted at cunning, not intelligence. His skin, weathered in wind and sun, had become an ocher color. I watched the small tics around his eyes and mouth, the directions in which he gazed, the movement of his hands and fingers for signs he was lying.

"You told me what you did for a living in Cuba before you came here," started Rafael. "Tell me again."

Quintana sighed but began, "In Cuba I no work for long, long time." Raising his shoulders in a shrug, he explained, "No job. Before, I work. I had job at tourist hotel. You know, a waiter." Then he added, "Head waiter." He looked down at his fingernails. A lie. "I leave Cuba. I get on boat at Mariel. Many, many people on that boat. Lot of vomit and *pipi*. Lot of boats. American boats. When we don't vomit, we sing." He grinned. I stared at him and kept any feeling I had about his tale away from my face and eyes. I wondered how Rafael was responding to this man's experience of crossing the waters.

Rafael looked down at the folder in front of him, knowing the next answer before he asked it. My folder contained the same information. I knew Quintana had been arrested for breaking into and entering an apartment in the Little River section of Miami where Cuban refugees, with no jobs and no experience in a non-communist society, crowded into rooms and under bridges. He'd committed battery during the robbery.

"Have you ever been arrested in the United States?" Rafael asked.

"I have no money. I have no food. I have no room," he answered. "Very difficult."

"That's not an answer," said Rafael, then repeated the question.

"One time," he said, and held up his index finger. "One. I go into room and take what she take from me." He didn't smile, but his eyes crinkled around the edges.

"What was that?" asked Rafael.

"A watch. My watch."

"Did you hit her?"

"I just slap her. She hit *primero*."

"What else?" asked Rafael. The photo showed a woman with swollen eyes, cracked lips, and black marks on one side of her face.

"I make her keep quiet." He looked down. "I hit her, maybe two times."

"You were sentenced, it says here, and served time," said Rafael.

"I no like jail. The social worker, she find work. I park cars. No more arrests," he answered.

"That job was at Bay's Edge Apartments?"

"*Sí.*"

"How well did you know Carla Reeves?" Rafael asked. I watched his face.

"Not so good," he said. "At night when she come home, I see. *Pues*, no every night. Sometime we busy, busy."

"When you saw her, what did you notice about her?" asked Rafael.

Quintana shifted in his chair so that he sat straighter, taller. "See, it's like this. I stand in parking lot and smoke cigarette. She drive in and walk by me. She no look at me. Like she's thinking, thinking. She hold briefcase and wear *muy* short skirt. All the time, short skirt." He showed us with the edge of his hand where her skirt stopped in the middle of her thigh. "I look. She go in back door."

"Did you ever go to her apartment?" asked Rafael. I watched Quintana's face.

"No. Never." He answered emphatically.

"Why not?" Rafael was probing.

Quintana shrugged again. "She never ask me."

"The manager has said you regularly visited the apartments of women. Did you?" asked Rafael.

"Some women, you know, like a visitor," he explained. Then he said, "I never," and he repeated the word, "never visit Miss Reeves. I never go to her apartment." And he shook his head as he said again, "Never."

"But you watched her," I said. "Did you see her anytime Thursday night?"

"No," he answered, and this time his eyes crinkled, "not Thursday. Busy, busy, busy. Thursday, Friday, Saturday. Always busy."

"Do you remember the man who came to see her at eight Thursday?" I asked.

"A lot of people come to Bay's Edge. Lot of visitors. I don't remember who come see who."

"Did you see Ms. Reeves come in later that night?" I asked.

"No," he said, and did his shrug again. "I don't know if she go out or come in. I only see her if she come in when I smoke cigarette."

"But you did see her when she was at the pool," I said.

"When not so busy, we look at the girls on video. We see Miss Reeves sometimes. *Qué linda!*"

"I think you're lying," I told him. "I think you saw her on Thursday night. I think you know more than you're telling us. If we find out you're connected to this, the court won't be so good to you this time."

He looked at each of us for a moment before he raised his hands, palms facing outward. "I tell you. *Pero* I know only one thing. She have same man visit her for many years, for all the time I am working at the apartment."

"Can you identify him?"

"I know how he look."

"Describe him."

"He old man. He skinny. He bald. He got funny voice. Like this." He demonstrated by speaking in a deep, gruff tone.

"Was he there Thursday night?"

"He came for a little time, then he leave. Before a lot of people come. I busy, busy after he leave."

"What time was that?"

"I think about seven. You check the book. You see I not lie."

"What time does it get busy at the Bay's Edge?"

"Sometime at eight. Sometime at nine. You check book. You see."

"We will. Now, tell us where you were last night," I said.

"Saturday night? At work. That a very busy night. Always Saturday night busy."

"Anyone see you?"

"*Sí.*"

"We'll need names. And after work. Where did you go?"

"I go home when I finish work. At two. I have *otro* job Sunday morning. I fix things."

"Did anyone see you at home?"

"*Mi esposa.* My wife."

Rafael told Quintana not to leave town and to be available for further questioning in the future. Rafael and I stood together at our desks, silent as we picked up the files for Edward Daniels.

"He was describing Bierman," I said.

"Bierman visited Carla Thursday after work, and she had another visitor at eight. Roy Jamison. And there is no information on a Roy Jamison," said Rafael.

"Bierman could have used that name. He could have come early, left early, and returned under another name. We've got to look at the check-in book," I said. "I want to confront him with this information. I want to see what I can get out of him."

"You were right to suspect Quintana had not told us everything. But you know, his kind do not divulge all they know right away. That is the way he has survived," said Rafael.

"Someone from the streets."

"And someone from a communist country," Rafael added. I would not have thought of that.

"I'll call Bierman," I said. "Tell him I want to talk."

In the interrogation room, I could look closely at Daniels. I wondered what about him had attracted Carla. From the back I saw his long gray hair, streaked with his natural brown. He held it tightly under control at the nape of his neck in a ponytail that hung halfway down his back. He wore a tiny gold circle in one pierced earlobe, and he wore black cowboy boots over his faded jeans. Gray body hair coated his arms below his short-sleeved shirt. He turned to face me. His veins showed blue underneath his pale skin. His file said he was thirty-five years old, but to me he looked quite a bit older. And I doubted he worked out.

"You must be hungry," said Rafael. "How about a burger?"

"I'm not hungry. I don't want anything," Daniels said. His voice sounded controlled with a hint of hysteria at its edge. It was a thin voice.

I took my time reading through his file. There wasn't much. I could see he had had no arrests, only traffic violations, and he worked at home as a computer programmer. I wished I were in the police station weight room instead of this stuffy closet-like space.

I heard tapping on the table and looked up to see Daniels drumming his fingers. They were long and slender, used to mastering the keys of a computer. As he flicked his fingers over and over again on the table, he stared at me. His eyes were an ice blue.

"I'd be glad to get you something," said Rafael.

"Nothing," said Daniels, his face set not to show any emotion.

I waited and watched him silently and then began. "I understand you and Carla Reeves dated each other for a while toward the end of last year and the beginning of this year. Is that true?"

"Yes, we met in the fall during a night class at the university."

"What was your relationship with her?" I asked.

"We saw each other once or twice a week for about six months."

"I mean, what did you two feel for each other?" I persisted.

"Feel? I felt nothing for her. She might have had some feeling for me. That's always possible." I'd hit a nerve. His voice became thinner and higher. "She was the one who always asked me over. I didn't ask to come."

"What makes you think she had some feeling for you?" I asked, remembering what her handwriting in her journals looked like. Different color inks, different pencils, different dates.

"I couldn't say."

"You were together for, what, six, seven months? You must have had some idea of what she felt for you."

"I discovered she was a clinging personality. And when I found out, I couldn't wait to get away from her. I did not want involvement." His voice sounded strangled, as if he couldn't get the words out, or wouldn't let them come out.

"Did she make you angry?" I asked.

"Wait a minute," he said. Finally, the anger overcame his self-control. He stood and shouted, "Yeah, she made me angry. But I sure as hell didn't kill her." When he became angry, his face reddened.

"Sit down," I demanded. "Maybe you felt like killing her, though. Do you have an alibi for Thursday night?" I asked.

"As a matter of fact I do," he said, calmer now that he thought he'd gotten the better of us. "I was with a woman and I'm sure she'll be glad to swear to that."

"How about for last night?"

"Last night?" He looked stunned. "Why are you asking about that? I was home alone, logged on to the computer. You can check the log-on and log-off times."

"We will," I said. "In the meantime, we'd like to take your prints and a blood sample. Do we have your permission to do that?"

"Take them. You'll find my prints all over Carla's apartment. That's no secret. She couldn't stay away from me. And what's the blood for? DNA? You'll find my DNA all over her."

"Why would we find any DNA evidence?" I asked. "You two broke up months ago."

"We had sex Wednesday night."

Whoa, I thought, then asked, "At whose instigation?"

"I called her. We did it every now and then. So?"

We took Daniels's prints and sent him to the lab to give a blood sample. We gave him the same instructions we gave Quintana.

"Boy," I said, "what did she see in him?"

"Maybe she liked them angry. Maybe she was down to the dregs. Do you think he killed her?" asked Rafael.

"That's a real possibility. He admits to having sex with her Wednesday night, and his alibi will have to be checked out thoroughly. If he felt trapped by her, as he seemed to, he might have killed her. He's got the intelligence to plan the murders and carry them out. But I'd be more likely to pin a murder of passion on him. I can see him overwhelmed with rage and plunging the knife in her again and again—not prolonging it," I said.

"Think of it this way," said Rafael. "What if he planned her murder in a way to throw us off his path?"

"Let's run his prints. He has no record locally, but we'll do a national search. That could explain the care taken to wipe off any prints."

"What about Janice Cantwell?" asked Rafael.

"One at a time."

Bierman had agreed to meet me at a coffee shop near the station. In the meantime, Craig checked through the names in the book at the front desk of Bay's Edge, and he'd call me as soon as he located Bierman's name. Or his alias.

The phone rang at my desk. Rafael answered it for me.

"It's Peter Bledcoe," he told me after engaging hold.

"Tell him I'm not here," I said.

I saw Bierman seated in a booth at the back of the near-empty coffee shop. I sat down across from him. There were few office workers downtown on a Sunday afternoon.

"I've got a lot of questions to ask you," I said after the waitress served our coffee. "You lied about your relationship with Carla Reeves."

"I've got a deadline coming up on *Florida Nights*. God, I wish Carla were here. I need her now. Don't know how I'm going to replace her," he said in answer to my accusation.

"Carla's sister Roberta says you had an ongoing affair with her since she began working for you. The doorman has described a man who looks like you. He said this person was her visitor for years, and he signed in as Ron Bearman. Carla kept a journal. In it she writes about a lover. His name is DonDon. Now deny you were her lover," I said.

I watched his face turn wary, looking at me as if he was deciding what to do.

"I already told you. I don't get involved in my employees' lives. My wife and I, we stick together."

"Who is DonDon?" I asked.

"I can't waste time talking. We've got a deadline to make, and I'm taking over all Carla's accounts until we hire someone to replace her."

"Answer me now, or I'll bring you down to the station," I said. He hadn't moved.

"It'd ruin my reputation," he said.

"I'm not concerned with your reputation. I want to find out who killed Carla Reeves. Did you kill her?"

"No, I didn't kill her," he said. "I loved her. And she loved me."

"Were you lovers?"

"Yes."

"She saw other men while she was seeing you. You were jealous, weren't you?"

"How could I make a claim on her?" he asked me. "I have a wife. I have a reputation. I belong to a church. She knew I couldn't marry her. But we loved each other."

"Did she tell you about meeting other men? Did she tell you she loved them? It's all in her journals," I said.

"No, she didn't tell me she loved them."

"The doorman has told us he saw her longtime visitor go up to her apartment and then leave after a few minutes on Thursday night, the night she was murdered. Did she tell you then that she was in love with another man?" I asked.

"No."

"You were there Thursday night. Did you kill her?"

"I did not kill Carla Reeves. I loved her."

I wanted to believe him. "Are you refusing to talk to us voluntarily? That's not going to look good." I stood. "We'll talk to you again, one way or another." I left him seated at the booth, staring at the window.

I went back to the station to prepare for a reenactment of Carla's last night alive. Then Rafael told me, "I did not receive the list of contents in Carla's stomach. Raja was busy yesterday in the decomposing lab. And today with Janice Cantwell."

"Elton attended Cantwell's autopsy for me. Thank God," I

said. "We can't do the reenactment without more information. We'll have to do it tomorrow night. That's better anyway. It's a weeknight. She was killed on a weeknight." I avoided the reenactment with any excuse available to me.

"Then I will see you tomorrow at seven-thirty," he said.

I hadn't told anyone yet that Janice Cantwell was a former girlfriend of my father's. Nor had I told them my mother knew her, too. I wanted to stay my fear that Bill might be involved, to make certain he wasn't.

At my parents' home, Fran took me out to Bill. She handed me a glass of cold white wine first, one like hers.

He gazed out into the night garden, protected by high oaks with staghorn ferns on the trunks and bromeliads in the branches, and made visible by the light coming from the house. Avocado and mango trees stood on the edges of the property with hibiscus and bougainvillea near the house. I smelled rotting mango on the ground, the last of the season. Avocados hung on branches ready to fall.

"I'll take some avocados home with me," I said. "And mango—do you still have the one you called about?"

"I'll pick some avocado for you. There might be a mango or two in the refrigerator. If there are, I'll put them in the bag."

I sat beside him. "You okay?" I asked.

"Sure," he said brightly. He raised his glass to his lips and drank, not looking at me, still gazing into the garden.

"Bill, talk to me about Jan," I said. I was interrogating my father as a witness, even though he wasn't aware of what I was doing.

"Anything you want to know," he answered. "Well, almost anything." He turned to me with his bad-boy grin.

"What was Jan like?" I asked.

"When she was a young woman, her hair looked like silken gold," he said, turning to face the oak. "Her eyes turned to the color of what she wore—bronze, gold, lioness." He was remembering. "She painted pictures of flowers to sell at the Coconut Grove Art Festival. When she wanted to start a floral design business, I helped. And she made a success of it, I heard."

"Did you keep in touch with her?" I asked.

"Not directly. Men at the club talked about her. Usually they were careful what they said in front of me."

"What did they say?" I asked. If I went too far, he'd get up to pour more Scotch.

"They'd say she was a good designer. And reliable," he answered. Then I waited while he sat, staring. "Every now and then I'd hear she was going out with this man, or another man. Unfortunately, they were often married men. I had hoped for more for her. She got married once, but divorced him in about a year."

"Did you hear anything about her lately?" I asked.

"Lately," he said, his voice sounding firmer, "the gossip about her lessened, and I didn't think about her. Until today."

"Do you have any ideas about who murdered her? Could it have been any of the men she knew?"

"Why would any of those men kill her?" he asked, turning to face me. "Jan didn't threaten men, even the married men. She didn't ask for more than a man could give. I've thought about that. Jan and I didn't talk much anymore. Unless we met at a party or a meeting. She was always special, though." He was quiet.

I knew I'd have to report Jan's relationship with my father, but I didn't burden him with that information yet. I was certain the man I deeply loved had not killed his former girlfriend, but his words reverberated in me—she didn't ask for more than a man could give.

Bill filled a brown grocery bag with hard avocados he'd picked for me and one mango from the refrigerator.

At home I placed the four hard dark-green avocados on the kitchen windowsill to soften gradually. I'd check their ripeness every day not to miss their peak. Standing over the sink I peeled the mango, a color that reminded me of the low setting sun or a rising full moon. My knife was sharp, and after I peeled it, letting the poisonous skin drop into the sink, I washed my hands and then sliced off slabs as I held the slippery, juicy fruit with one hand, and placed the slices in a bowl. I washed and dried my hands and arms again, and I took the bowl of mango and a fork and went onto my patio where I sat and ate in the dark.

Only after I finished did I go over to the answering machine to listen to my phone messages, the red light having faithfully blinked all day. I was waiting for Rafael to call me so we could go to Bay's Edge to check out the activity at the main door.

There were reminders from the laundry and the library. I'd reserved two books, one by P. D. James and the other by James Lee Burke, and I'd taken in my black pantsuit to be cleaned. Rafael hadn't called yet. Peter had.

"What the hell," I thought. I decided to put an end to his calls. He didn't answer. I left a message on his machine.

"Do not ever call me again," I said, carefully enunciating each word. "I do not want to see you again, not here, not at my parents, not in court. Do you understand?" As an afterthought, I said, "Don't bother answering that." My heart felt empty. I loved Peter. If he had called me at that moment, I would have invited him over.

Gilda barked. She was in the patio. How did she get in there? Annoyed that I'd left the screen door open, I went outside and saw her standing by an opening in the screen enclosure around the pool.

"Bad dog," I said, and bent down to inspect the screen. I held her collar and ran my finger over the edge of the screen, hoping I'd be able to press it easily back into its molding. But the screen had not been pushed in by a dog eager to come inside. The screen had been cut. Sliced at the edge of the frame that held that section of screen. Sliced neatly with a sharp instrument for a length of about three feet.

"You're not a bad dog," I said to Gilda, and scratched behind her ears. "You're a good dog for showing me this."

I called the Neighborhood Environment Team, police and planners and city employees placed out in sections of the city. A hands-on approach. When the sergeant who answered found out I too worked for the city, he was open with me.

"Patrol hasn't reported any vandalism on your street. There's two or three reports closer to LeJeune Road, but they have to do with stolen property and broken windows. I'll send a patrol out to look at your screen, and you can talk with him."

"Don't bother," I said. "Who knows how it happened or when. It could have been cut weeks ago and I just noticed it. I'll get it fixed."

"Call if you have any more problems," he said.

"There's one other thing you might want to know about," I said.

"What's that?" I pictured him poised, a pen in his hand held above his page recording calls that night.

"I found a dead kitten in the yard. Or my dog found it," I told him. I didn't go into details. I would if he seemed alarmed.

"Mother cats carry out the runts of the litter, the ones that are going to die anyway," he said. "A dead kitten out in the yard is not unusual."

"That's a relief," I said. I thought to myself: This mother cat wrapped her runt in a cigar box, tied the string, and slipped a flower on top. "Obviously a dead kitten is not related to my cut screen."

"I doubt it," he said.

I opened my refrigerator to get a glass of cold water and, when I saw it, refused to touch the small box wrapped in a plastic bag.

CHAPTER 10

LATER Rafael called to tell me to meet him at the Bay's Edge. It was past nine on a Sunday. I doubted the lobby was as busy as Quintana had described. Craig had looked at the check-in book. The manager had given us permission, which saved us time. We wouldn't have to get a court order.

It was late when we arrived. A long hot day coming to an end. And true to Quintana's word, the lobby was busy.

The doormen, two men in black pants, shoes, and ties and white shirts, worked the front. One took keys and tickets and ran to get a car. The other greeted people and opened car doors as they drove up. They were both about my age, a little older than Rafael. I peered inside the glassed-in area where the doormen waited during quieter periods. There was one swivel stool. Three black-and-white television screens alternated views of the back door, pool, docks, parking lot, side door, and delivery bay, changing every five seconds. No one was keeping an eye on the screens.

I went out to the parking lot beside the building. The south Florida night air almost touched me with darkness. And the moon and its reflection on the water were hidden that night behind clouds. I watched the doormen run back and forth and heard a distant clanking of lines against masts from the apartment building's dock out back. A security guard weighing a good two hundred pounds sat in his golf cart, half hidden behind the wall of the apartment's trash dumpster. I smelled cigarette smoke. A woman pulled up to a parking spot, got out, and walked toward the back door. She wore white shorts, and the security guard watched her walk across the lot. The doorman outside at the time looked in the direction of the back door only when it clicked shut.

"Did you see anything on the monitors?" I asked Rafael, when I returned to the lobby.

"You mean the woman coming in the back door?" he asked. "I saw her head. They've got the camera positioned at the back door so you see the tops of heads. Notice the pool view. Full frontal."

We waited around for a few minutes. The doormen raced back and forth and the elevator door at the side of the lobby dinged to indicate it had opened its doors. People walked out of the elevator. I saw people wearing jeans, shorts, a satin evening dress, and suits, and each went to the doorman, handed him keys, and waited for cars.

"They don't stop for a second," I said.

We had checked the lobby and the book the doormen used for each visitor. We had seen how the security tapes worked.

Or didn't work. Probably Quintana had told the truth about not noticing who had come to see Carla Thursday night.

"That's it for today," I said. "I'm going home."

I set my clock for five-thirty and slept fitfully. My dreams were of my father with Janice Cantwell, and she was nude. The slices under her breasts gaped and leaked. Blood spurted like a fountain from her neck, and her spun-gold hair reached to her feet, streaked with the wet blood. I saw my father reaching for her, and she reached for my father. At that moment, she turned into the kitten. My arms wouldn't move; my mouth wouldn't speak. I woke panting, with my heart pounding, and unsure of where I was. Gilda sensed I was awake and she stood on the floor beside the bed. I walked with her to the cut screen and saw it was the same as I had left it. Back in bed I reached over the edge of the bed and touched her fur and left my hand on her neck as I drifted off to sleep again.

When the alarm rang, I dressed for a run, and as I ran with Gilda at my side I watched the sun clear low clouds. Still too early for the heat to oppress every living thing. I showered, dressed in my classiest and only clean pantsuit with my eggshell blouse, and drove through the streets as early morning traffic steadily increased. I arrived at the station by six-thirty. Before I went to my desk, I dropped off the cigar box coffin to the gang unit.

I made the first pot of coffee for the day. As the brown liquid gurgled down into the container and I looked on, apparently fascinated by the process, Commander entered the unit. She carried the load of paperwork she'd taken home.

"Did you see the papers?" she asked, and dropped the morning paper near my feet. I picked it up to see the paper folded to show Al's story. It had made it as far as the front page of the local section, not all the way to page one, first section. He'd obtained photos of both Carla Reeves and Janice Cantwell. I scanned the story, turning to an inside page to finish. He'd honored my pleas and presented only the known facts and blamed the police for omitting details of the killings, citing the nature of the investigation.

"I've already had calls from the city and county mayors, two commissioners, the head of the tourist bureau, and the chief," she said. "The chief has heard from these same officials, plus more commissioners and irate citizens. Did you see the news last night?"

"No."

"PIO sent out a release, a release that was not sensational. But," she emphasized the word, "the TV news people obviously got hold of the paper's early edition. Public information got lots of late calls, all from television reporters. The chief wants the whole unit on the case. You're to remain lead. But if there's no movement on the case, he wants me to take over. We're having a unit meeting this afternoon. You ready?"

"I'm all dressed up for it."

"Cut the smart-ass bit."

"I'm ready. Anytime. I'll bring everyone up to date," I said.

"I'm calling Quantico," Commander informed me. "I want to know if they've had any reports on similar murders elsewhere. Write up a report on both cases and get the autopsies. We'll fax them up."

"I have to call Cantwell's brother before he leaves Philly," I replied. "Then I'll get everything you want together. And I've got to talk to you about an unusual development."

"Talk to me now."

"Janice Cantwell was my father's girlfriend more than twenty years ago."

Commander didn't say a word. She stared at me, her rich black face impassive. Neither welcoming or cold. When she stared at me with that expression, I felt like I was dangling and a wrong word would drop me into the pit. I operated on gauging the behavior of others. Homicides did that. We had to. And Commander knew that need to gauge behavior only too well.

"There's more," I said, barging ahead, not willing to show my uncertainty in the least. "My mother knew her through charity work and socially. In fact, I met her fairly recently at a Red Cross meeting."

"Do your parents have alibis?"

"They had a dinner party," I answered. "I was there." The unit had slowly come to life as we talked in front of the coffee machine. Those who'd arrived during our conversation listened.

"Who's going to interview them?"

"Someone besides me. Elton?"

"Elton," said Commander to my partner, who had walked up to the coffeepot, his cup still empty, "verify Suze's parents' alibis. She'll fill you in." She turned to go to her office.

I took my cup, finally filled it with what was left of the coffee, and started a new pot.

I told my team about Bill and Fran and Janice Cantwell, then said, "Elton, check out Bill Cannon and Fran Cannon." That's what they were waiting for. Elton, Craig, Rafael, and anyone else in the unit who'd come in early stopped staring at me.

I dialed Philip Cantwell and let his phone ring. And ring. After about three minutes, he answered.

"I'm packing my suitcase. The flight to Miami leaves at eleven. Can't this wait?" he said. He sounded irritated.

"When you arrive in Miami, you'll read how this killer may have murdered another woman in the same way. We think he'll do it again."

"I've already read about it up here," he said. "I'll give you a minute."

"What did she talk about when she called you the day she died?" I said.

"She'd just had an offer from a major florist in Miami to buy her company. For a lot of money. She called to talk about it."

"Who was the prospective buyer?"

"Manuel Flores Company. Her contact was the owner, Jules Manuel. They met a number of years ago when they'd both bid on a big wedding."

Jules Manuel's name appeared in the newspapers frequently as one of Miami's major contributors to the arts.

"Do you think she went out with him the night she died?"

"No. Not him. She would've told me. And Jules, for God's sake, wouldn't have killed her."

"What did she tell you about her date that night?"

"Nothing, really. She was in a dreamy mood. She said if she sold her business, she'd retire." Then he said angrily, "Look what she got. A psychotic bastard." I didn't say anything. "I can't talk anymore about this now," he said. He hung up.

I had to stand up and walk around the unit. I wished I'd brought my apples. All I needed was to chew on something with mouthfulness.

Later in the morning, Commander took over my presentation, doing exactly what she loved to do. Our team stood beside her.

When she permitted us to speak, Elton, Craig, Rafael, and I each shared what we had dug up about the case, even though most already knew we had two homicides with the same MO and a possible third in Homestead.

"From what you've told us," said a female detective, "we've got to be on the lookout for a man with medical knowledge, who owns or has access to a scalpel, who is charming enough to get some smart cookies more than interested, maybe has some scratches on his face and upper body." The chief and Commander looked at each other.

Gradually, the men and women left the unit if they weren't on duty or if their duty called them outside. A few stragglers went to their desks and checked messages or wrote on forms or leaned back in their chairs to look out the window at the expressway and think through their cases. Logical, clear thinking was a requirement. As were intuition and gut feeling. I felt more relaxed, knowing the entire unit would work with us to pool bits of information and seemingly insignificant clues and, with our combined experience and skills, maybe, just maybe, we'd find the killer.

That same afternoon, after I had faxed reports on the two murders, Commander spoke with Quantico. She put me on the phone with Dr. Casey Horowitz, FBI's criminal behaviorist at the Behavioral Science Unit.

"We've had reports of cases not exactly like this one, but similar enough for me to think the killer in both areas may be the same one," he said. "About seven years ago there was a case in Boston where the perp killed the victim after raping her. After death he cut her—on the breasts and neck."

"Are these two cases similar enough to make a link?"

"Yes," he answered. "And I think he could have refined

the technique over the years. Also, like this case there were no fingerprints and the weapon used was a scalpel."

"Were they able to identify the weapon?"

"No. I don't believe they tried. Send us all your ME reports and photos of the wounds, and we'll compare them with the ones Boston sent us," Horowitz said.

"I'll get those materials out to you this afternoon by overnight mail," I said. "What worries me is that even if there's a match, we don't have an identity."

"But then it won't be a local problem." He laughed as he said this. "And we can put out a bulletin. Some witnesses may come forward."

"We've already started looking for witnesses or anyone who may know anything related to the murders," I snapped. "What else?"

"There is more than one type of serial killer. Some are very sloppy and act without much of a plan. The type you have down there, neat and precise, usually has a pattern of injecting himself into the crime scene. This one's probably already done that. You may have seen him, talked with him, interviewed him, and not known who you were dealing with. He'll pass himself off as ordinary and unremarkable," he told me. "Additionally, what you've learned about the method leads me to think this fellow had some medical training. Maybe a doctor or former medical student. You'll find he's from a middle class or upper middle class family."

"Yes. Our ME thinks there's been medical training," I said.

"Naturally," he said, then added, "There are two factors I find fascinating about this case. One is the way he draws out the seduction, dates the women. Very unusual. Apparently he makes these women comfortable enough to have sex with him willingly, if the observations you sent me are reliable." Of course, they're reliable, I thought.

Horowitz continued talking, oblivious to my silence. "He takes the time to gain complete control. In a sense he has prolonged the foreplay. This means, to me," Horowitz said, "he needs more and more stimulation in order to get his sexual gratification. And I think this need for stimulation is related to a second factor. The fact that there are two murders occurring close together, both in time and space, is interesting. I can't quite figure out why, nor why he's gone public by picking prominent women and leaving them in sites where they'd be easily found. Probably he has extended the need for sexual gratification to 'afterplay' by taunting and manipulating the police. Very intelligent. You're going to have a hard time snaring this one."

I had asked Commander to listen to our conversation on her speaker phone. Horowitz assented. She strode to my desk after Horowitz hung up.

"They never give us any information we don't already have," she said. "But the point about taunting the police. That's good. Any evidence he's doing that?"

"I'll put that on my list of things to do," I said. "I'm headed down to Homestead, and I'll get back to you on the police issue." I rose. Commander stood, blocking my way. She had one more thing to say.

"The very fact you haven't solved this murder yet means he's one step ahead of you. He's taunting the police until you solve it."

When I arrived at the Homestead Police Department after a forty-five minute drive down the turnpike, Detective Dominoe was waiting for me in their Homicide unit. He was a short dark man, and his head was completely bald. He wore a mustache covering his upper lip. And his eyes continuously smiled.

When we had the dead case file open in front of us, he said, "When the story of this murder appeared in the paper, a woman named Kitty O'Hara called to say she knew the victim. She said she talked to the victim the day before she was murdered—or the day before we think she was murdered—and the victim had told her she'd found a new boyfriend. The victim was an owner of a rare fruit business. She specialized in star fruit and lychees."

"Were you able to get more specific details about how the man met the victim Valerie Hunt?" I asked.

"O'Hara said that one morning her friend Valerie Hunt called her. During the course of the conversation, Hunt told O'Hara about a man who came up to her at a grocery where she sells some of her fruit. Hunt also told her friend she was going out with him the night of their conversation. That was the last O'Hara heard from Hunt."

"Carla Reeves also dated a man who was not known by any of her friends and family," I said. "But we believe the killer could have been someone she already knew."

"That is true in this case. Hunt was not missed for about ten days because she had a business out of her home and she was the sole proprietor. She hired workers to help when a crop needed harvesting or the trees needed trimming or spraying. Most of the time she did the work herself. O'Hara said growing fruit trees is not labor intensive, until harvesting time, and it wasn't unusual for Hunt to stay at home for days."

"And she could have been murdered by one of her workers," I said.

"Right. We must keep in mind that when the police found

her, she was in bed, nude, and slashed. That is very like the Miami murders."

"Yes, it is. What else?" I asked.

"The killer covered her body with a sheet and left it there. The slashes were on her chest, and there was a small slash in her neck."

"Were there any prints?" I asked.

"The police found many prints. So far none of them lead anywhere. None of them are on file or in the computer. And none matches with any of the day laborers."

"Were you able to get all the laborers?"

"Well," he said, "you know how easy it is for a day laborer to disappear. We got all the prints of the laborers we knew about."

On the drive back to Miami, I felt deep disappointment that the Homestead murder gave us no new clues. Except this one—the killer had killed before, at least once. Somehow or another this case wasn't coming together. There were suspects: Bierman, Simonton. Thank God my father was out of the picture. Simonton was strong enough and had the equipment. The means. And Bierman. I doubted he was strong enough. In Carla's case he had a motive. Was he involved with the other women? Who else? Anybody, I thought. Anybody could have done it. I could tell I was starting to get jumpy.

Rafael came over to me when I walked into the unit. He'd been coordinating activities to give us greater access to each other's information on the murders. Both Craig and Elton had taken calls prompted by the newspaper articles, then checked them out.

"Want to do the reenactment tomorrow night?" I asked. He looked over at me before answering.

"You've had a long few days. Tomorrow is fine with me, or the next day would be okay, too."

"We'll find someone who saw Carla and her date, won't we? Assuming she was killed by her date that night. Now there are two more murders. You know that the Homestead murder is probably related."

Commander saw me talking to Rafael and walked toward us.

"I just got back from Homestead," I told her. "I am almost certain, as certain as I can be without corroborating evidence, that the murder there is related to the Reeves and Cantwell murders. Call up PIO again, and we'll put out another release."

"Go home, Suze," Commander said. "You look awful. Rafael will take care of PIO. This place won't collapse if you take tomorrow morning off. And I have no doubt you'll come back ready to solve these murders." I wished she hadn't laughed as she walked away. She turned back to say, as if she were reminding me work would be here waiting for me, "Dr. Horowitz is calling tomorrow afternoon. You won't miss that, will you?"

 MORNING off. I needed that. Already I felt better. At my desk I dialed the number Harry had left a few hours earlier. I had forgotten to return the first call and didn't look forward to talking with him.

"I'm returning your call," I said.

"Come on, Suze," Harry said. "Try to forgive and forget. I've sold the house and the lawyer says you've got to sign more papers. Lawyers. Always wanting to show us they earn their money."

"Sign more papers?" I said. "You got the house when we divorced."

"I'll bring the papers over to you. No trouble," he said. "Sold the house. Need the money to settle a lawsuit. Some old lady sued. I told her the dogs were trained to bite. Expensive guard dogs, too. They put them to sleep."

"Come by tonight. I'll sign whatever needs to be signed. And then you can be on your way again."

I thought about the days, and they seemed like yesterday, when we'd trained together in the police academy: three-mile runs every day in the heat, never ending push-ups, sweat dripping down my chest and back and neck, my hair wet from the sweat, shooting practice at the range, where noise resounded in my head, and I couldn't hear for those seconds after each shot.

One of the first women on the force, I helped prove we could do it. We were like men, we thought. Harry offered me refuge from the real-man's world where I couldn't permit tenderness, where my femininity became an unfair weapon in the men's eyes. Day after day, after the grueling sessions, I followed him up to his rented room and was grateful for the tenderness he showed me. In his shower we stood under the water together and he'd rub the soapy sea sponge over my body. And he rinsed me by dripping water he squeezed from the sponge. Together we'd fix cold rum and Coke drinks and eat pizza or Chinese food or whatever we could order in. Then he'd begin by kissing. Sometimes starting on my neck, sometimes on my ankles and toes. His sheets stayed rumpled and damp all summer and fall. We married the day after we joined the police force together. The marriage took place at the courthouse downtown, a couple of rookies on the force in attendance. My parents refused to come.

Harry was my love. He had proved he loved me by kissing me and stroking me and making love whenever we could. I wouldn't let my parents' objections come between us. He may not have been good enough for them, but for me, he was perfect. And that lasted more than a year. It lasted until I discovered Harry kissed and stroked and fucked many women other than his wife.

Harry was waiting for me when I arrived home about dark. I pulled up in my drive and saw him sitting in his parked green Mercedes, his legs out the open door, feet on the black macadam, leaning on his thighs. He glanced over at me as I parked my car behind his.

"You're still walking sexy," he said as he came up behind me. Inside Gilda pranced around, happy to see me, darted in to sniff Harry's feet and checked with me to see if he was safe.

"You know him," I said to the dog as I petted her to calm her down. "He's a good guy. Sort of." I let Gilda out the kitchen door to roam in the backyard.

"What a case," I said to Harry. "Liquor's in the cabinet to the right of the sink, Coke's in the refrigerator. Are these the papers?" I pointed to a folder he'd placed on the dining room table. I took out the papers inside, each marked with a red X at the bottom, signifying where I was to sign. Before I fished my pen out of my purse, Harry returned to the table with glasses of cola poured over ice. He carried the bottle of rum.

"May I do the honors?" he said, with his mocking smile.

"Pour," I said, looking down at the papers. He handed me my drink and kept his hand on the glass a moment longer than necessary. We touched. He badly wanted me to sign.

I pulled the glass away and earnestly scanned and signed papers. Harry leaned both arms on the table. The late afternoon sun shone in through the patio doors, gilding the blond hairs on his arms, still the warm dark tan I remembered. I drank the cool drink he'd made and pushed the papers in his direction, finally looking him in the eyes. Blue. Like the sky at three in the afternoon. Harry was a better looking man than Peter. And he was charming. I saw what made me fall in love with Harry, and fall out of love. But Peter? How could I have let that man treat me as badly as he had? Maybe the older one gets, the more desperate one becomes.

"That didn't take long," I said. "You're done."

"Closing's tomorrow. I'm using the money from the sale of the old house for the new house. I'll run over to the next closing and hand them the check I got from the sale. High finance."

"You didn't tell me you were buying a new house," I said. He traced a line around my fingers holding the glass. I set the glass down and put my hands in my lap.

"Why'd you stay single all this time?" he asked.

"Why not," I answered, and got up to go out to the patio. I opened the sliding glass door and Harry followed me.

"I'm getting married," he said. "She wants a house I haven't shared with another woman."

"Harry," I said, "you're not the marrying type. Does she know that?" I'd had just enough rum and Coke to give me a warm feeling. I didn't want to think about the case anymore.

"You're a damn sexy woman," said Harry, handing me my glass.

"Still know how to make a girl feel good," I said, not really jesting. "About time for you to get back to your wife-to-be?"

He moved over to where I stood next to the screen, far enough away from the house to catch a slight breeze. He put his hand on my arm, and when I didn't move he started to kiss my neck. I didn't push him away.

"Harry, no," I said. I wanted at that moment all that I believed he'd given me when we were in the academy together. I wanted to feel his skin against mine and my lips on his. I wanted to feel loved and to love. He stopped.

"Really," I said. "And you're getting married."

"I'll call," he whispered. "Soon." He turned and walked back in the house to pick up the papers on the dining room table and walked out the door.

Like he thought I believed him.

When the door had shut behind him, I walked over to the pool. Gilda had come inside the screen opening and pranced beside me. She knew the routine.

I left the lights off. Though it hadn't turned night yet, the evening darkness hid me. I took off my clothes and jumped into the cool water. Gilda jumped with me. I swam back and forth until I had to stop at the shallow end to catch my breath. I leaned backward to lower my hair into the water and stood straight again until my wet hair lay back, slick on my head. I cupped my hands under my breasts and looked down at them rising above the waterline and for a moment felt: Yes, I can still attract them.

The water soothed me. Gilda jumped out of the pool and barked her way across the patio. She stood at the screen, where it had not been cut, and barked as if she had cornered something out there in the increasing darkness. I lifted myself out of the pool with my arms and edged toward the screen. I was naked.

I heard shuffling in the debris, but that could have been a small animal. A raccoon or squirrel. Then I saw a figure silhouetted against Tina's and Mrs. Hathaway's lighted sliding glass doors. The figure was there for just a second, and as soon as I had spotted it, it disappeared. I ran into my bedroom and grabbed the T-shirt on the bed, pulling it over my head as I slipped out the patio's screen door. The shuffling sound drifted to my left and I began to follow it into the next yard. Gilda still barked. Then I heard a woman's voice call, "Tina, Tina." Mrs.

Hathaway was out again. I turned in the opposite direction to go toward to her, and yanked my T-shirt lower to cover my butt. I began to believe the sound I'd heard was Mrs. Hathaway walking around.

Through the underbrush and her screen, I could see into Tina's house. She had not closed the drapes and she sat facing her television. I took Mrs. Hathaway by the hand and led her once again to her home. This time I didn't speak to her. I felt angry. And worried. Tina was seated alone in the room, the cold glow from the television absorbing her. I returned her mother to her and advised her to check how she was getting out of the house.

The phone was ringing by the time I was in hearing distance of my house. I rushed in to answer it. Peter.

"Don't hang up," he said. "Please."

I said nothing but listened.

"I know you're very busy. I know you've got a big case that's driving you crazy. But don't break up with me." This was the come-on part. Then when he got me, he'd kick me.

"Give me a good reason why I shouldn't," I said.

"I find you extremely attractive. We have good sex. You have a great pool." Then he added, "Face it. You need me."

"There's something you didn't mention," I said, and hung up. I don't know why I expected him to love me.

The message light blinked. I had missed a call while I was outside. Martin. He'd left a phone number where I could reach him and asked me to call. Since in the message he'd said the number wasn't his home number and he wouldn't be there long, I didn't expect Martin to answer. But he did.

"How about going out for a late dinner tonight?" he asked.

"Too tired," I said. "I've got tomorrow morning off, though. Want to go canoeing? Early?"

"I've been waiting for just that," he said.

Early the next morning, Tuesday, I drove down to the Everglades with my Nikon beside me in its bag, which I'd packed with a couple of lenses, one a 125mm zoom. I'd agreed to meet Martin at one of the waterways for our early morning of canoeing.

The image of white herons perched in the bald cypress forest had recurred to me in the past few days over and over, and I wanted to try again to capture it on film—the herons and whatever else came into view. Some of my best photographs were those accidental shots, taken at the moment they appeared. Focusing on the image through the camera viewfinder shut out pictures of dead eyes and blood and murder. I wanted to remind myself there was a universe oblivious to man's insanity. Though not unharmed by it.

At a little after four in the morning, I saw Martin in the distance standing beside a Jeep when my headlights shone on the other four cars already parked beside the road with their canoe racks emptied. This site was popular with canoeists who liked to glide silently deep into the Everglades waterways—natural waterways, not the man-made ones that drained the park. I saw in the headlights that Martin wore jeans and a white T-shirt with an unbuttoned long-sleeved shirt over it. He had had the sense to protect himself from mosquitoes. He raised his hand and smiled as I pulled up beside him. I leaned over and rolled down the passenger window.

"I've already got the canoe in the water," he said. "All you have to do is get your gear and climb aboard."

As soon as I got out of my car, I first sprayed myself with mosquito repellent, even covering my cotton long-sleeved shirt and jeans, despite the unbearably hot and humid air. Martin came over to where I stood. "Want some?" I asked, and held up the can.

"I've already sprayed, but bring it along. We'll need it. Here," he said, reaching into the open window of my car, "let me help you with your gear." He took the water bottle and sack of sandwiches. I carried my camera gear.

"I've got to get back to the station before lunch," I said, as we bent under the low opening in the mangrove, a billowing canopy of dark green leaves, black in the dark morning hour. Underneath the leafy cover, the tree trunks looped and curved down into the two- to three-foot-deep water where they anchored in the bottom. If you didn't know this was a canoe drop-off point, you'd drive past and wonder why all those cars were parked beside the road.

"Don't worry." He smiled when he said this, and in a natural movement he reached over and touched my arm. "I'll get you back in plenty of time. It's early yet."

"The drive back takes about an hour, and I have to stop by the house first," I said.

"Trust me," he said.

At the edge of the opening, Martin leaned over and reached down to grasp the side of the canoe, then slowly swung it parallel to the embankment. I held the flashlight as he climbed in first. He held each side and walked bent over toward the stern to steady the canoe. Then seated solidly, facing the bow with his knees spread to balance the canoe, he motioned for me to climb in. First, I set down my camera gear packed in its waterproof bag, then I entered the canoe just as he had. I seated myself on the cross bench aft of him. Also facing the bow. We were settled. He shoved the canoe away from the bank and paddled, first on the right, then on the left, three strokes on the right, three on the left. While we were still underneath the darkness of the mangroves, I directed the flashlight onto the short, compact, dark fur of an otter as it rolled underwater close to the canoe.

We left the cover of the mangroves and entered open water about the size of my yard. The sun rose by inches, and I saw a flock of egret roosting on mangrove trunks. They were skittish and flew up at any movement we made. They quieted when we were motionless and roosted on trunks a few feet farther away. Slowly, I attached the long lens to the camera body and raised it to see the birds in a morning light still soft and misty. I engaged the motorized shutter and pressed the shutter release. I must have gotten fifteen shots before they all startled upward because of the camera noise.

By eight-thirty, Martin paddled over to a sloping embankment covered in low, sparse weeds. It was bare of mangrove and in the heavy sun the weeds covering it had grown yellow. We had paddled past several alligators, two of which I photographed as they were slipping into the water. None were sleeping in the spot where we chose to rest.

I was ready to stop. The sun had risen to a height that would make any photos shot in its bright light washed out and faded. I also needed to put on more mosquito repellent, drink from my water bottle, and eat. I was about to tell Martin I'd had enough for the day when I saw his eyes. I had thought I couldn't see in them when I first met Martin at my parents' party. That morning they were a deep, almost navy blue.

"Water?" I offered, after I'd taken a swig. He took the bottle from my hand and drank till he emptied the container.

"You don't take water with you when you go out?" I asked.

"I left my jug in the car," he said. "I forgot about all my plans. I stood out there looking for you instead." He looked over at me.

"I spent a good part of my childhood out here. It's like coming back home and filling up on home cooking," I said.

"That's what your dad told me—how you loved the Everglades—trekking out through the saw grass, taking pictures. That's what attracts me to you. You go after what you want—through saw grass and over limestone and in mosquitoes. You're fearless."

"Not always," I said.

"Probably not," he agreed.

"You know a good bit about me from my father," I said. "I only know you're a ranger out here. Tell me some more."

He smiled before he spoke. "Are you ready for this?" he asked. "I've been stationed in most of the national parks. All over the States. I got married right out of college, but in a few years she left me. I don't know where she is now."

"I'm sorry," I said.

"Don't be sorry," he said. "It was hard at first, but after all these years I've gotten over it." He looked at me when he said, "I'm not an exciting man, but there's good things about me. I want you to get to know them."

"I'd like that. I'll have time for a cold drink at Flamingo before I go back to work," I said. "Want to go?"

Martin had flirted with me. He was good-looking, sincere, and eager for life. I was flattered. And the more time I spent with Martin, the more I liked him. Peter was different, I told myself as I listened to Martin and thought about Peter, who was more like an Old World renaissance man. Not jaded exactly, but certainly experienced and loving it. I loved it too.

"How did you become a park ranger?" I asked Martin later as we drank a soda at the Flamingo Marina. "I often thought if I had to do it over, I'd become a naturalist and lose myself in the weeds. Not that I don't lose myself in weeds already. City weeds."

"I studied science in college and then specialized in the environment. First thing I did when I left college was head out to the wilderness. And I've been here ever since. I suppose that's why my wife left me."

"The wilderness or the Everglades?" I asked him. It would be unusual for a national park ranger to be stationed at one site for a long period. Moving around from one national park to another was one of the job's perks.

"The wilderness," he answered. "I've traveled around a lot."

We were seated near the water again, this time on a small dock with a store that had once sold tackle, bait, hooks, lines— all the gear deep- and shallow-water fishermen wanted. Now tourists who drove the length of the main park to the south-western point could find convenience items in the store. Martin and I bought sodas and cheese crackers to slake our hunger. No one else sat at the wooden tables that morning, tables marked by years of exposure to the sun, rain, and wind. Seagulls settled their rotund bodies on a dock or a post, facing into the small wind like sailboats, and flew up each time a boat pulled in or someone walked by. Fishing boats had already left for their day out. One tour boat remained, waiting for its last passengers to board. Its engines provided a low growl as background, and I smelled gasoline and oil instead of salt water and marsh.

"I hope they hurry up and leave," I said, pointing to the waiting boat with my soda.

Martin looked at his watch. "Any minute now, and they'll glide right out of here." He was right, within five minutes. I opened the crackers and offered him one.

"No thanks,"' he said. "I won't eat till lunch. You go ahead."

I did. And I began to reach down to scratch at mosquito bites. The wind had died down a bit, and my repellent had become diluted by my sweat.

"I don't think we can sit out here for much longer," I said.

"While you're finishing your drink, you can tell me about your job. Do you see lots of dead people?"

"Of course. It's not as bad as it sounds, though."

"How did a woman like you end up as a homicide detective? You don't seem like a tough cop."

I laughed. "I myself wonder how I ended up in the murder business. But I came down here to get away from the mess up there. Let's not talk about it." I tried to brush Miami away with my hand. "Tell me how you came to be interested in the natural world."

"My father let me help him with his animals," Martin replied. "He was a veterinarian and we sort of bonded with animals. He showed me they can be lots of fun."

I thought of my childhood, then said, "My father's first years were spent on trips out to the Everglades, before it was even designated a national park. My grandfather loved every inch and knew it almost as much as he loved it. I'll bet my father could tell you stories about his father."

"I'd like that," Martin said.

"Next time we go over there I'll remind him to tell you some of his stories." I didn't mention that despite his early exposure to south Florida's natural environment, Bill Cannon today was partner in one of the higher-priced law firms, representing corporate clients who couldn't care less about the environment.

I slapped another mosquito. "I'm afraid I can't sit here any longer," I said, as I rose to leave. "I've got to go to the station anyway."

Martin drove me back to my car. He stood beside me for a moment before he said, "Let's go out. I mean really out. Like on a date."

"I'd like that," I said.

He turned to walk back to his car. I watched his strong back. Then, facing me and walking backward, and said, "I'll call you and set up the time."

I hadn't photographed the white heron that day, but had accomplished much more.

CHAPTER 12

I FOUND a message from Horowitz at the station that afternoon.

"Any news?" I asked him when I returned his call.

"There is a theory I am developing since you faxed the information to me on the Homestead victim. It may be somewhat overblown, but nevertheless I am bound to discuss it with you." I pictured Horowitz in my mind as a rotund man in a three-piece suit, his vest buttoned, his hair gray, thickly spilling over his head, seated at a desk piled with papers he'd read or needed to read. "Some of the details you sent us point to a highly unusual mind, and therefore highly unusual motives."

"I'd like to hear what you have to say," I told him, "even if you think it's overblown."

"First, before I begin, I think it is imperative that you not overreact. Do you agree?"

"I've been in Homicide too long to overreact to much anymore. Feel free to speak."

"Remember I told you the perpetrator leaves the bodies of his victims where he knows they'll be found quickly—in their homes. These are active, prominent women. And I told you that suggests he is engaging in a kind of after-play."

"Yes, I remember." I saw Rafael watching me, and I knew he was puzzled by my end of the conversation.

"I believe even more strongly now that he is taunting the police."

"Why do you think that is so?" I asked.

"He wipes anything he has touched, yet he leaves fingernail scrapings and hairs caught in blood spread out over the torso. In other words, he deliberately leaves traces of himself. By doing so, he is taunting you. He is playing a game and bets he will win. He bets you can never catch him to link him to the murders through DNA."

"It looks like he's winning," I said. "We have suspects, but they are tied only to the Carla Reeves murder."

"That is not all. He is engaging in a game to the death. I believe he wants to trap you."

"I'm not sure what you're getting at," I said. "Please be more specific."

"When I say you, I don't mean the police in general. I mean you."

"Me? Suze Cannon? You must be joking. I don't think that's a viable theory at all."

"I hope I am joking," he said. "Please be careful."

"Tell me why you say I'm the intended victim." I said. I thought about the kitten in the cigar box, the screen, and the silhouette. My heart pounded. I didn't want the unit to see my fear.

"I think he has you targeted because you are the type of woman he must have to satisfy his fantasies. I think he has killed in Miami before, and he has somehow laid his trap for you. You are a strong, independent woman. Like the other women. I don't know what you look like, but there may be some kind of physical characteristics that are similar to the victims. And I think, as I said before, his fantasies have become more elaborate over time, and they now include the need to taunt the very group that so far has not been able to stop him. The police. And you are a female homicide detective. Is that enough for you?" he said.

"I'll discuss your theory with the appropriate individuals here."

When I placed the phone in its cradle, I shook my head. The three men came over to me and stood around me. They had listened to me.

"Horowitz, FBI whiz, thinks our killer is after me," I said. I looked at each of the men in the eyes, allowing no fear in mine. "What's been found out about Simonton?" I asked to change the focus.

Elton spoke. "We're waiting for transcripts to come from Tampa Bay University, which he says he attended. But I already spoke with the registrar. After some sweet talking, she told me he dropped out of school in the middle of his sophomore year—which confirms what he told us. But what he didn't tell us may be more important."

"Which is?" Craig asked. He'd shaved his head for one of

his son's wrestling tournaments. His glasses emphasized his baldness.

"His declared major was pre-med," Elton said.

"No kidding," I said. "What about his alibis?"

"They check out," said Elton. "The bartender swears he was where he said he was Saturday night and that he left with a woman named Gloria. I tracked her down. I threatened to bust her for prostitution if she didn't talk. She swore Simonton was with her until early Sunday morning. You read the interview transcripts?"

Simonton had been interviewed Monday morning. Elton had immediately tracked down Gloria. In the transcripts Simonton said he'd been with his mother until eleven, a Saturday night routine, and left to go to a call-girl bar, also a Saturday night routine.

"I reviewed them," I said. "Of course, both the bartender and Gloria want his continued business. We need to know if there are corroborating witnesses."

"You know Auntie Blue's, the bar he was at, is a hooker bar, don't you?" Elton asked.

"Come on, Elton. Everybody in the department knows that," I said. "What about scalpels? Did you find any at his warehouse?"

"There are three styles there," Elton told us. "The ones we found were encased in plastic and in velvet-lined boxes."

"Let's take them to Raja and get her opinion on whether any of them could have been used in these murders. Also, search Simonton's apartment."

"Should we read him his rights?"

"Not just yet. But put a watch on him," I said.

———

After our meeting, I called Al at the paper. I expected to find him there.

"How about meeting me for lunch tomorrow?" I said.

"At one," he said. "No later."

"We'll meet at the station and go over to that little Cuban place you like on Flagler."

I didn't call Peter before I left the station. He hadn't called me. I wondered if my anger would hold out.

That night I sat on the dark patio with a glass of cold seltzer, Gilda asleep on the concrete beside me. I thought about the canoe trip and vowed to go into the Everglades more often. Every moment in that space, no matter how mosquito-infested, gave life back to me. I'd forgotten to take in my roll of film to be developed that day, but would drop it off on the way to work the next day. If one of the egret shots turned out, I'd blow it up and give it to my father for his birthday.

Then I heard steps in the underbrush outside my patio. Horowitz's theory. I was sure the steps came from the front of the house, not from Tina's. I sat up and the chair creaked. Gilda raised her head and turned in the direction of the sound before she bounded to the screen and barked her warning bark. I slipped through the sliding glass door from the patio into my bedroom. I opened the drawer of the night table where I kept my gun, then closed it without removing the Glock.

This is silly, I told myself. I walked to the patio light switch and flicked on the inside and outside lights. I saw a black malamute dog standing on the other side of the screen, growling at Gilda, who continued to bark. I hadn't seen the dog in the neighborhood before. It wore a collar studded with iron points.

The dog looked up at me and snarled. The screen alone separated us. I heard a whistle, and the dog stepped back into the darkness.

I was shaking. And ashamed that I was shaking. Gilda sat looking up at me, panting. The malamute would have mauled her as well as me. We had no defense against that power, except for my Glock, and I had left it in the nightstand. Horowitz's warning surfaced. I made the decision that these threats had no relation to the murders. They were unlike anything to do with the murders. But someone wanted to scare me. And someone had.

I was angry. I was frightened. I couldn't stand to be alone. I dialed Peter's number as if my fingers thought for me. There was no answer. I realized I'd never gotten Martin's home number. I dialed my parents' number. No answer. I sat motionless for a moment, my hands still shaking. I had to quiet myself. I didn't want to go outside to the patio. I didn't want to swim laps.

You are overreacting girl, I said to myself. Don't think. Keep busy.

I called Rafael.

"Come over," I said. "I have some ideas about the case. You'll like them."

"Right now?" he asked. "We've been working almost nonstop since Friday morning. Except you. You had a morning off."

"I've got ice cold beer and wine and rum."

"How can I resist such an elegant offer?" he asked.

When he came, I gave him a beer and poured myself wine. We sat on the patio by the pool.

I began. "Horowitz thinks there's a connection between this murder and one that occurred years ago in Boston," I said. "Both he and Raja have said the perp had medical knowledge."

"Right," Rafael said.

"Both of them have said the killer is a charmer. He might be a doctor. Or maybe he attended medical school and didn't finish."

"That might explain why he was cautious about fingerprints. Do they fingerprint in medical schools? What if he committed a crime while he was in medical school and then the police fingerprinted him?" said Rafael.

"That's what I'm getting at," I said. "What if he was fingerprinted in Boston? What if this perp is connected to the unsolved rapes and the murder in Boston?"

"Let's go to Boston," he said.

Rafael and I high-fived each other. We both went inside to retrieve more cold beer and wine. Rafael sat opposite me on the patio, light coming in from the living room onto the left side of his face. His arms were placed on the armrests of the chair and his feet were solidly on the concrete.

I leaned toward him, my forearms resting on my thighs, and said, "What if we find a real Boston connection?"

"We need prints," he said. "We have not found any that would allow us to make that connection."

"We have to keep looking," I said. "He has to slip up at some point. Though from what Horowitz has told us, a slipup by the perp won't be accidental."

Rafael listened to me. I believed his eyes registered understanding. His eyes were black and bright that night.

I said, "We need to be ready to go up as soon as a print is

found. I think we should survey Boston-area med schools to see if any have prints or records from, say, ten to fifteen years ago."

Rafael spoke. "Horowitz said the Boston murder took place seven years ago." He was going to go along with me.

I sat back in my chair and smiled. "Fine, from five to fifteen years," I answered.

"It's worth a try," he said.

He took off his jacket and folded it neatly across the back of his chair. We sat in the dark by the pool where a light breeze cooled us.

Rafael raised his bottle to his mouth and drank. I watched his throat muscles tighten. I turned to gaze at the water. We both sat quiet for a few minutes in the dark.

Then Rafael spoke, breaking the silence. "Your father and mother have an unusual marriage."

"I'll say. When I was a kid I thought all families were like us."

"How old were you when your father had an affair with Janice Cantwell?"

"Sixteen. She wasn't much older. He was old enough to be her father," I told him.

"I have thought quite a bit about that situation," he said. I gripped the arm of my chair. He continued, though I'm sure any homicide detective would have noticed my hands grasping the chair arms. "There was a lot of that kind of behavior in your family?" he asked. I nodded. "Then," he said, "I understand better how you can be such a good homicide." I waited.

"You have learned how to block out feeling." I stared at him. He didn't break my gaze. He waited for a response.

I got up and spoke as I left the patio for the kitchen to refill my wineglass. "Don't you? Don't all good homicides?"

"Oh, yes. That is why we have such a high divorce rate. The trick is to block out feeling at work and allow it to be present in our private lives. I have been wondering if you are able to do that." Again he waited for a response. By the time he finished speaking, I was seated in my patio chair with a full glass of wine.

"As long as I'm a good detective, as long as I can do the job, as long as my partners can count on me to be there for them, it doesn't matter what I do in my personal life," I answered.

"It could matter," he answered. "On the job, for example, think about your reaction when we found that little girl in Overtown. You were out of control."

"This job gets to you every now and then. All of us. Doesn't it ever get to you?" I asked, brushing aside his implication that my experience with my family had anything to do with my life now.

"Sure," he answered. "Forgive me if I am getting too personal."

"No problem," I told him. "You're about to stop, aren't you?"

"I will," he said. "Let me tell you what else I have been thinking, and I will stop."

I sighed. "Get it out of your system." The moon was beginning to rise and its light was still muted. I saw one lamp on at Tina's house in back of my patio.

"I am embarrassed to ask this," he said.

"Then don't."

"Here goes. Have you ever felt what it is like to be loved?"

I was stunned. By his frankness. By his daring to probe.

I answered him with a steady voice. "Rafael, these kinds of things have nothing at all to do with our job. And I don't want to talk about them. *Comprende?*"

He smiled over at me and answered, "*Comprendo.*"

I closed the door after him. My grandfather loved me, I

thought. When I turned from the door, Gilda stood before me, looking up at me, wagging her tail. I bent forward and placed my hands on either side of her head, rubbing behind her ears, and said, "You love me, don't you? You saved me from a big bad dog." I hadn't told Rafael about the malamute.

CHAPTER 13

I WAS at the station early Wednesday morning. Raja returned my call from the previous day.

"You called?" she asked.

"Horowitz told me something yesterday that even he admits is somewhat overblown," I said. "I want to know what you think of it."

"FBI wants in on this," she replied.

"No," I said. "Actually, he was calling on his own, not as FBI. He says he thinks these murders of these particular women point to a darker motive."

"What's that?" she asked.

"This is the laughable part," I said, hoping to cover my concern. "He thinks the killer is actually after the police."

"That's one way of thinking about it," she said. "The other side of that theory is that the perp wants to be caught."

"Specifically, Horowitz says the perp may have targeted me."

She was quiet. I didn't wait long before saying, "Isn't that ridiculous?"

"I don't know if it's ridiculous or not," she said. "I've been thinking about this case and its implications. I've come to theorize he's trying to involve the police as part of his fantasy. He did not move his victims from the site where he murdered them. He could have taken them away to the Everglades, cut them up, and dumped them, only to be found months or years later. Others have done that, as we know."

"So true," I said.

She continued. "And he's murdered two well-known women, both single and both known as independent achievers. Possibly a third. However, each of those women must have had a trait that made her vulnerable to this killer."

"From their profiles, I'd say they were looking for the usual—love. They were lonely," I said. "And they were sexually active. At least both the Miami victims were. This scenario happens all the time, only most women don't get murdered."

"These women were not pickups from a bar," she said. "He got to know them. He got close enough that these independent women let their guards down. He knew their weaknesses."

"And what weaknesses does he target? What did all these women have in common? These are our questions," I said.

"I think he honed in on their neediness. That was their vulnerability," Raja said. She always had an answer. "Now, if the killer must have ever greater challenges to satisfy his fantasy, he's going to push to the edge further and further to get his kicks. The risk of getting caught could be a challenge. And targeting the police is certainly risky. You've got to admit that if he plays with the police and wins, he's going to feel extraordinarily powerful. Power is what he must have."

"But that has nothing to do with me."

"I don't know, Suze," she said. She now had the tone of voice I heard when we went out to dinner and talked about the men in our lives or our parents or the crime rate. "He needs an individual, a person, a woman, to satisfy his sadistic impulses. But if he's targeting police, I'm not sure what Reeves and Cantwell and maybe the Homestead victim have to do with the scenario. I haven't figured that out yet. And maybe we're totally wrong about his motives. Keep an open mind."

"Very comforting," I told her.

"I wish I had a more definite answer."

"Don't discuss this," I told her.

"I won't. However, if you're personally in danger, you've got to ask for help."

"I'm already shaky as it is," I said. "I've gotten to the point where I see threats in shadows. I hear sounds. I'm spooked."

"I would be, too," she said.

"There's no way I'm going to have everybody looking in those shadows for the fading wisps of my spooks. No way," I told her.

"You're funny," she said.

My next caller was Peter. "Suze," he said. "I'm calling about the other night."

"What about it?" I asked him, wondering which night he spoke of.

"I'm trying to make up with you, and you leave nasty messages for me. You won't talk to me. You hang up in my face."

"You don't seem to understand what I'm telling you," I whispered. I didn't want to be overheard throughout the unit.

"This time I'm finished with you. I'm not going to come back for a few fucks and then have you turn away from me. I'm tired of your unwillingness—no, that's not it—your inability to get close to me."

"You'll get over it," he responded. "You'll come back."

"Damn you, Peter." I pushed the OFF button.

After the usual office stuff, Al met me for lunch as I asked him to. We walked three blocks to the *cafetería* on Flagler from the station under umbrellas in a rainy-season downpour.

Inside the storefront Cuban *cafetería*, Al ordered his favorite. *"Arroz con pollo,"* he told the waitress. *"Y tú?"* he said to me.

"Lo mismo," I answered, *"y tostados."* When I turned to Al, I said, "We need more publicity on these murders."

"What do you expect will come from that?"

"Both Raja and Horowitz have said, and this is off the record, that the killer not only wants the feelings of power he gets when he controls and sadistically murders an individual woman, but he's looking for an even greater surge. And that includes taunting the police." I didn't go into details.

"He kills the women. What do you mean, he taunts the cops?" asked Al.

"The theory they've proposed is that by killing these women, the perp is aiming at the ultimate target—the police. In a sense, he's luring us into his milieu. By writing about the murders, keeping them out before the public, he'll feel he's accomplishing part of his ultimate goal—taunting the police."

"And then?" Al asked.

"I hope he'll get sloppy, and we can nab him before he kills again. If, that is, he's killing in order to bring attention to himself. If not, then we've got to try something else." The waitress brought the *tostados* and *arroz con pollo*.

As I crunched on the *tostada*, I told Al, "Horowitz thinks the killer's seduced by the thrill of the chase as well as of the kill."

The *tostados* were fried and crisp and salted the way I like them. A banana species suitable only for cooking, *tostados* are made by cutting cross slices of green *platanos*, which are then fried, pressed to flatten, then fried again.

Our Cuban coffee, thick, sweet caffeine, came in tiny cups. The rain had passed. We walked out of the *cafetería* holding our wet, folded umbrellas. Al walked east toward the *Herald* building on the bay. I walked west and south toward the station on the expressway.

As I walked I called my team members. We arranged to meet at the unit within half an hour. Janice Cantwell hadn't left behind any clues to her killer. Carla Reeves had. We had to concentrate on Carla Reeves. If this was the same killer, she'd lead us to him.

I'd already decided how we'd divide the work among us when we gathered around my desk.

"You're as big as Simonton," I told Elton. "You follow-up with him. Go as far as you can when you question him." Elton smiled.

"I want to go through the evidence thoroughly. Again and again. There must be a clue there. Something to lead us to the killer. Craig, check the evidence again." He nodded and wrote on his notepad.

"I think it's time you and I went through a reenactment," I said to Rafael. "Let's sketch out a plan and get on with it." He and I hunched over our desks and wrote a skeletal outline of Carla's last evening. As we reenacted the steps she'd taken, we'd fill in the outline with specifics.

"I'll start from her office," I said. "You meet me at Carla's apartment as if you and I were going out to dinner. About an hour from now."

Wednesday mid-afternoon Coconut Grove traffic was already heavy. Cars drove through the Grove from downtown heading south. In the other direction, cars drove from the southern end of the county heading to the Beach or the community college or one of the shopping malls up north. And cars headed to the Grove—to go to the movies, to eat, to hang out.

Coconut Grove was a separate community from Miami proper in the early part of the century, and people rode horse-drawn buggies to travel between the city and the outlying community. Grove land here cupped a bay, a haven for sail-boats, and was settled by south Florida pioneers and Bahamian workers.

As the city of Miami grew, it gradually enclosed the Grove. By the middle of the twentieth century, artists found cheap housing in the Grove close to the bay, and sometimes in house-boats on the bay. There were musty bookstores and dark gal-leries and framing shops and a hardware store with its counters open and spilling over with tools and screws and oil and wires and a drugstore where people sat at the counter to order lunch and meet whoever came in that day.

These days, that Grove was gone. Restaurants filled every space not occupied by a shop. The streets were crowded with men and women who wanted to see and be seen, new faces by the day and week. Cars drove through the Grove bumper to bumper. Men and women rode them looking for love. Their radios blared as they drove past the streets and other cars, and they gazed out, searching.

The day I drove to Carla's for the reenactment, traffic was

backed up at the center of the Grove, the three-street traffic light on Main Highway, McFarlane, and Grand. It took four light changes for me to drive through to the other side of the intersection.

Even then the cars moved slowly while drivers and passengers checked out the scene—store windows showing swimsuits, eyeglasses, Indian cotton dresses, Italian men's pants and shirts, a Christian Science Reading Room, books, ice cream, the theater, and storefront restaurants with their tables and chairs set up on the sidewalk, girls in jeans, boys in jeans, men and women dressed in shorts and T-shirts. I picked out the theater patrons. Men in suits and ties and women in dinner dresses. They had arrived early for preperformance dinner.

After passing through the commercial part of the Grove and driving past the Taurus, the tearoom turned bar and steak house on the edge of downtown Grove, I continued down Main Highway, heading toward Carla's apartment building.

Main Highway was a two-lane winding street where ferns, hibiscus, frangipani, and Surinam cherry spilled outward the whole way. Where live oak, ficus trees, and tropical almond trees formed leafy canopies. And where walls and hedges blocked views to estates meandering down to the bay. I drove around these streets when I turned sixteen, with my new driver's license and my father's car, a menace to the then-quiet neighborhood. Today my house was on the other side of town, you could say, on the side of Main Highway closer to U.S. 1 and LeJeune Road. Carla's apartment building was on the bay side of Main Highway.

I pushed Carla's parking-lot card into the slot to open the barrier and drove to her space, situated halfway between the front and back doors. The doormen had told Rafael that Carla usually came in the back way. They watched her on the security video. They were watching me use her key to open the door and walk to the elevator. If they were looking. Had they watched Carla and Roy? Did they see him leave late Thursday night or early Friday morning?

I walked down the empty hallway. Sounds of kitchen utensils and televisions and stereos and words came from behind closed doors, and I could hear the soft padding of my shoes on the carpet. No people to hear or see me. It was as if I were invisible. I used Carla's key to open her door, entered a stifling hot apartment, flicked on the air conditioning, and looked out the floor to ceiling windows where the curtains had been left open. No cat jumped out or rustled the curtains. Roberta had taken the black-and-white cat. She said its name was Nancy. The sun dropped low in the afternoon sky so it shone directly into the room and into my eyes. The sky was turning the subtle hues of afternoon and soon the sunset would turn the sky and clouds into reds and oranges and fire and blue and green. I wished I could sit and watch it. I wondered if Carla had.

Air had begun to come cool from the vent and I stood near so it'd blow over my face and chest. I turned to feel it on my back. Rafael should show up in half an hour.

Carla must've showered with heat such as this waiting for her in the apartment, I thought. I turned on the shower and went to her closet, bypassing the bed where Carla had lain in dried, darkened blood. Clothes, shoes, and handbags crowded Carla's walk-in closet. Some of the clothes still had tags on them, tags identifying them as from her mother's shop. The shoes were tumbled around the floor, and when I opened the top of a shoebox pushed to the back of the closet, I saw fresh tissue around a pair of shoes that had never been worn. I lifted the lids of others underneath that box and several next to it and saw that none of the shoes in boxes had been worn.

Her drawers had new items neatly folded with the pins still in them. All of her drawers in the bedroom were filled with brand-new items. Bras, panties, socks, hose, and bikini bathing suits were strewn in baskets on her dresser. Those were the items she wore. I opened a jewel box behind the baskets and found bracelets, earrings, necklaces—her jewelry—brass, silver, gold, colorful plastic, strung beads. She'd hung a few earrings from hooks on the lid.

By the time I returned to the bathroom, the mirror had fogged. When I opened the cabinet to the left and above the bathroom sink, I recognized the shot taken by the crime photographer. Small bowls and baskets held her lipstick, mascara, pale powders, eye pencils, and eye shadow. Bottles and jars stood beside them. A gentle fragrance wafted from the cabinet. Carla's fragrance.

Peter liked my fragrance, especially after I'd showered. He said it was sexy. And I remembered his fragrance.

The phone rang. I was glad to run away from Carla's bathroom to answer it.

"Detective Cannon," said the voice, "Rafael Hernández is here. Send him up?"

"Yes, send him up," I said.

CHAPTER 14

"D ETECTIVE Susannah Cannon?" Rafael said when I opened the door. "Detective Rafael Hernández reporting for dinner duty." He stood outside the door, not as tall as Elton, but taller than I, dressed in one of his expensive suits and shirts. He didn't have many, I'd noticed, but those he had were the best. My father would have approved, if Rafael had been an upper-class Cuban. Uncharacteristically, that night he wore no tie, and I saw the edge of his chest and some hairs, soft and black and loosely curled.

We'd decided to go to a restaurant (one Rafael had picked out based on the contents of Carla's stomach) and work out a timeline as we looked for witnesses.

"The Homestead and Cantwell murders complicate the case," I said. "We can't assume they are linked until we get the evidence they are. At this moment all men tied to Carla, and only Carla, are our suspects."

"DNA testing takes so damn long—four weeks at least," said Rafael.

The head waiter at the restaurant confirmed he was on duty Thursday night. He didn't remember seating a tall, red-haired woman and her date. I showed him a photograph Patricia Reeves had given me. Carla stood beside a pool, the painted sides making the glittering water appear aqua, as if it were an accessory to highlight Carla's eyes. The sun washed out her other features.

"We have many people come in at dinnertime," he said proudly, sorrowfully. "It's hard to remember each one."

It was one of those restaurants where desserts lay in a glass case beside the front door. Noise bounced off the walls and ceiling and each tap of a glass or touch of a fork on a plate reverberated. People yelled at their companions and music came in through speakers. Every now and then I heard snatches of jazz.

"Why this restaurant?" I asked Rafael after we were seated. He leaned toward me, across our two-person table. He talked in normal tones, and I leaned in close to hear him. We sat like this throughout most of the dinner.

"I finally got Raja to send me a list of the stomach contents. They were not digested, and she identified them easily. During free time over the last couple of days, I called restaurants in the neighborhood and asked them to read their menu from Thursday night. This one had a dish that matched the contents," he said.

"And the list included?" I asked.

Before he answered, our waiter came and asked for our drink order. I showed him the picture of Carla smiling in the sun beside the pool. He didn't remember her.

"How about it?" Rafael said.

"We're working," I said.

"The stomach list included pasta, broccoli, basil, tomato, and oregano," he said. We looked over the menu and found a pasta dish with those ingredients.

"Here it is," I said as I pointed to an item on the menu. "I'll have this," I told the waiter.

The waiter left. I leaned forward again. I told Rafael the details I'd seen in Carla's journals.

"I could see that the woman was deeply depressed," I said. "She actually looked for men who would be certain to leave her. I couldn't say she knew she was doing that, but that's what happened. That's also what her sister told me."

"There is no doubt he will do it again," Rafael commented eventually.

"We have to find the guy first," I said.

"Pray to God," he said. "Bring in a psychic, invoke Santería. You never know what will work."

The waiter brought our dinner, pasta spread out on large, hot ceramic plates. I looked at my watch.

"It's been an hour and a half since Roy Jamison arrived to pick up Carla," I said. "That would put the time at nine thirty. And we've just started to eat." The dinner before me looked good, and then I pictured what Raja had seen in Carla's gut. I couldn't make myself eat it. I reached for the rolls.

Neither of us spoke, but we sat back and looked at each other, the table, and the room full of chattering diners and clanking dinnerware. The waiter saw we'd stopped moving and came over.

"Everything okay?" he asked.

"Everything's fine," I said. When the waiter left I turned to

Rafael. "I answered your questions about my family the other night," I said. "They were not relevant to Janice Cantwell's murder. And they were personal."

"I am sorry if I was too personal," he said.

I ignored him. I wanted to know about his life. I asked, "Tell me how a Cuban boy ended up in Kentucky, one of America's more un-Cuban places."

He smiled simply and openly. "I can tell you that," he said. "My parents couldn't get out of Cuba. It was 1972. Some friends of my parents planned an escape on a fishing boat. I remember the night. *Papi* woke me up, told me to get dressed, told me to kiss *Mami*. She cried." He looked over at me and said, "I cried, too. *Papi* walked with me, stopped at the edge of each house and peered down the streets. The streets were empty. I could tell we were going in the direction of the fishing pier. There was no moon and no other light, and to a scared boy, the night was black. But *Papi* took me fishing on the pier many times and the smell of fish came stronger and stronger as we walked that night. All of a sudden, *Papi* told me to jump. A rough hand grabbed my arm and pulled me over. *Papi* turned around and walked away without a sound. I could see only his shape. The man holding my arm whispered, 'Don't cry. Don't make any noise.' I had just started school."

I hadn't heard, maybe I hadn't listened to, the personal story of someone close to me about escaping from Cuba. I wondered how he managed to live with the memory. I wondered what the memory did to him in the present. Then he spoke again.

"The Coast Guard found the boat in a few days. Remember, this was before the 1996 rule to send back to Cuba anyone found in the water. I don't know how many were in our boat. I was thirsty and hungry. One of the Coast Guard men took papers out of my pocket. The social worker looked for the people named on it. When they could not be found, I became an unaccompanied minor. They placed me with a foster family in Lexington, Kentucky. That family was one of the volunteers with the Catholic church. And there are not many Catholics in Lexington, I can tell you."

He added with a smile, "That is how a Cuban boy ended up in Kentucky."

"A little Cuban boy."

"*Sí*. At first I was miserable. I wanted my parents. I did not speak the language, did not like the food, did not like the rules. I did not have light hair and blue eyes. But the family who took me was kind and devout—and patient. They let me alone. I learned to speak English, with just a little Southern accent."

"And your parents?" I asked.

"Eventually I understood they wanted me to have a better life than the one Castro offered, and they suffered when they sent me away. And I did have a better life.

"But when I turned eighteen, I told my foster parents I wanted to come to Miami to find *Mami* and *Papi*. We used to light a candle at church for my real parents in Cuba, and I have never forgotten my Kentucky family. They gave me money to get started on my search. We did not know that my parents had not gotten out of Cuba yet."

I knew Rafael had a lot more to tell. Living alone in a rooming house with other refugees, attending the junior college where he was pushed toward further education by a professor who recognized his innate talent, the ceaseless search for his parents, the scholarship to St. John's College in Santa Fe, where he began his "great books" studies, the partial semester he attended St. John's, and the sudden return to Miami when his parents finally arrived in the United States.

"You'll tell me more another time," I said. He nodded. "Think they had dessert?" I asked.

"No sign of it in autopsy."

"Damn. Get the check."

I verified the time. "It would be, let's see, two and a half hours from the time they left the apartment. That's about right if we can depend on the man next door and his television news. Or did he go upstairs with her?"

"Come on, witness," Rafael said. "Show up. One person is all we want."

Rafael drove around the block twice till a car pulled away from the curb, leaving a space down the block, away from the front of the building. We entered Carla's apartment building through the back door, which was really a side door and the entrance from the parking lot, at a time that would have put Carla's return after dinner a little after eleven. Mimicking the crime scene, I poured two glasses of wine from a bottle I'd put in the refrigerator, carried them into the living room, and placed them on the table in front of the sofa. I seated myself there, pushed off my shoes with my feet—Carla's shoes had been under the coffee table—as we timed the actions.

I stretched my legs in front of me and leaned my head against the back of the sofa, thinking.

Finally I said, "My take on this is that when she got back to her apartment—with or without her date—she drank more wine. She and whoever killed her sat here drinking, maybe pre-sex. She knew the guy well enough to prepare her bed with new black sheets before she went out—her mother said Carla told her she couldn't talk on the phone because she had to make the bed up with her new sheets—and that's where she expected to end the evening."

"You are assuming she didn't use black sheets all the time."

"Yes. In this scenario. We can check her linen closet to see what her supply looks like. If the sheets are all black or satin or some kind related to sex, then the guy could have been picked up anywhere. And she had a full-blown death wish—as Roberta insinuated."

"And then we start over." Rafael said.

I continued with the first scenario. "Okay. They drank. Pre-sex. Went to the bedroom and undressed. She expected to have a good time. She was drunk—I don't know how she expected any pleasure with that much alcohol."

Rafael smiled. "Go on," he said.

"After things got going, she became aware of pain. She fought to push him off. Hence skin fragments under her finger-nails and broken wrists."

We were both silent for a moment, analyzing the steps to her death.

"That's the scene if she knew the killer."

Rafael added, "And if she didn't, then the guy broke in, raped, cut, and strangled her."

"But if you think about it," I said after stretching my legs some more, "the break-in is not likely. The murder was meticu-lously planned. The bedroom shows no signs of struggle. They were already in bed when he cut her and strangled her. She knew her killer." The sofa felt soft and comfortable. "But we don't."

"However it happened, the perp's a sadist," said Rafael. "That uniquely human characteristic."

I wanted to drink the wine I'd poured, but didn't.

"If the perp's the same as in the Homestead case, then either the break-in or the known-assailant scenario is possible. Blood was all over the scene there, a real struggle. But there are the same pattern of cuts under the breasts and marks on the throat. I'd hate to have attended that autopsy," I said. "The possibility in Homestead is that Valerie Hunt knew her killer and realized what was about to happen before he got her to bed."

Rafael finished for me, "But he refused to stop what he had started and fought her to submission. Or unconsciousness."

I thought about the kind of man who needed to slowly, sadistically murder a woman for his pleasure.

"Let's close up," I said. "We've already checked the door-men. Try to get hold of the security video, the tapes from Thursday," I told Rafael. "We'll look for Carla coming home—with or without someone—even if there's not a clear picture of her companion. At least we'll see the top of his head and find out whether she came home with someone. Meaning the possibility increases that the person who killed her knew her."

Rafael sat close to me. We spoke in low tones.

Part of me wanted to place my hand on the back of his head and draw him to me. The other part said, Don't.

I stood. "Write this up, will you? I have to take care of things at home. Like the dog."

Rafael joked, "We're not going to reenact the rest of the evening?"

"If we did, we'd have to tell Elton the details," I responded.

* * *

That night I finished my swim and shower and was getting ready for bed. The phone rang. I was called to the Peneles house.

No, I said to myself after Commander had brought me up to date with the news of the most recent murder bearing the Carla Reeves MO. This has nothing to do with me. Please don't let it have anything to do with me.

Then I repeated to myself, like a mantra: I am a homicide detective and I will go on the call. The case is mine. I am performing my duty to uphold the law. No one wants to get to me through these poor women. And we will catch the bastard.

One by one, the team met me there.

Ed Peneles traveled all over the world as he researched for his investing business. That night, he came home unexpectedly from Belgium and found his wife, Conchita. He told me how he'd found his wife. He sat slumped in the kitchen. His face was marked from acne scars, and he had a paunch. His thick black hair was interspersed with gray. Whenever he lowered his head, the flesh of his neck folded under it. His nose made a straight path from his eyebrows.

"She was very disappointed I didn't come home more often," he said, eyes red. "I got free today and decided to surprise her." He wiped his eyes with his tissue. "I took a cab from the airport."

"And what did you find?" I asked.

"I unlocked the front door and stepped into the living room. Right away I smelled alcohol. Liquor. I've got a good sense of smell. Our candelabra was on the coffee table. The candles had been burning, but they were out when I saw them. The wicks were black. The wax had dripped. I saw Conchita's shoes on the floor. Her dress was next to them. And I thought, *Ay, Dios mío!* What is happening?"

"And then?"

"I called her name, 'Conchita!' Believe me. I didn't want to walk in on anything." He paused and squeezed his eyes with his thumb and forefinger. "I picked up the dress and shoes, and I called her name again. And I walked toward the back of the house. I said to myself, 'Maybe she's in the office.' We have a room we use for an office."

"Did you see anything unusual at that point?"

"When I got to the bedroom, it was dark in there. Only a light from the hall. I couldn't see the blood then." He stopped talking. His chin folded downward, forming new chins. He shut his eyes. When he started talking again, he raised his head but kept his eyes shut. I could see his lashes then, long and dark and curled.

"The bed was rumpled. The sheets looked bunched and tousled, and I thought she'd taken someone to bed with her. She'd cheated. I could have punched her. I threw the dress and shoes I carried into the closet. Just threw them down. Then I went over to the bed. I was tired and upset and wanted to lie down. I had worked hard all day and made a special trip across the Atlantic to see her for one night. I began to straighten the sheets." He took a deep breath. "The room was dark. I lifted the top sheet up to straighten it out." He opened his eyes. "And she was there."

He sat in a yellow kitchen chair, his legs crossed, his arms across his chest, the muscles in his face tense, his eyes full of bewilderment. The curtains in the window were white, simple. They cupped a window that let in the black night. The countertop held a bread machine, blender, and coffeemaker. The sink was empty. The walls were painted to match the chair. The cabinets were a natural maple. The whole effect of the room was one of warmth and little use.

"Please wait here for a moment, Mr. Peneles," I said. Craig stayed in the room with him. I walked through the crime scene.

Raja was already bent over the woman's crotch, performing the ritual required by the rape kit. Blood had spurted this time onto the wall opposite the dead woman's neck. It dripped across gray carpet from the side of the bed. It flowed around her body. Blood smeared over her torso. The cuts under her breasts gaped. Her black hair spilled over the pillow. Her lips had been bitten until a piece hung down the side of her face. Her dark eyes were open. I leaned over to examine them. Red stippled the whites. I saw that her neck was scratched raw in several places. Raja saw me looking.

"That's probably where she tried to pull his arm off her neck. She clawed herself. This one didn't go easy," Raja said.

"He's berserk," I commented. "When you compare this body to Carla's, you get the impression that he's in a frenzy. He gets more vicious each time."

I checked out the room. The bed took up most of the space. Pillows covered in shades of red, and sometimes the woman's blood, lay on the gray sheets and floor. The few pieces of furniture in the room were of Scandinavian style. On top of the dresser was a wedding photograph of Eduardo and Conchita. She had been a stout woman. She wore her dark hair in loose curls falling to her shoulders. I checked the woman in the photo against the one on the bed. I could see the photo had been retouched to erase her age. She was forty, her husband had said. She looked it.

I opened the drawers to the dresser. Husband and wife shared it. She used the top three drawers for her jewelry, underwear, and nightclothes. He used the bottom three for underwear, socks, and T-shirts. In the walk-in closet I saw the dress and shoes on the floor where Peneles said he'd thrown them. The techs were busy brushing down the bathroom for prints. I looked inside to see a counter lined with a basketful of soap cakes, a box of bath powder, and bottles of lotions. A towel lay folded on the edge of the tub.

Before I returned to the kitchen I went to the bed again. Her battered, torn face amidst the blood told a story. And I couldn't understand it. You can't understand the force that wants to destroy life, wants to destroy hope, wants to instill fear. But you can fight it. And I intended to do that.

Back in the kitchen, I said, "Mr. Peneles, this is horrible for you."

"Who does this kind of thing?" he said. "Who'd want to hurt Conchita this way? I don't understand." He shook his head. "Why?"

"I wish I knew," I said, and continued my questioning. "You work out of town?"

"Yes."

"Your wife worked here in Miami?"

"Yes. I told her to get a live-in maid. She was alone too much. She didn't listen."

"Tell me about your wife's work."

"She was a financial planner at Madson Madson," he said. "I have a seat on the stock exchange. My clients live all over the world. Conchita and I are in the same field. That's how we met—two years ago. We fell in love and got married right away. It was the first time either of us got married." His shoulders began to shake. He put up his hands to cover his sobs. I waited until he settled himself. The next questions were going to be difficult.

"Were you two happy?"

"Very," he said, quiet again. "Very happy. I couldn't wait to come home."

"What about your wife?" I said. "Was she happy also?"

He looked at me, a puzzled expression on his face. "Yes, she was. That's what I don't understand. He must have forced her to bed. And then he murdered her."

"Is it possible she knew him?"

"No."

"And invited him into the house willingly? We've found no signs of forced entry."

Before he answered me, he stared silently, fury welling up in his eyes. "Damn you!" he shouted. "You don't know anything about her. How could you even think such a thing? Ask anyone who knew her. I'll give you names." He stood up and continued to stare down at me. "Damn you to hell." This time he didn't shout. He spoke with such controlled anger that spittle showered down on my face. I stumbled as I stood. When I turned toward the doorway, I saw Rafael standing there.

"Detective Hernández, Mr. Peneles will give you the names of people who knew Mrs. Peneles, where she worked, and how to contact her friends and coworkers."

Peneles put his hands over his face again. "I hate all this," he said. "Why won't time go back another day? I want my wife. I want you people out of here."

"I understand, Mr. Peneles," I heard Rafael say. "It's a great misfortune. But believe me, we want to help you. Do you want to call a family member or a friend to be with you for a while?"

I entered the hallway leading to the master bedroom and bath. I heard a tech call out, "We've got a print."

Later, when I came out of the house, I could see neighbors standing outside the yellow crime-scene tape—onlookers waiting for a glimpse of the gore. They'd see a black body bag wheeled into an ambulance and men and women walking into and out of the house with boxes, bags, briefcases, and toolboxes. I looked slowly at each face to see if I recognized anyone.

It was about three in the morning. Back at the station, Rafael, Elton, Craig, and I moved our chairs close to each other.

"Count on it," said Elton, "she brought the guy home with her. She didn't think Eduardo would come home unannounced."

"The perp is pushing the limits," said Rafael. "He has now left behind a print. Raja said leaving behind a print confirms what she told you—that he is daring us to catch him."

"Or maybe he's driving fast down the middle of the road. This was a frenzy," I said. "She was mutilated, not carefully carved like the others. Was this the same perp? And if so, what's going on in his mind? Why this increase in brutality?"

"A preliminary check of the print with the deceased shows it doesn't match her. The techs will get the husband during the day," Rafael said.

"Why is this taking so long? What about Simonton, Daniels, and Quintana? We've got to check them, too," I said.

"Stay calm. I went through the tapes after the reenactment," said Rafael. "I found Carla. She appeared on the tape at the back door at twenty-two forty-five, according to the clock on the tape. She held someone's hand. I saw a dark jacket sleeve in the corner of the tape. I saw the top of her head."

"You're not even sure it's Carla," I said.

"I am not certain."

CHAPTER 15

THE newspaper had been opened on my desk.

"Al wrote a story about the murders again," Rafael said. "Have you seen the paper?"

"He couldn't have gotten information in about Conchita Peneles," I said. "It happened too late."

"No, not Peneles. But the others."

"Look at this," I said, the layout spread before me, "a feature. Reeves, Cantwell, Hunt. Even a little map. And he's gone into the perp's probable psychology—his need to frustrate the police."

"And he's been gracious enough to tell everyone that he has indeed frustrated the police," said Craig.

"Has Al called about the Peneles murder this morning?" I asked.

"They're handling it at PIO," said Elton.

I looked over at Commander. She was reading the newspaper. I expected her to come roaring out of her office at any minute.

She didn't roar. She sauntered. She carried the newspaper folded under her arm.

"You've read it," she said when she reached us. "I want to know what exactly you're doing to solve this case. I want to know right now. No more delays. I want the next story to be that we've caught the killer—before he kills again." She didn't sound pleased. I told her about Horowitz's linking the killer to Boston and my theory of finding a match with the fingerprint at one of the medical schools.

Commander listened, and when I'd finished, she said, "No more theories. Results. Results. Results. I'm warning you, Suze. I'm taking over if you don't close in on this son of a bitch."

The report from the Florida Department of Law Enforcement computer search had found no matches with the partial from the Peneles scene. And—a big disappointment—there was no match with any of our suspects. They weren't in the clear yet because, I thought, the print might have nothing to do with the murders. The FBI's files and the med school search were our next hopes. I hadn't given up a suspicion that either Simonton or Bierman, or even both, were involved in all the murders. Maybe as accomplices.

Rafael had made the coffee. Craig loped over and picked up his mug to fill. Elton strode up to us with a towel draped over his neck.

"You've been working out," I said to him. "I can smell it."

"I'm taking my shower right after our meeting," he said.

"Want to join me?" I ignored the big guy, though I was curious.

Craig came back carrying his black coffee.

"Where's mine?" I asked him.

"I thought you were one of us." he said. "A real man. You know where the pot is. Get it yourself."

"I've made a list of Massachusetts med schools and high-lighted the ones in the Boston area," I said. "We're looking for an individual who either attended or was kicked out five to fifteen years ago. It'd be a bonus if there were documented criminal charges. Call these schools, see if any keep old records. Commander has given us four hours to make sense of this."

Rafael, bless him, said, "It might work."

Elton looked at his watch. "It's a little early. Let's wait till eight-thirty, when the damn places open up." He got up to talk with a colleague about the previous night's game. The one he'd watched before he had gone to the Peneles murder scene. He wasn't going to be rushed by me or Commander.

We all waited for med school office hours. I called Horowitz and told him, "We've got a print and no matches in Florida. I'd like to send it up. I want you to look for matches nationwide."

"Most certainly," he said. "Modem it up to us. If there are any matches, I'll come up with them."

"We're checking with med schools in the Boston area," I said. Then I reminded him, "You said there was an unsolved murder case there. And like our case down here, that murder pointed to someone with medical training. The MO in Boston was similar to that of our killer down here. If our print and the Boston print match, we'll get closer to identifying the killer. Especially if we can find a link in the medical schools."

"Most of the med schools have photographs of students on file," he told me. "You may identify the killer through their photos."

The med school calls took longer than I expected. I begged Commander for more time. She grudgingly gave it to us. Lunch came and went. We ordered in an extra large pizza and Cokes.

At about three, Horowitz called back. "We have a match on the print," he said. "It was collected from a rape, let's see, twelve years ago in Boston. The offender was never identified or caught, and the case is still open."

"Thank God," I said, probably louder than I intended. The men turned to look at me.

"Don't get too excited," he said. "We only have a match with the print found in Miami at your crime scene and one found in Boston. We do not have the identity of the individual. There is still quite a lot of work to do."

"Yes, yes," I said. "And we are doing everything we can to narrow the search. Thank you for your help." I felt impatient—with the man and with the pace of our discovery.

I leaned over the partition between me and Rafael, Craig, and Elton. "FBI found a print match in Boston. It's an unsolved case and still open. They have no ID. Shit," I finished.

"Harvard has fairly complete files to well over fifteen years ago, all on microfilm," said Rafael. "During our calls, I talked to the dean, who said I could search through the files if I came up to do it myself—and if I got the Boston police to cooperate."

"Go up there," I said. "Call Boston PD."

"They should be happy to cooperate," said Rafael, "if we catch their rapist."

Commander and the chief would cooperate. They'd send Rafael up. I hoped.

I returned calls. Among the stack of messages were ones from Peter and from Bierman. I called Bierman at his office.

"The insinuations about me and Carla Reeves in the newspaper are disgusting," he said. "You have no proof one way or the other that I am the man she had an affair with. You will find my fingerprints in her apartment because we worked there sometimes. Putting out a magazine is labor intensive, and I went to her apartment many times."

"You already admitted you were there," I said. "Previously, in an interview which we have on tape, you said you and Carla loved each other."

"You are disgusting," he said. "I never said that."

"You did, and we have proof. But the point is moot. We have a partial print from a crime scene. Yours does not match. But that does not put you in the clear. You still could have murdered Carla. Did you?"

"Never. Never!" He shouted. He was out of control. I was glad I was not in the room with him. He ended the conversation with me suddenly. "Never," he was saying when the phone went dead.

I visualized for one moment the stacked clouds over the flat landscape of the Everglades. And then the wind moving through the saw grass. And the heat of the sun. I felt the phone vibrate under my hand and heard it ring. I answered.

"Detective Cannon here."

"Hello, my dear." It was Peter. Why, I asked myself, did he keep calling me? Did he count on me giving in again? Oh, Lord, I hoped I wouldn't. "You are under tremendous pressure right now. I know all about it."

"You've been reading the newspaper," I said. "You're usually not interested in my activities."

"Maybe I was more interested than you knew," he said.

"I think your only interest is in controlling me," I said. "Why do you keep calling me when you know I don't want you to, especially at work."

"I thought I would help you with your work. Solve one of your cases for you. One of your bloodier cases. The one I've been reading about in the papers. The one your little friend Al Miranda writes about. Wouldn't you like some help?"

"Not from you. Leave me alone." I hung up. When I could think again, I saw Commander looking over at me. She came my way.

"Boyfriend troubles?" she asked.

"How can you tell?"

"I've had a few myself," she said. "Keep strong. Don't let him sweet talk you back. You're doing fine without him." She knew the gossip about me and Peter.

"I'm trying," I said. "Trying real hard. But he wasn't exactly sweet talking. It was more like a veiled threat."

"That kind will try anything. You be strong." She walked away. I smiled, then I thought about what I'd said. Veiled threat.

I had to see Peter again. I had to know how veiled his threats were. I thought about the kitten, the sliced screen, and the malamute.

I turned my back to block Commander's view of me at the phone and dialed Peter's number. He answered immediately.

"I've changed my mind," I said. "Meet me at the Taurus. I need to see you."

Funny. As soon as I showed a need for him, he pulled away to leave me dangling on his thread.

"I'll get there as soon as I can. I'm finishing up on a project that can't wait. It won't be long."

I passed through the commercial part of Coconut Grove, and on the far edge of the congested streets, I came to the Taurus. I parked in front under an overhanging tropical almond tree. I was glad this wasn't a Friday night, which could be rowdy and rambunctious. I sat at the dark wood bar in the room off to the side of the restaurant and ordered a Chivas Regal, rocks. My father's favorite. As I waited for Peter, I thought of him as an arrogant and cold man. I thought such a man might be capable of killing a kitten to frighten me. I thought of the kitten in the cigar box. Of the screen cut by a sharp instrument. I kept turning toward the door behind me, waiting for Peter to show up. I hoped I'd see him first. A man seated at a table on the other side of the room came to sit beside me. I would have been flattered on another night. But not that night.

"Lonely?" the man asked my reflection in the mirror facing us. I ignored him for a while but he kept repeating the word "lonely" as if I hadn't heard.

Finally, to keep him quiet, I answered to the mirror, "No. I'm waiting for a friend."

"How about I keep you company while you're waiting?

You shouldn't be alone in a place like this. Being blond and all."

"I'm not blond." I hoped my tone sounded unfriendly. But I watched in the mirror as he turned toward me to look at my hair, then back to the mirror.

"You're blond," he said. "And mighty pretty."

"See this?" I said to his ear. I'd reached into my jacket, taken out my wallet, and flipped it open to show my police ID. "Undercover. Get lost."

Peter finally arrived. Before I saw him, he kissed the back of my neck. I felt him. I smelled his fragrance, as I remembered it. I forced myself to think of the malamute.

"You look positively frightened. Sorry." Peter actually sounded concerned. He looked down at his watch. "Don't be mad, but I've got to leave in less than an hour."

"Do you know how weird you are?" I asked.

He laughed. "I'm weird all right. But you like that, don't you?"

"I don't like dead kittens left in my yard for Gilda to find," I said. The more I thought about it, the more I was convinced he had pulled those tricks on me. He wanted to frighten me.

"Kitten?" he asked. "I don't know about any kittens, dead or alive. What are you talking about?"

"I'm talking about you," I said. "Actually I think you're dangerous. I don't know how dangerous, but I intend to find out."

"Talk about weird," he said. "I think you've gone too far in weirdness." He sat on the stool next to me. He turned to me, one hand on my seat back, one on the counter in front of me. The background music, deep basses and rocking rhythm, pulsed through me.

"You get like this, Susannah. The case is getting to you. You always get over it."

I reminded myself he was setting me up for another knockdown.

"You are sick," I said. "You are perfectly capable of killing a little creature to scare me. I wouldn't be surprised if you were equally capable of killing larger creatures. Didn't you say you were in pre-med before you went to law school?"

"This is going too far," he said. "I'm leaving. When you've settled down, call me."

"I think we've already gone through this scene several times," I said to his back.

I sat at the bar alone. The man on the other side of the room had left. I drained the glass of Scotch, ice cubes knocking into my nose. I had picked up my photos from the Everglades canoe trip during lunchtime earlier that day. Though I felt drained from the encounter with Peter, I wanted to go home to look through them.

I left my empty glass on the counter and stopped at the Grove grocery before heading home.

In my kitchen, before I opened the container of take-out tuna salad and pita bread, I leafed through the photos. I saw the Everglades morning through the lens of my Nikon: white sunlight on the birds and blue black water, a deep sky with white clouds, the morning mist softening the edges of curving mangrove trunks and roosting birds and bent saw grass. I discovered I had accidentally included Martin in the last frame. It was one of the shots I'd taken of the great egrets in flight. I thought it'd be a good idea to get it copied, when I had the time. It wasn't a great photo, but it was a memento of our first date. I could give him that.

I sat on the back stoop eating from the Styrofoam container while Gilda ran around in the backyard. I couldn't eat. I imagined Peter killing the kitten. I closed the container and in the kitchen poured myself a glass of cold water.

CHAPTER 16

I GRABBED the envelopes with the Everglades photos and stuffed them in my purse early Friday morning. I called Al from the car.

I told him, "FBI matched the print with a wanted rapist in Boston."

"Do they have suspects?" he asked, sounding like I'd just awakened him.

"They had a description from the victim," I said, "but after they got the description, no arrests. The offender disappeared. And it's a twelve-year-old case. There's also the rape and murder in the same area. That one happened seven years ago, and the MO is similar to ours, unsolved."

"How is this a good lead? All you know is he's been to Boston," Al said.

"I'm sending Rafael up to Boston. He's going early today

before the med school offices close at five. We expect to find links to the prints and the crime. And a name." I hoped.

"You're searching for a photo in old medical school records."

"Trust me," I said, irritated. "The perp has medical knowledge. He probably has some medical training. We're looking into old records at Boston med schools because that's where the matching print is from and where the rapes and murder occurred. If we're lucky, we'll find med school records, a photo, or other leads. You know, his background, his application form, his family."

I sensed that Al had sat up by the change in his tone of voice. "Do you think Rafael would mind some company?"

"The press following along on a manhunt? I'm not even sure the department will send Rafael up to Boston," I told him.

"This is a big story. You know I'll go whether it's with Rafael or on my own. You'll be better served if Rafael and I go together," he said.

"And you'll get an inside story."

"True," he said. "I'll be at the station in an hour.

Except for Commander, I was the first one in. She walked over to me as I filled my mug with the coffee she'd already made. "What's this I hear about sending Rafael to Boston?" she said, before I'd taken my first sip.

I explained it all again. "I'll stay to coordinate with the rest of the department. If we get any ID, I want to cover this city with police. We have a good chance to close this case."

"You have a good chance to mess up," she told me.

"Look," I said, "it's one man for one day. It's worth the risk. All of us back here will continue to work on other aspects of the case. No time will be wasted."

She stared hard at me for a second and said, "One day." And she turned to go to another desk.

I spoke again before she had stepped too far from me to hear. "Al wants to go along with Rafael." I waited for a reaction. She hadn't turned around again. "He's going to go whether we allow him to accompany Rafael or not. I think it'll work out okay." I held my breath.

She turned slowly and stared at me again. "Are you crazy?"

"If we sanction his trip to Boston with Rafael, the reporting will be more evenhanded," I said. I tried to sound firm and decisive.

"One thing's for sure," she said, "we can't stop him from going. But that's as far as I'll go." I didn't intend to tell Al that Commander was furious, because that was nothing new.

Rafael walked into the unit carrying an overnight bag. He'd already made reservations. He never expected to be turned down. "The reservations are for nine," he said. "Let's go."

"Al's going up to Boston. He wants to cover your search," I said.

"What?" he said, his eyes wide, showing disbelief. "Oh, great. Some reporter following me, as if I do not have enough to do already. I suppose he will want to be in the same hotel, eat meals with me, same flight."

"You and Al work that out," I said. "He's on his way."

Al walked in. I looked up to see Commander watching him as he stood by our desks. "Something wrong?" he asked.

"No," said Rafael. "We leave now."

"Right on," said Al. "I've got my backpack in the car. And my notebook computer."

"I'll fax up whatever you need," I said to Rafael.

"How did he know about this?" he whispered. Al had run down to get his backpack and computer.

"Excuse me," I said as coolly as I could. "I updated Al on the print on the way in this morning. He informed me he was going, like it or not. Now, you can either let him come with you and like it. Or you can refuse to cooperate and find out you sure won't like it," I said in low tones.

I drove Al and Rafael to the airport in time for the flight, the first one out. Neither had luggage to check. Al slung his backpack over his shoulder. Rafael had his own bag and a nylon briefcase.

Then he spoke to me, not looking at Al. "Do I have to tell him it's off the record every time I don't want him to report something?"

"Don't ask me—ask him," I said.

They walked away from me through the terminal's glass doors, the two men side by side. I couldn't hear what they said to each other.

Elton called me at the unit to say he was interviewing Conchita Peneles's friends and coworkers. I found a message from Fran. She wanted me to call her, something about Bill. No call or message from Peter. Had I frightened him away? Or was he feeling guilty?

Because I had dropped Rafael and Al at the airport and hadn't dug into my work yet, I decided to return Fran's call.

"Bill is depressed," she told me. "Ever since you told him about Jan. And you know her brother called here, don't you? After Elton Hall interviewed Bill to get his alibi and complete all that paperwork."

"No, I didn't know," I said. "We haven't talked with Cantwell since he left Philly. We haven't been able to find him."

"Bill kept telling him, 'I loved her, she loved me, I took care of her.' He finally said, 'She broke up with me, you know. I only wanted the best for her and tried to give it to her.' He sits on the back patio and stares out into the dark. And he drinks till he falls asleep. Come over. He needs your company. You're his favorite person in the world, you know."

"Isn't he his favorite person?" She didn't answer me. "Yes, I'll come. But I'm going to find out what's going on with Philip Cantwell first."

"Thanks, Susannah, I've always been able to count on you."

Commander turned to look at me. She came over. "Suze, you're not going to be able to handle this case, are you?" Commander said when she stood next to me.

"Why are you saying this?"

"You've got too many family and boyfriend problems," she said. She'd overheard my conversation with my mother. I was making too many personal calls.

"Would you say the same thing if you heard a man talking to his wife or his mother? I doubt it. It's perfectly acceptable for a man to have a life. But a woman? No way."

The corners of her mouth turned up slightly. "The lady's got some spunk, after all," she said. "Praise be."

"I hope to God I do," I said. "I'm going to crack this case. I'm going to eat it, sleep it, drive it, even make love with it. Even if it kills me."

"Honey," she said, "why do you think I got married three times and I'm still single? You've got to be a little crazy to do this job. And every now and then that crazy part pops out."

Commander sat down beside me. We went over the notes my team and I had gathered on the case.

"Okay," she said. "I fully understand why Rafael had to go all the way to Boston to check old school records against the print we found. But tell me, has anyone bothered to check the hospitals around here? If the perp has medical knowledge, he's probably employed in the medical field. *Around here*. That means you're about to begin checking area hospitals."

"Right," I replied. "I'm on the way." She shook her head as I grabbed my shoulder bag, pulled out the package of photos, dropped them on Rafael's desk, and left the unit.

There were several hospitals near the dwellings of Carla, Janice, and Conchita. I didn't figure Valerie Hunt into the equation. Her house had been far south in Homestead. The first three hospitals I went to wouldn't give me access to employee records without a court order. The commander contacted the DA, and we would get the order the following week.

Miami Medical Hospital, a public hospital near downtown, employed thousands in numerous categories, ranging from the woman who mopped floors to a doctor in charge of a department. I was lucky. The former Homicide receptionist had moved on to become manager of the hospital's human resources department. Even though she, too, insisted the police had to go through legal channels to check the prints, she shut her office door while I scanned lists of employees that she'd handed me. I searched for surgeons and surgical nurses. I spent all day at the hospital while the department manager Xeroxed lists of names.

Supper at my parents' home, I decided, would take care of two tasks. It would provide me with calories for energy to keep working. It would nurture my father. I talked to Rafael while I drove from the medical center to Coral Gables. Our best hope for identifying the perp would come from files in Boston.

Rafael was driving out of the med school parking garage when I reached him. "We looked through the cold case file at the station," he said. "Boston cooperated. The murder and rapes have nagged them for years. I talked to the detective who was on the first rape case."

I drove past the Coral Gables Biltmore Hotel and its golf course. "I'm driving past the Biltmore as we speak."

"And I just pulled into the hotel in Boston. It is cool up here and the leaves are beginning to change."

"Bring home some leaves," I said.

"I saw the crime techs' reports," Rafael said. "They got prints from the rape victim's neck. The perp strangled her to unconsciousness and then he raped her. She regained consciousness, struggled, and screamed. He ran away. The victim said her attacker was a fellow med student named Dwight Arnold. They were alone in a hallway late one night. He was never arrested because he disappeared, never showed up for class again. This happened twelve years ago."

"Did you find information on the rape-murder that occurred seven years ago?" I asked.

"I examined that file also. They found no usable prints, but there was semen in the vagina. There is a sample in their crime lab here. The cuts on the woman were similar to our murder victims, but there was a difference. They were surgically precise but more extensive than the cuts on the Miami victims."

"How so?"

"The throat was cut, as if by a surgeon. But the puncture of the jugulars alone did not occur."

"If we have the same perp," I said, "it sounds like he's refined his technique. Horowitz, and I think Raja, said that would happen. What have you found out about the perp's background?"

"The police checked out the parents. The mother. The father was deceased. The mother denied having seen the suspect after the rape. She said she would call if she did. That is all the information on the perp they have in the files."

"Have you located the victim?"

"No. The victim refused to talk to the police after the initial charge, which was dropped. She said she couldn't take time from her studies."

"Can you locate her now?"

"We're following up on that. She graduated from med school and went to a residency in North Carolina. We'll have to wait till Monday to call the Duke offices to find out where she went after residency."

"What about the mother? Have you located her?" I asked. "Any photos?"

"It seems that someone cleaned out the police file. No photos. But we found the mother's phone number. We finished at the med school before the offices closed. Coincidentally, the microfilmed file does not have a photo of the suspect. We found the mother's phone number on his application also. Same number. We'll try to locate the mother. If we get a photo from her, I will return to Miami tomorrow night. I already booked a return. I can go back up to Boston on Monday if necessary."

"We're checking local hospitals," I said, "in case the perp's actually working in the medical field. I have been building lists of surgeons and surgical nurses. Very slow work. Raja's examining Simonton's scalpels. She'll give us an opinion whether any of those types could have been used on the victims."

I heard the crunching sound of my tires rolling over gravel. We ended our conversation as I parked in my parents' driveway.

Rafael said, "Al is not as much of a pain as I expected. I am surprised, but he is helping me out. Two heads and four hands."

CHAPTER 17

T HE deep green and fuchsia of the plants and the yellow cast by the inside lights enlivened the appearance of my parents' house. Bill stood behind the screen door to wait for me. I presumed he'd been there since my tires crunched the gravel. The house hadn't been air-conditioned all day. Heat and heaviness and stillness filled the space.

"Turn on the air. It's sweltering in here. Doesn't it bother you?"

"I hadn't noticed," Bill said as he followed me into the house. "Your mother has the air on in the studio, and I didn't fool with it in here."

I hadn't sat in the living room for a while. I usually headed straight to the kitchen and dining room from the front door. Or I joined a group of people standing around with drinks in their hands. Sitting then in the living room, I remembered Fran worrying over swatches of cloth and tile samples for this room and the transformation that had come when her colors were in place. There were two plump chairs covered in chintz patterned with an array of tropical fruits—star fruit, mango, kumquat, loquat, banana—all on a sand-colored background and still vibrant after all these years. A rattan sofa with dark green cushions separated the chairs. A low rattan table was placed in front of the arrangement. My mother collected conch shells, driftwood, limestone weathered on the beach, and colored glass ground to a rough finish with edges rounded by pounding waves. These she placed on the mantel. One piece of her sculpture, a figure of a nude male lying on his side, took its place beside the fireplace. I don't remember who modeled for it. Bill and I didn't look at each other but through the expanse of window beside the fireplace into the back garden.

"How about a glass of cold wine for your overworked daughter," I said to Bill. "What are you drinking?"

"Scotch and soda. Smooth, tall, cool. Perfect for this time of year," he said. His blue eyes brightened.

"Something smells good," I said. "Fran in the kitchen?"

"No. She's in the studio. Dinner's on the stove. She said we can eat any time we want," he said. "I called that young man and asked him to join us. Jimmy and Carol might come, too. You know how your mother is. Once she gets started, there's no interrupting her. But we'll have fun anyway."

Jimmy and Carol rang the bell. I was glad to see people in the house. "Your mother's working?" asked Carol, as she kissed my cheek. Bill poured drinks for the couple.

"She's getting ready for a show in Tampa," I said. The doorbell rang.

"You go answer it," Bill said. "It's your dinner companion."

Martin greeted me at the door with a kiss on my cheek, just as Carol had.

"So we meet again," I said. "I'm glad you could make it tonight. I hoped we could do something this weekend, but I'm going to be extremely busy."

"Too bad. I was planning to call you so we could go out on our real date," he said. "Unfortunately, you won't be available. Is it work?"

We talked as we walked back toward the kitchen. I heard Bill, Jimmy, and Carol talking. Occasionally a burst of laughter punctuated their conversation.

"Yes, it's work. You know, I don't have your home phone number," I said. "I wanted to call you the other night. I thought you could come over to keep me company."

He smiled. "I would have enjoyed that," he said. "I'll be sure to give you my number tonight. I don't want to miss an opportunity like that in the future."

We all stood around in the kitchen. The air conditioner finally began to cool off the house. The meal was informal, a last-minute gathering of friends. In the kitchen we ladled out green beans and scooped up baked dolphin and pinched off pieces of French bread. And we talked.

We placed our plates on the table. Fran had set the table this time with a sienna red tablecloth and deep blue napkins. Bill lit candles. He brought out two bottles of cold white wine and cans of Coke for Martin.

We ate dinner and drank the wine and Coke. I looked at my father sitting across the sienna tablecloth. He picked up his wineglass with delicate fingers, the back of his pale hand marked with brown spots and a few dark hairs. When he didn't smile or smirk, his skin dragged down at the corners of his mouth. Dark circles under his eyes dominated the face I'd touched and kissed and gazed at over the years. His body that I thought of as lean and youthful a few minutes earlier looked old. I knew only the part of him he allowed me to know. I turned away from his visage to look into the living room. I saw colors and life and the past in there.

Martin leaned over to whisper "You look like you've gone away from us."

"I'm thinking about the case," I said. "Sorry."

"I don't know what you're working on," he said. "Whatever it is, you are consumed by it. Will you have anything left for me?"

"You'll have to be patient," I said. "We're about to crack this case. After that, I'll have a great deal of time for you. And more."

We smiled at each other.

Eventually I shooed all the guests out. I was ready to go home. Eager to go home to prepare myself for the next day. I was sure by then we'd nab the perp. Jimmy and Carol and Martin had left the house. Bill and I were alone. I helped him stack the dishes in the dishwasher. We packed plastic containers with leftovers. He drank all the wine from every glass before I washed them.

We walked out back and sat on the open-air patio. We talked about the plants and the rainy season and how it had affected the avocado crop. Before I too left the now quiet house, I said to him, "Are you going to be okay?"

"I always am," he said with his smirk.

"Don't get depressed over Jan Cantwell and what her brother says. When you start to feel bad about her, I want you to remember that Fran and I love you." It was hard for me to say "I love you" without putting in Fran as a buffer.

At that, he said in a steady, sure voice, "You love me, Susannah. That's all I know. Your mother gave me you. That's the best thing she ever gave me."

As soon as I entered my house that night, I sensed a change. Gilda had scraped at the glass door with her paws, leaving tracks of her nervousness. She ran between me and the patio door when I came into the house. My Glock in my hand, I flicked on the patio lights and the pool lights from the switch on the wall beside the door. The water slapped idly against the sides, as it did when I jumped in. Its color, usually made to appear aqua from the paint on the sides of the pool, had turned a watery red. I opened the glass door and stepped onto my patio, checking all corners for any movement. Nothing. I moved closer to the pool and saw the dark form on the bottom, the form of an animal. Standing there, alert to any sound or movement, I dialed 911 on my cell phone. I identified myself. They knew not to turn on the siren. In minutes, flashlights appeared around the side of the house. They shone into the screened patio and onto the sliced area. It had been pushed in wide enough for a human to come through it.

Two cops immediately went inside my house to search for intruders. Gilda stood beside me, her body shivering in excitement. Maybe fear.

"There's an animal on the bottom," I said to the cop standing beside me. He shone his light down there. "Get a diver out here. We've got to retrieve it, whatever it is," I said. I heard him talk on his cell phone, requesting a diver. "Don't touch anything," I reminded them, as if they needed reminding. "Fingerprints." I called Homicide on my phone. "We need crime techs," I said, and gave my address. I wanted to catch Peter. I wanted to get his prints. I wanted proof he'd done this. I wanted to vomit the dolphin and green beans and bread and wine. I gagged.

Tina had walked through our backyards when she saw policemen on the patio. I wouldn't let her inside and, after I briefly explained the situation, I asked her to stay away until the area had been cleaned. She left without saying a word to me.

Late that night, after the diver had left, after the crime techs had gone, after the dead dog had been carted away, I sat inside. I closed all the curtains and doors and windows. I turned up the air conditioning. I did not want to see the bloody water. Nor did I want to smell it. I didn't even want a drink. I wanted numbness. Sweet numbness.

Blood had dripped over the side of the pool. The blood there indicated the dog had allowed the person who killed it to get close. When the divers had brought up the malamute, it still wore its studded collar. The slash to its throat had been above the collar at the jugular. The dog bled profusely into the water, and when it died it either fell or was pushed into the pool. Whoever had done it had entered the screened area through the opening made where the screen had been sliced. The opening gaped. I needed to call a pool cleaning service the next day.

I woke at four in the morning. I went to the kitchen, flicking on the lights. I was still cocooned by air-conditioning and drapery. I didn't want to take Gilda outside until there was light in the sky.

By six, I drove down U.S. 1. The road was nearly empty on a Saturday morning.

During our conversation the previous evening, before my father's dinner party, before I found the dog in my pool, Rafael had told me that Al planned to have a story of the Boston search in that morning's paper. The story would help me forget the dog for a while. I walked a block from the station to the Miami-Dade County building to buy a paper. During the weekdays, I had often gone to the mezzanine food-court level of the fifteen-story building to buy a second breakfast. I heard the hum of a MetroRail train as it arrived on its track above the street level. Weekdays, the trains came one after the other. Then they emptied scores of men and women, who all seemed to be hurrying. I liked to watch these people riding the long, crowded escalator connecting to the street level.

The *Herald* had papers in its wire stands out on the street. I read the paper on the walk back to the station. There was nothing in it about the Boston trip. Al hadn't made the deadline. I was sorry. I had hoped his story would put more pressure on the killer. And I had hoped more pressure would force him to make a mistake.

Commander called me into her office. "What's this I hear about a dead dog in your pool?" she asked.

"It's true," I said.

"Do you think it's the perp?"

"No," I said. I didn't want Peter to be the perp. "This is not the first incident I've had at my house. They have all come since Peter, my boyfriend, and I broke up. I think he's trying to scare me back to him."

"Good God," she said. "Is he threatening you? Do you want a restraining order?"

"I don't have the proof," I said. "As soon as we get the results back from the lab, I'm sure I'll have something to tie him to the death of that dog. I'll pull him in. I'll arrest him. I'll make him pay."

"You sound like a mad bitch. And I don't blame you," she said. "I'll do everything I can to support you in this. You don't have to put up with that kind of abuse, you know. Not a bit."

"Unfortunately," I said, "I've allowed myself to be Peter's victim. He doesn't hit or that kind of thing. He completely undermines me psychologically. I'm pulling out of the relationship. His response is to keep chipping away, to ratchet up the intensity, to make me need to crawl back to him." I told her this, and I cringed inside. I'd revealed too much.

"Abusers do that," she said. "When you refuse to play their sick game anymore, they try to make you cower. After all, that's what you've always done."

"Is this from one of those cop psychology courses?" I asked. "Or from personal experience?"

"I don't think I'll tell you how I know that," she said. "Bring me up to date on the case. Start with your search at the hospitals."

"My opinion is that looking for the perp at the hospitals could take us years. We have to wait for the court order. That'll take forever."

"You never know where the hospital search will lead," she said. "You might find useful clues."

"I've been making a list of surgeons and surgical nurses who live in the south part of the city. That's where all the murders have occurred. If this Boston search turns up nothing usable, we'll interview individuals on that list."

"You can eliminate the women right off," she said. "They wouldn't deposit semen in the vaginas. When's Rafael coming back?"

"Tonight," I said. "If he can't find leads this trip, he'll go back Monday."

"We'll talk about that when and if he hasn't got the goods," she said. "But he better come up with the goods fast."

CHAPTER 18

AFTER Commander and I talked, I took the time to phone several pool services. At one, a man agreed to clean the pool of all traces of blood. He didn't ask how they got there. I wondered if blood in a pool was a common occurrence. The pool man and I decided we could meet at my house by six that evening.

At noon, Rafael phoned. "We called the number we had for the mother of the suspect. In all these years, the phone number has not changed. That was a relief. When we talked with her over the telephone, she said she had not seen her son since he left med school. She told us we could come to her house. I believe she is willing to talk about her son."

"Where does she live?"

"Outside of Trenton, New Jersey. We will fly home from Newark, not Boston."

"I can't believe there's no photo in the Boston PD files. Somebody tampered with them," I said.

"I agree," he said. "The BPD is starting an internal investigation."

"Let me speak to Al."

"What's new on the case down there?" Al asked.

"We're checking local hospitals. If the perp's employed, he could be in the medical field. We're collecting names of medical personnel with surgical skills. He could be leading a respectable life. His victims haven't been afraid of him. They've brought him into their homes," I said.

"That's not off the record, is it?" he asked.

"No," I said. "You can publish that, but not with attribution."

"This story is Pulitzer time for me. My editors are excited about the series. Think of the papers it'll sell."

"Think of the lives it'll save," I said. "Your story focuses on the perp. Let's hope someone recognizes him."

Rafael came back on the line. "I'll call you after I talk to the mother. Al is writing as we go along. He is using his laptop, and he sends his copy over telephone lines. He said he can even send it from the plane. *We* should have such high-tech equipment."

"We should. He'll get the story out fast. And that's exactly what we need him to do."

I went directly to the hospital after the call. Craig met me there. The manager who'd worked with me the day before had agreed to meet us there on a Saturday. She made sure I was aware she was taking extraordinary liberties to help us.

"We're looking for names of all employees who have surgical skills," I said to her as she pulled files.

"Let's also look for those who have access to surgical instruments," Craig said. The manager looked exasperated.

"We'll collect prints of the men who are suspicious in any way. At least we're not twiddling our thumbs waiting for court orders," I said. "Thank you so much," I said to the manager. She smiled.

Later both Craig and I began phoning names we'd collected up to that point. Male names. We expected to be able to find the men at home on a Saturday, though we knew many hospital workers had their days off during the week. I dialed the numbers on my list. When there was voice mail or a person to take a message, I left my name and number and asked for a return call.

Many of the men were not home. A man answered the fifth number I dialed. I went through my script, identifying myself and asking for permission to question him. He agreed.

"Where did you get your training?" I began.

"In Vermont," he answered. Then he said, as if he had second thoughts about my motives, "I'm not sure what you're doing and whether I should answer questions from you."

I explained we were looking for an individual who had medical training and who had been in the Boston area five to fifteen years ago. I didn't tell him why we wanted the individual.

"I can save you some trouble then," he said. "I was in Boston twenty or so years ago. And not since then, except for concerts."

The next man I spoke with said he'd been in Boston during that period. He'd lived there. By the time we finished, we had a list of seven men who'd admitted to being in Boston during that period.

"We're making some progress, Craig," I said. "Let's go out

---

to interview these men in person. See if any fit our profile. And we'll ask for prints."

During that day at the hospital, Elton called in to tell me he had spoken with Raja. Our scalpel strategy had reached a dead end with her. She'd told him she'd tried but couldn't differentiate between the scalpels and the marks they'd make. She suggested we send them up to FBI.

I told him we'd send them to our own crime lab.

Elton told me Raja wanted to speak to me. He gave her the message that I'd call her later.

By five that day, Craig and I had gone as far with our list as we could. After leaving the hospital, I stopped by the unit. I saw that Commander was in her office. I went in. I wanted to talk about the case. I wanted her to share my sense of urgency, though I wasn't sure whether mine came from the sight of the murdered women or from Horowitz's warnings that I was the target. I didn't know if my anxiety was relevant to the case. I didn't want her to know I was afraid.

I told her, "I'm worried. Reeves was murdered Thursday night more than a week ago. Cantwell was murdered two nights later, Saturday night. Peneles was murdered four nights after that, Wednesday. There've been no new murders in the case for three days. If the killer is on a rampage, he'll kill again soon. Tomorrow or the next night or the night after that."

"And he might not," she said. "We must find him so the DA has her turn. He'll face the justice system then, and they'll determine his guilt or innocence. And while we're concentrating on apprehending him, we will do everything in our power to stop him from killing again." She faced me for a few seconds before she said, "Are you becoming emotional again? Are you letting your feelings take over? You know we can't have that. Good homicide detectives don't let their feelings cloud their thinking. You don't do that, do you?"

"No feelings. Intuition," I said. "We work on intuition as much as on logic. I don't intend to shut down my intuition." I thought I was hiding my fear from her.

"I don't expect you to shut down intuition," she said. "I expect you to shove your feelings aside. There's a difference between intuition and feelings. One can give you a direct line to a solution. The other muddies up your clarity."

I left the Commander to take Rafael's call from Boston at my desk. He and Al had taken a shuttle flight from Boston to Newark, rented a car, and driven to Trenton. The mother's property was located on the outskirts of the city.

Rafael told me, "The mother, Lily Arnold, lives on an estate about seven miles outside the city. It is in the countryside and has a wrought iron fence around the property. There is a formal entryway with brick columns and a gate and lamps on the columns. It looks like the old Batista estates in Cuba. But it is in much better condition."

"This is the mother of the suspect?" I asked.

"Lily Arnold is the mother of the man whose print matches ours and who at one time was wanted for rape in Boston."

"Did she cooperate?" I asked.

"Yes, she did. Willingly. She seemed to be glad to talk to us. And I did not expect her to give us as much information as she did."

"What did she tell you?"

"Her son is named Dwight," Rafael said. "She said she has not seen or heard from him for years. She told us she is seventy-one years old. To me, though, she looks sixty. She is slender and tall with brown streaks in her gray hair. She has the skin of a middle-aged woman. You will probably look like her when you are seventy."

"Forget what she looks like. Tell me what she said about her son."

"She said he has a great deal of money, but it is sitting in his trust account earning interest. The trust account became available to him when he turned twenty-one, the year he entered med school. The money is her mother's. The suspect's grandmother set up the trust for her grandson. He took out enough money to pay for med school tuition for one year. When he ran away, he never touched it again."

"He didn't want to be traced through the trust fund. He has self-control if he hasn't touched it," I said. "What else did you find out?"

"She gave us a photo, an old one that was taken for his college graduation. Undergraduate. She said he disappeared before any others were taken. She knew about the rape charge and that he was a suspect. She wanted to know if the case had reopened."

"What did you tell her?" I asked.

"What we know—there have been a series of rapes and murders in a short period of time. I told her that we found her son's print at one of the crime scenes. And I said we want to question him. No more than that."

"That's the legal truth. How did she react to what you told her? Do you think she'll continue to cooperate?" I asked, not expecting a mother to hand over a child, even a grown child, to the law.

"Yes. She wants to cooperate. She said she's been afraid of her son since Dwight was a young boy," Rafael began.

"Did she say why she was afraid?"

"Yes. She told us. I taped everything she said," he replied. "She started her story with Dwight as her little boy. She said he was like a china doll, delicate, sensitive. She said when Dwight turned nine or ten, his father lured him away from her control. And the way she talked about his father, you know that the family was very troubled."

"What did she say about him?"

"The father, according to Lily Arnold, came from a family where the men were expected to be real men. They cut the limbs off lizards and iguanas, burned cats alive, and watched how they reacted to the pain. She said once the father opened up a pregnant horse while the mare was tied down. He watched the mare struggle to get to her foal even while her insides spilled out. Dwight watched it, too. Lily Arnold said the father told Dwight over and over again that the men in his family were real men because they didn't flinch. Real men enjoyed making others squirm. Real men had no feeling. She blames the father for whatever her son is today."

"Blame," I said. "Did she talk about the fact that her son didn't turn away in disgust when he was old enough to make up his own mind? Did she talk about the way she treated her son like a girl? Talk about confused. To me it is another case of a person who won't take responsibility for her actions."

"We will have to let the good investigative reporter explain the moral consequences of the perp's background. He will write about the relative importance of genes and environment," he said. I heard Al clearing his throat in the background. "Or a lawyer looking for a mental competence defense will explain it all. But no matter what, we cannot get the father's side of the story. He committed suicide shortly before the son disappeared. Lily Arnold, I think, seems to expect her life will end soon. She said she wanted to tell this story before she dies, and she does not want us to blame her son for what he did."

"Not her, not her son, but the father who's not around to give us his point of view. Wouldn't it be neat if we could blame at least one of our parents for our traffic violations?" I said. "What now?"

"We'll be home in time for Al to get his story into tomorrow's paper. His editor is saving space for it. Send someone to the airport to meet us. We're arriving on the eight o'clock flight from Newark."

"I'm expecting his story to get results—from people who think they know the perp. Who knows, we might even get a reaction from the perp himself. Good going. We'll all meet at the station tonight when you get back."

I leaned into Commander's office and told her what we'd learned.

"I'm meeting the pool man at my house," I said. "I won't be long. I'll be back in time to meet with Rafael and the team tonight. You'll be here?"

"I'm always here," she snapped, and waved me away.

The tag hanging on my front door was visible from the driveway as I drove up to my house. I checked the time before I got out of the car. Six thirty. The tag said, SORRY WE MISSED YOU. "Damn," I said out loud. I dialed the pool service's number on my cell phone while I unlocked the door. I didn't expect an answer at six-thirty on a Saturday night. And I got none.

Gilda did not greet me at the door. I called her. I heard scratches at the kitchen door and looked out the window to see my dog outside.

"How'd you get out?" I said. "Did I forget to bring you in

this morning?" Her muzzle was wet and red. She'd been drinking from the pool. Probably she'd been licking the dried blood on the side of the pool.

"I'm cleaning this mess up myself," I said. Gilda looked up at me.

I changed into a T-shirt and shorts and went barefoot to screw the hose into an outlet on the patio. I squirted a stream of water on the dried blood on the side of the pool and watched the reddened water gradually turn lighter until it washed clear. I decided to drain the pool little by little. The neighbors would not be happy to see bloody water running down the street and into their yards. I brought out a scrub brush as the water drained from the pool. For a little while, it would sink into the ground. I planned to stop it from draining when it reached the street. I scrubbed the dried blood and watched the water flow. It didn't take long for it to reach the street.

Then the doorbell rang. I ran to answer it before I stopped the pool from draining. The pool man must have returned. But when I opened the door no one was there. I decided I hadn't heard the bell and returned to the pool and stopped it from draining.

While I worked on the pool, Gilda went outside through the hole in the screen. She loved water and stuck her nose and paws into what was streaming from the patio. She played in the bloody water as if she were attacking an intruder.

"Don't drink that," I said sharply to her. She looked up at me and continued to play. There would not have been much chlorine left by this time. She'd be okay, I thought. I turned off the water draining from the pool and brought out a towel to dry my dog.

We were in the kitchen when I heard a knock at the back door. I opened it to find Tina standing there.

"What happened last night?" she asked.

"It's gruesome," I said. "Someone killed a dog and put it in the bottom of my pool. A kid's prank, I expect." I didn't mention Peter.

"That's frightening," she said. "My mother is anxious today. She saw all the police around your house. I couldn't coax her to go to bed until every last one of them left."

"I'm sorry," I said. Her mother would be unsettled for days. She'd be even more difficult for Tina to control.

"It's not your fault. I'm worried those kids will bother us, though. Are the police keeping a watch out in the neighborhood?"

"I'm sure they are," I said. "If you call the NET—you know, the neighborhood patrol—they'll put a watch on our streets."

"I'll call," she said. "Look, I can't stay. I wish I could help you clean up, but I left Mom alone."

I heard a sound and turned to see Mrs. Hathaway's face at the door. "I'm looking for Tina," she said. "Have you seen Tina?"

"She's right here," I told her. Tina hurried outside to take her mother by the hand and lead her away from the pool.

Rafael's plane would arrive at eight, less than half an hour away. It'd take a while for him and Al to get out of the airport. I planned to get back to the station around nine.

I opened my refrigerator and found a loaf of bread and mayonnaise. I felt the avocados on my windowsill and pressed them with my fingertips until I found one that was beginning to ripen. I halved it, let the pit drop into the sink, sliced a peeled section onto the bread where I had already spread mayonnaise, and covered the sliced avocado with the other piece of bread. This was a favorite sandwich, one my grandfather had taught me to make. I sat at the kitchen table with my sandwich and a can of iced tea. Gilda hovered at my feet. She wouldn't lie still. She was anxious, too. I read a news magazine as I ate.

When I finished eating I headed toward the back of the house and my bedroom, Gilda at my heels. I needed to shower and change before I went back to the station. We passed the hall bathroom, one I never used, the window of which opened onto the patio. Gilda stopped at the closed door. I figured I'd left the bathroom window open. She had smelled the blood from the patio. No matter how hard I pulled her, she wouldn't budge from her stance.

"Okay, girl," I said to her. "I'll show you there's nothing in here." I swung the door open wide, keeping my eyes on her for what I expected would be a bewildered reaction. Instead, she jumped into the room, barking wildly. I looked at where she was headed.

A man stood in the shower behind the clouded-glass doors.

CHAPTER 19

PETER," I said. "For God's sake, stop it." Gilda growled. Her lips were pulled back. Her reaction was stronger than if she'd known the person. I told myself she was on edge. She smelled the blood.

The door slid back slowly. The .22 aimed at Gilda was all I saw. Then I heard the shot. The sound exploded in the tiled room. She sank to the ground, yelping two times. Then she was silent.

"What have you done?" I shouted. Then I saw that Peter was not Peter. It was Martin. "What are you doing here? Why in God's name did you kill my dog?"

"Better the dog than me," he said.

I kneeled down over Gilda. She was breathing. I couldn't figure out what all this meant. The facts didn't compute. The person standing in the tub reached over and grabbed me by the hair. He pulled me to a standing position till I looked squarely in his face. His gun pointed at my heart. It was Martin. The expression wasn't the Martin I knew at my parents' or in the canoe. My mind raced.

"Why did you hurt Gilda?" The words tumbled from me.

He laughed. "I already told you," he said. "It was either the dog or me. I have plans. The dog would have gotten in the way. I don't let anything get in my way."

"Way of what?" I said. He yanked harder on my hair and stuck the gun next to my neck. He was strong. "I don't understand. And I don't know who you are. You're not Martin. You are somebody else. A stranger." I began to think. I had to get control of the situation. "You're in the wrong house. Get out of here. Now." I estimated my chances of overpowering him, knocking his arm with the gun. He must have felt me tense as I thought of the act. He jerked my head back. I thought my neck would break. I tried to knee him in the groin. The edge of the tub was in my way.

Again he laughed. "I'm exactly where I want to be," he said. "And I like it when you bitches think you can control me. You have absolutely no control over me. None. I'm the one. I'm the controller. You'll see." He pushed me backward with his gun. "Turn around. I don't want to stay in your tub."

I turned away from him, my back to him, and I could see Gilda. She raised her head. It fell back down on the floor into the blood surrounding her. Not once had he let go of my hair. He held the gun's muzzle on my spine. He led me by the hair and by pushing me forward with the gun. We went into the living room. I had left the drapes closed. No one could see us. Nor could we see outside. The room was growing dark as the sun set.

He pushed me over to a chair at the same table where I had

signed papers for Harry. He told me to sit. He took from his pocket a bright yellow nylon cord, the kind used on boats, the kind Martin had used on his canoe. He stood behind me and poked his gun into the top part of my spinal cord.

"Put your hands back here, or I'll shoot. You won't move then, will you?" he said.

My mind was clearing. I made a decision. I wanted to come out of this alive. I'd cooperate until the chance came to kill the bastard.

I put my arms in back of me, behind the chair. He held the gun at my spine and worked with one hand. He placed my wrists together and wrapped the cord around first one wrist, then the other, yanking tight each turn around. Only when they were secure did he take the gun away from my back. I heard a slight movement of cloth and guessed he'd placed the gun in his pants pocket. With two hands he knotted the cord around my wrists. My hands felt swollen. The cord had been tied like a tourniquet.

He walked around the chair. He'd taken the gun out of his pocket and pointed it at my knee.

"Put your ankles against the legs of the chair," he ordered. I was slow to move. I heard the sound of the gun thud as it hit my knee. I moaned. He pulled the leg to where he wanted it and wrapped the cord around it and the chair. He did the same with the other leg. My knee throbbed. My hands were numb.

"How much control do you have now?" he asked. I didn't answer. I stared at the face I had thought I'd known. It was at that moment I gave myself a task. One task. I wanted to live and to do so I needed time. Keep him talking.

"Who are you?" I asked.

"Shut up."

I ignored him. "Bill and Fran and Jimmy and Carol and a lot of other people at my parents' house know you as Martin Benson."

"Shut up."

"Then who are you?"

"You don't know yet?"

"No."

"You are a dirty, disgusting female. I don't know if I want to touch you."

"Then don't."

That kind of answer was a mistake. He lifted the gun to the level of my knee—my other knee, the one he had not disabled. I recoiled. He liked that. He lowered the gun and laughed.

"I can smell blood on you. And your fingernails. There's blood underneath them. All you women are alike." He stared at me a moment. "One time my father opened the belly of a horse, and he took out her foal. It wasn't ready to be born, but he took it anyway. The mare tried to get up to get her foal. Her guts spilled out of her. Her womb, her intestines. It was disgusting. My mother was there. Dad told her to stand there. While that mare tried to stand up with her guts spilling out, my father shoved Mother into the next stall. I heard her say, 'No, no.' I heard slaps. I heard him grunt. And that mare tried and tried to stand up through it all. I was there." He talked.

"I know who you are," I said. "You're Dwight Arnold."

"Good. Very good. You said you were about to crack the case, and that's why I had to get you by surprise. No time to waste courting you."

"We spoiled your plans, didn't we?"

239

"Not really," he said. "You found out a lot about me. And none of it's going to help you."

"The police know who you are. You won't get away this time."

"I like that. A bitch who thinks she's smart, but isn't as smart as me. I prove it to them every time."

"We know"—I emphasized each word—"who you are."

"No you don't," he said, also emphasizing his words. "You thought I was Martin Benson. You thought I was a man your father and mother and their friends liked and admired. You thought I was the man you'd fall in love with and I'd be so happy when we were lovers. You didn't know anything. You didn't know I was the one in control. I was the one who created Martin Benson, the man everyone loved. I knew what you were doing every minute. I chose to capture you when I did. You had no choice in the matter. You were totally under my control."

"Why me?"

"I picked you out one time when I stood outside a crime-scene tape. That was a few months ago. You were lead and you acted like the bitch you are. But I saw your eyes. I could see in them what you were really like. I can see those things." He smiled and waited till I looked up at him again.

Then he continued. "You were hungry for it. I know your kind. You never stop searching and you think you'll never find it. Love. You know why? Because you don't really believe you're good enough to get it. And you don't even know what love is." I turned my head away from him.

He stopped talking and laughed. Then he said, "You bitches. Always trying to prove to the world—to your mother, to your father, to your lovers—that you're worthy. And you think that when you prove you're good enough, they're going to love you. You can't do it, can you?"

He began to gaze at something over my head. "That's the kind of woman who falls for me. A woman who knows deep inside her that she's never going to find someone to love her no matter how hard she tries. No matter what she does. The kind who lets a man push her into a horse stall to fuck her. And she thinks that man is going to love her."

"You don't know anything about love," I said to the man who had sadistically murdered at least three women.

"I know a lot," he said. "I know love is the biggest hoax of all time. There is no love. My mother can tell you that."

I responded angrily. I should have maintained control over my emotions. I didn't. "You are sick. Love is all around you. It's there when you see a heron flying or an alligator float in water. It's there when you feel the water's freshness on your skin. It's there when birds feed on berries in the backyard. It's there when people of the world come together to send food to the starving in the desert. It's there when our city feels calm and orderly." I stopped. Then I said, "I love my city." How weak I must have sounded.

"You talk too much," he said.

"And Bill? How does he fit into your plans?" I asked.

"I discovered the old fool through you," he said. "I despise fools. A creepy romantic fool. Bill thought he loved Jan. So I chose her and knocked the old fool off his feet."

"You chose her just to hurt him?"

"You stink," he said. "You need a shower. You smell like that dog in the bathroom. I'll bet she's shitting all over herself right this minute."

I wanted to shout, Stop! I willed myself to focus on my one

task. Don't get emotional, I said to myself. Keep him talking. Every minute alive was a minute closer to his capture.

"You're changing the subject," I said. "Why Janice Cantwell?"

"You are too curious," he said. "You'll have to wait while I get something to drink." He walked to the kitchen, keeping me in the sight of his gun the entire time. He walked backward, glancing three or four times to make sure he wouldn't stumble. I waited for him to stumble. He didn't. He opened the refrigerator and grabbed an open bottle of white wine. He came back, holding the bottle by the neck.

He sat in a chair in front of me, flicked the cork with his thumb, raised the bottle to his mouth, and drank.

"Jan was easy," he said. "To her, I was a former associate of your father's, a young lawyer who'd worked in the firm for only a few months before going out on his own. My name was Danny. Markowitz. Polish name. Good Catholic. I bought flowers every day, personally picking them up, for my mother. Jan liked the young man who had worked in her benefactor's firm, her former lover's firm. She liked his ambition. She liked his devotion to simple things—God and mother. She especially liked his attraction to her, an older woman." He lifted the bottle to his lips again and drank.

"You knew she was my father's former girlfriend?"

"A perfect choice. She gets me closer to you."

"I can see how you might think that," I started.

He interrupted me. "Not *might* think," he said. "She was my choice. And I did get closer to you."

I began again. "Yes. You did. You hurt my father. And my mother."

"Exactly," he said. "You're not as stupid as I believed. But you're not as smart as I am."

"Then explain how Carla Reeves and Conchita Peneles got you closer to me."

He drank the last of the wine from the bottle. He backed into the kitchen again, holding the gun on me, aimed at my head. "Where's the liquor?" he yelled.

"In the cabinet next to the refrigerator," I called out to him. His drinking could be dangerous for me. Or it could cause him to pass out. I watched him grab a bottle of rum from the cabinet and return to me. He'd already taken the top off. He raised the rum bottle to his mouth. I wished I could shove it in his face, but I was tied tightly to the chair.

"Tell me how Carla and Conchita got you closer to me," I said.

"You already asked that. You are bothering me by talking too much," he said. He raised the empty wine bottle above his head as if he meant to smash me with it.

He liked me to cringe. I cringed. "I'll be quiet," I said.

He lowered the bottle. "You want to know about Carla and Conchita. Carla was a lovely woman. She really liked to be mistreated. And I gave her what she wanted. She met me through her magazines because I called her. I'd seen her at some bar all by herself. She looked like she wanted to cry. I spot that kind right away. The bartender told me she worked at the magazines. Later we had drinks at the Biltmore, where Jan had her shop. I came on to her, I kissed her till she hurt, and she wanted more. She wanted to love me. She wanted passion. She wanted me to hurt her and leave her. Same old story."

"I still don't understand how killing her brought you closer to me," I said. He lifted the bottle to swing at my face. I cowered and said in a little girl voice, "Don't. Please don't." The victim role stopped him for some reason. I had touched something in him. What?

"I'll be quiet," I said in the same voice. He put the bottle down. I watched his every move as he came toward me. He extended his hand as if to caress my face, but immediately pulled back before he made contact. He raised the rum bottle to his mouth and drank.

"You know what Dad said to me when he gutted that horse and took Mom into that stall? He said, 'You little sissy. Look at you crying over a horse. You're no man, thanks to your mother.' And he pushed her down into the horse's guts. I'll never forget. Never." He drank from the rum bottle again. He wasn't drunk enough to take on his father's role. I picked out one more task. Stop him from getting drunk.

"You never drank liquor at my parents' house. Now you can't get enough," I said. I tried to whine. By the end of my comment, I'd forgotten to play the role. I spoke in my normal tone.

"I'm fierce when I drink. I tear houses down. I wreck cars. I rip animals apart. I cut women to pieces and fuck them to death." He laughed and laughed. "I'm a bull with big balls."

I kept asking questions. I wanted him to talk. "Were you drunk when you killed Carla?"

"Oh, yeah, baby. That was good. She fought, and the bull subdued her." He stopped talking to drink more rum.

Come on, I prayed. Talk some more. Don't drink.

"You want to know how Carla brought me closer to you? I'll tell you. I had already picked you out months before when I stood outside the yellow tape, like all the other gawkers. Then I just waited. Till you were lead and you were looking for me. I knew Carla lived in your area. When I saw in the paper that you were lead detective on the case, I had you. That's how Carla brought me to you." He drank from the bottle.

"I'm thirsty," I said. "And my hands are numb. The cord is too tight."

"What do you want me to do about it?" he asked. "I don't care how thirsty you are."

"Please," I whined. "Please give me some water." I heard Gilda give a weak bark from the bathroom. "Please," I said again.

He came over to where I sat and leaned down to gently stroke my face. I couldn't picture him tearing and slicing and beating the body of Conchita. "I'll get you some water." He brought back water. He set it on the table while he untied my hands. He massaged my hands till feeling came back in them. He was kind. I did not trust him for a second.

I held the glass and drank the water. He drank more from his bottle of rum. He'd picked up another one while he was in the kitchen. He drank and he watched me. He finished the rum in the first bottle and threw it near the front door where it smashed to bits.

"In case anyone has an idea about rescuing you," he said.

He began untying the cord around my legs. My hands were free. I pushed him away from me. He fell backward. My legs were still bound to the chair. I half stood and shuffled toward the drapery cord. First one leg forward. Then the next. I had taken three shuffling steps toward the drapes. He put his arm around my neck from the back and pulled me down till I fell to the floor. My legs were still strapped to the chair.

"I like it when the bitch comes out. She was hiding in there, wasn't she? She wouldn't stay hidden for long. They never do," he said. I grabbed his leg and tried to pull him off balance. I'm strong. I thought I could do it. He stood stock still and laughed. "Remember what Conchita looked like when you found her? You're going to look like that. She fought. Or she tried to fight. I taught her a lesson. Want to know how Conchita is connected to you? You'll find out. Your mother hasn't figured it out yet. She's not in touch with the outside world much. Conchita is your mother's portfolio manager."

I said nothing. He was talking, not drinking. The full bottle of rum was on the other side of the room.

"I've been killing you slowly. Through Jan and your father. Through Conchita and your mother." He thought a moment. "And I'm going to destroy your mother and father through your death. Not bad for a sissy. My father would be proud. I have no feelings at all. I am a bull. I destroy." He took the gun out of his pocket and pointed it at my face. He took a metal object out of his other pocket and with it he cut the cords he'd tied around my legs. He ordered me to stand up. Though I had tried to walk while tied to the chair, I hadn't paid any attention to my knee then. When I tried to stand, I could hardly place my weight on it.

But I stood there as he pointed the gun at my forehead. I saw him replace in his pocket what I then saw was a strange, small knife. Then the phone rang three times. The answering machine picked up. He watched my face, smiling. We listened to the message left for me.

"It's me. Raja. Why didn't you call sooner? I've been in the decomposition lab. The Miami-Dade cops brought in a body found in the Everglades. But listen," she continued, "your crime lab guys asked me to look at that dog they found in your pool. I'm working this weekend, so I went over there to check the dog. That's what I wanted to tell you."

His smile turned into a grin. I smelled the liquor on his breath. He was drunk. Mean drunk. His gun didn't budge from my forehead. I calculated my chances of getting my hands up to knock the gun away from him before he got a shot off. Not yet. Mean drunk. But not out-of-it drunk.

"I'm worried about you," Raja spoke as if I were on the other end of the line carrying on a conversation with her. "The dog's jugular was pierced with the same kind of precision as we'd expect from a trained surgeon."

He laughed. With his free hand he pointed at his chest. He mouthed the word *me*. As if she could have heard him.

"You told me not to tell anyone about Horowitz's warning, but I don't know. You need to let the others know, Suze. You are the target. I'm sure of it."

He nodded his head, affirming what she'd said. He mouthed the word *stupid*. He was drunk.

"I called you at the station. They said you were at home. Call me as soon as you get this message." Raja hung up the phone.

"Am I smart?" he asked. "Smarter than any of you cops? Smarter than any woman pretends to be?" His breath stank.

"*You* killed the malamute," I said. "*You* put the dog in my pool. *You* sent the dog over to threaten me. *You* sliced my screen. *You* butchered that kitten and put it out for my dog to find."

"Scared you, didn't I?"

I said quietly, "You. Not Peter."

"No. Not your lover, Peter. Me. I saw him at your parents' house, at that party. You looked like you were so hurt by him.

You wanted to believe he'd do anything to get you back. He was the one you thought had to love you. You didn't have the willpower to look at the reality. You are weak."

I raised my arm suddenly, intending to knock the gun out of his hand. He jumped backward, more quickly than I'd thought a man as drunk as he was could.

HE laughed.

"What do you know about love," I stated. Had I loved my baby? I loved my son. I couldn't die now. What if he wanted to find me? His real mother? I would never have told my boy I loved him. I was too young when he was born. I didn't know anything about love then. I had nothing to give when my baby was born. I had much to give him as a grown woman. Didn't I?

"You're a helpless bitch," he said. "I know enough about love to make you sorry you ever heard the word."

The phone rang again. The answering machine picked up. There was no message. No voice from the outside world. Then I heard the cell phone. It too stopped ringing.

He stepped closer to me, the gun in his right hand, a knife in his left. I dared not move, but I stared at the knife.

"That's my cutting instrument," he said. "My father lived

down here in Florida on a cattle ranch after my mother sent him away. One night he went to a shack on a back road way away from everybody else. The man who lived there made knives. Not just knives, but skinning knives, killing knives. He made this one. See?" He thrust it toward my neck and touched the skin. But he didn't break the skin—that time.

"You won't find a knife sharper than this one," he said. He brought it up to my face. I looked at it—even though I couldn't focus, he held it so close to my eyes. "These kinds are the ones used to skin catch—no matter what that catch is." He drew it back far enough for me to focus. I saw the knife. He held it between his thumb and forefinger to show me the entire instrument. The handle had been a tooth, a large animal's tooth. It had been patterned with an indigo dye. I saw the picture of a wild boar stabbed with a knife like this one. The blade was of a highly refined metal, a stainless steel. It had been sharpened to a point, and the edges were as thin as razors.

"What is the metal?" I asked.

"My father gave the man one of his scalpels," he said. "Did I tell you he was a veterinarian? He specialized in large animals. Farm animals. Dumb animals. That's why he was in Florida."

"Did all his scalpels look like this?" I asked. I'd ask questions as long as he was willing to answer.

"His scalpels looked like ordinary scalpels. He told the man to hammer this out like a skinning knife. And he did."

"And he gave it to you."

"Yes, he did. For my twentieth birthday. Before he died."

"How did he die?" I asked, though I already knew he'd committed suicide.

"He died the way he wanted to die," he said. He was quiet. "You bitch. Stop asking so many questions."

"I'll be quiet," I said in my little girl voice.

"You don't fool me," he said. He circled me and came up behind me and placed his skinning knife at the front of my neck, below my chin. "Put your hands back here."

I moved only my arms and hands. Otherwise I stood stock still. He took both my hands in one of his and raised my arms high behind me. I bent forward to relieve the pressure, forward into the knife. He raised my arms higher, and I felt a crack, and I moaned.

When he lowered my arms, I stood straight. Tears came to my eyes. I kept them wide open to prevent any from falling. I prayed. All I wanted was time. Minutes. Seconds. I didn't know what time it was. I couldn't see the sky. I couldn't see whether it was light or dark outside.

When I'd bent forward, he'd kept the blade pressed against my skin. Standing straight again, I felt warmth cover my neck. Don't panic, I told myself. Surface wound.

I wanted to sound normal, as if there were nothing unusual going on. "Would you mind bringing me a towel? I don't want to drip on the floor."

"You are stupid," he said. "You sound like my mother. Believe me, you won't be around to worry about how your floor looks."

We began to walk toward the back of the house. My knee was not as injured as I feared. As we moved I flicked my eyes toward the rooms we passed. I had closed all the windows to keep the air-conditioning from leaking out. All venetian blinds were down and closed to fend off the heat from the sun and to hide the pool in the back.

When we were at the hall bathroom, I said, "There's a towel in there."

He surprised me when he turned the two of us toward the bathroom, knife still on my throat, my wrists held in one of his hands. I'd begun to think of his hands as massive.

"You women are all alike," he said.

I had expected he would let go of one of my wrists. I imagined I'd be able to pull his hand holding the knife away long enough to overpower him. But he didn't let go. Instead he led us to stand in front of the towel rack. Gilda lay at our feet. She didn't move. She didn't raise her head.

"Bend down and wipe your neck on this towel." I did as I was told. He shifted the knife to my spine. When I rose from the towel rack, he moved the knife to the front of my neck.

"Thanks," I said, as if he'd offered me a glass of iced tea. "That feels much better." I felt his breath. I smelled his stink.

We reached my bedroom. He walked us over to the sliding glass doors. I'd closed the drapes the night before, and I hadn't opened them since. He let my left arm go free from his grasp, but he kept the knife at my throat. My left side, the injured side, was toward the door. "Pull the curtains open." I raised my arm to grasp the pulley and felt the deep pain waiting there for me.

"I can't lift my arm," I said to the curtains.

"Do it," he said to my ear.

I edged us closer to the pulley and with short movements gradually opened the curtains. Outside the day was sliding into darkness. Tina had not turned on her lights.

"Open the pool door," he said. "I'm going to leave by the back way. I've noticed how private you are here. You go swimming in the nude even and fuck your lovers with the bedroom door open. Nobody will see us or hear us. We're going to have fun all by ourselves. Sorry you won't be around to say good-bye to me."

"I have to get closer to the door," I told him. "It's heavy and something's broken in my arm."

"Be sure you don't move suddenly. I don't want this knife to slip. Yet."

I slowly edged closer to the door handle and raised my left hand to unlock the waist-high catch. In the same short movements, I grasped the door. "I have to go backwards," I said. "I'll pull the door open."

Each tug on the heavy door tightened my arm muscles. Sharp pain radiated from my shoulder. The door was open. My house was dark. Tina's house was still dark. Gilda was silent. See me. See me. I willed my neighbors to see into my house. I heard only crickets in the lowering dark.

He pressed the knife more deeply against my throat. I felt warmth rolling down my neck again. Only surface cuts, I told myself.

"Bring your left arm back slowly, slowly, to where I can hold it again." I heard a voice call.

"Tina," called Mrs. Hathaway. "Tina. Are you in there?"

He glanced over his shoulder toward the screen. I felt his breath and smelled it. He whispered, "Tell her to go away."

"She's not here," I said. "Go away. She's not here."

"Tina," called Mrs. Hathaway. "I see you. You're a naughty girl."

I heard Tina's voice say, "Come on, Mom. I'm right here." Mrs. Hathaway mumbled something to her daughter. She wouldn't see us in the dark room through the screen. I heard them walk away, their bodies brushing against palm fronds.

He held both my arms behind me again. My left arm caused

the most pain. I was aware that any plan I made had to take that injury into account. I knew he needed to torture me before killing me. My time was down to seconds. Every second meant I had that second to figure out how to survive. And I intended to survive. I had reasons.

He guided me toward the bed until my thighs were at the edge of the mattress. He pushed me down, face-first, holding my arms behind me. He held the knife pressed to my throat till my face almost touched the bed. Then he shifted the knife to the side of my neck. It was at my jugular. I thought of how Carla had looked as she lay on her bed. Carla and Conchita had fought. I wondered if Jan had. Perhaps she had been more compliant. Perhaps she thought that would save her. I assessed compliance and whether it would save me. Then I assessed the value of rebellion. Time. That was what would give me a chance to survive.

"Turn over," he said, holding the knife point a fraction of an inch away from my neck as I rolled over. I looked him in the eyes when I faced up. I saw at first a deep sadness. Then I saw a brief smile and crinkled eyes as if he was merry. I wasn't sure I'd seen either emotion. Or any.

"Did you have medical training?" I asked. Make him talk, I reminded myself.

"Don't you ever shut up?" he asked. Then he answered, "I've taken anatomy. And my father made me work in his operating room. I know where every vein and organ is in your body, and how to find it." He placed his fingers on my neck, feeling for a pulse. "There," he said, and held his fingers steady. "That's your jugular." He smiled, this time showing triumph on his face. I remained quiet and thought about my gun in the nightstand drawer. It was on the right side of my bed. The other side of the bed.

"Take off your clothes," he instructed.

"I'll have to stand up," I said.

"No, you don't," he said. "I want you to struggle."

I awkwardly took off my T-shirt and shorts, using my right hand and arm, the pain in my left shoulder stabbing outward with every move. As I wriggled out of my clothes, I also wriggled myself closer to the night table. In increments. He held the knife above me, pointed at my neck, ready to plunge it into me. I didn't want to make a suspicious move. I wanted to reach the gun.

"No bra," he said. "That's how I like it. Now your pants," he said. I used my good arm to remove my pants. By the time I lay there completely nude, I had maneuvered myself to the middle of the bed. He didn't notice.

"Unbutton my shirt," he said.

"I'll have to sit up to reach it," I said. "My left shoulder is badly injured. I'm going to roll to my right and push myself up." I looked down at my shoulder and saw it had swollen to twice its normal size.

When he did not object, I turned to my right. My back to him again, I felt the knife pressed against my spine. For a moment, I felt hopeless. I wouldn't be able to roll over to the floor, take the gun out of the drawer, pull the spring, and squeeze the trigger. It wasn't even loaded. I'd have to load it first.

You are not helpless, I told myself. There is hope as long as you are alive.

The room gradually grew darker. The moon had not yet

risen. I decided to wait for complete darkness—just a few more minutes. I'd kill him.

My left arm was almost useless. I raised myself, pushing myself up with my right arm. I turned toward him, looking up to his face, unbuttoning his shirt with my right hand, a position of lovemaking. Peter had lain passive on the bed as I made love to him. Passive for a while.

"You didn't force the other women, did you?" I asked as I unbuttoned his shirt. "You didn't have to."

"At some point, I always used my magic skinning knife." He pressed the blade harder against my neck. He pressed it into the wound he'd already made. The blood ran. The pain was raw. He wouldn't kill me for a while, I told myself.

"Have I told you about the magic?" he asked.

"No," I said. "Tell me."

"The man who made this knife lived outside the urban life most of us know. My father said he was ancient looking. His shoulders were bent. His whiskers were white. My father stayed with the man while he made the knife. The man sang a chant the whole time, and made a dance with his feet. A step this way, two steps that way. A magic dance. Then he lit a pipe, a long pipe with a wide shallow bowl. I don't know what he put in it, but my father said it didn't look like tobacco. He smoked the pipe, chanted, and danced. He had a shelf full of the teeth he used for handles. He reached up, said my father, and put his hand on one, picked it up, inspected it, and nodded. That's when he put the two pieces together. The blade and the handle. At the end, he blew smoke on the finished knife, said a few words, circled the room, and handed it to my father."

"An old man made this knife? And you say that's magic?" I asked.

"Not any old man. A shaman. A man who knows magic. He knew what my father wanted the knife for. And he gave it the magic it needed," he said. "That's why you'll never catch me. I catch you. I control you."

"This is the knife you use on the women you kill?"

"Yes. And it is magic. Women do not know what I'm doing. They are under my spell. I love to see how far I can get before a woman wakes up from the spell and realizes I'm killing her. Women are fools." I had unbuttoned his shirt. He slipped it off his shoulders, and it fell to the floor.

"The pants," he instructed. Slowly, with my right hand, I undid his pants. First the belt, the button, the zipper. He let his pants fall to his ankles, and he stepped away from them. He wore no undershorts. He, too, was naked. I looked at his penis as it lay against his testicles. It was neither swollen nor erect. I looked up at his face. He was in the dominant position. I saw out the door to the patio behind him. I saw beyond my yard to the lights in Tina's house.

"Lie back," he said, the knife touching the skin at my throat. He had begun to mumble. He was drunk.

I talked. I tried to sound matter-of-fact, not the least afraid, calm and relaxed. Not driven to survive.

"You've had a lot to drink. I don't think you'll be able to perform tonight. Shall we put this off?"

"You're crazy. You'll give me satisfaction tonight," he said, "If you don't, I'll have to find someone who won't get me this drunk."

"I got you drunk?" I asked.

"My plans got changed because of you. I would have gone out on a date with you. And you would be the one drunk. But you persisted. You had to find out who was killing these women."

"This is my fault," I said.

"Damn right," he said. "But I think our foreplay will get me excited enough."

"What do you mean 'foreplay'?" I asked.

"You want to know what I mean?" he asked. "Remember how Carla looked? Jan? Conchita? That's my foreplay."

"Are you saying that slicing up a woman, suffocating her, raping her, brutalizing her—these are the ways you get excited? Is that the only way you get a hard-on?" I probably sounded angry. He hadn't moved his knife from my neck. I lay flat on my back. He sat on the edge of the bed, on my left, facing me.

"Shut up," he snorted. "You don't need to know. Let's say killing you slowly and painfully gives me one terrific hard-on." He poked my throat with the knife and stretched out beside me. When he did, I maneuvered my body so I lay to the right of the middle of the bed. Darkness was almost complete. The moon would rise soon.

In the darkened room, I sensed he had raised himself to lean his upper body over me. The knife no longer touched me. I felt his forearm press downward, downward. I coughed and pulled at his arm, and I couldn't pull it away. I coughed. And did not breathe. The extent of my world was his arm on my throat. Such a heavy, strong arm. That's what I remember thinking before I lost consciousness.

When I opened my eyes again, for a second I was confused. Had I awakened in the middle of the night? Was this Peter? It was dark. I smelled sweat and blood in the room. Why was my shoulder hurting like hell? I turned my head. I felt around the bed with my right hand. I touched, rather than saw, Dwight's thigh with its curly hair. He was seated on the left side of the bed.

"You took a long time to wake up," he said. "I was getting bored. Who knows what I would have done if you'd been out any longer."

He grabbed my left hand and placed it on his penis. The pain jolted through me. When it subsided, I thought to myself, What a floppy little thing. As soon as he'd placed my hand on his penis, I pulled my hand away. With the second jolt, I arched my back in pain. I heard him laugh. The odor of his alcoholic breath reached me in the middle of the bed. I felt nauseated. From the pain. From the smell.

But for that one second I was free from him. I couldn't let him find me in the dark. I twisted toward the right side of the bed. I rolled off the bed onto the floor. It must have been the adrenaline. I moved like a cat. I saw like a leopard.

With the same motion of rolling off the bed, I grabbed the nightstand drawer handle with my right hand and pulled it out on the floor with me. I scooted backward and dragged the drawer with me. I had to bring my legs close to my body, then push back. On the second push, I lifted the Glock and the magazine from the drawer. I held them both in my right hand, and scooted naked and silent, having let go of the drawer. I headed to the far corner of the room. In the darkness, I was invisible. The sky would not light up for a few more seconds. I did not feel anything. No pain. No fear. I did what I had to do.

I heard his feet pat on the terrazzo as he ran around the foot of the bed toward the sound of the drawer. But I had left the drawer in his path. He stumbled against it, shoving it across the room, away from me. He tripped forward toward me, knocking into me as he fell. I had put the gun in my left hand, and I worked with my right, where I held the magazine. But I hadn't pushed the magazine home. I dropped the magazine on the floor, and it clattered. Pain swirled through me.

I knew he couldn't see me clearly. He grasped the first thing he felt when he fell against me, my left arm. Involuntarily I gave a sharp cry. I moved my right hand around the floor for the magazine I had dropped. I didn't stop searching even though he pulled on my left arm to increase the pain. I found the magazine. I reached over to my left hand, where the gun lay cupped in my open palm. He brought up his knife to the place he grasped, my upper left arm. I felt him slice my arm, though that pain was minor compared to the shoulder pain, and I shoved the magazine in where it belonged.

The gun fell from my hand, and he let go of my arm to reach toward the sound for the fallen weapon. I knew exactly where the gun landed: right beneath where my left arm hung, now covered in blood. I picked up the gun and raised it with my right hand. "Move back. Now!" I shouted. I heard no movement but felt the blade touch my belly. He was going to gut me. I squeezed the trigger. One time. Two times. Three times. I wanted to make sure. He hadn't made a sound.

I rested my head against the wall. I felt wetness beneath me. I didn't know if it was his or mine. I smelled gunpowder and sweat and coppery blood. I figured I'd bleed to death before any damn fool found me.

A tree frog croaked and crickets ratcheted. These were the only sounds I heard after our cacophony: the drawer banging on the terrazzo, it scraping on the floor, his feet, the click of the magazine as it went home, the shots. How beautiful the frog and cricket sounds were.

Blackness spilled around me, surrounding the sounds. I

faded from the sensible world. I saw my yard at twilight. I walked there with a cool drink in my hand and Gilda beside me and the pines silhouetted against the sky and the scrub palmetto brushing against my legs. Someone was walking toward me in this twilight scene. Someone I knew but couldn't see clearly.

Suddenly, beside me, glass crashed onto the bedroom floor. A strong light beam shone down on the two of us. I couldn't figure out what all that red was on the floor. Was it the pool water? I saw a naked man lying in the red. Who was breaking my windows? Someone was breaking into my house. Why wasn't Gilda barking? Who was that naked man? People were shouting. I wanted to go to sleep.

"Raise your hands high or we'll shoot. Don't move. Don't move or you're dead meat." They shouted and shouted.

"Don't move."

"Raise your hands."

"Keep your hands where I can see them."

The bedroom filled with men and women in black. Someone had turned on the lights. I could barely see them.

"What the hell took you so long?" I said, and closed my eyes and drifted in and out of the noise around me.

A cop leaned over me, holding his weapon close to his chest with both hands. I hurt. "Detective Cannon. You're hurt bad. We've called emergency rescue. They're on the way." I felt something tied around my upper arm and pulled tight, tight.

"Look over here," the cop said. "She shot him. He's dead."

"I shot him," I said, and my head fell back on the wall again, overwhelmed by the effort of saying those three words. I wanted to sleep.

"Stay with us, Suze. Don't go to sleep." Someone kept slapping my face.

"Stop it," I said.

"She's going to live," Raja said. I heard voices and boots walking up to me and then away. I heard the shutter of a camera clicking. Crime scene shots.

I heard Raja's voice. "Hold on, Suze. Hold on. The doctor's almost here." I felt her place her hand on the back of my neck and slowly edge me down flat on my back. I heard the clatter of someone rummaging through small things. I felt a needle go into a vein on the inside of my right elbow. I began to sink into a deep sweet calmness, hearing Raja's voice say, "Hold on, hold on, hold on, Suze. You're going to live."

CHAPTER 21

I OPENED my eyes in a hospital bed. I tried to turn over and felt layers of pain in my left arm. Deep bone pain and sharp skin pain. I felt the tug of a needle in my right arm. I opened my eyes.

Rafael stood beside the hospital bed. He looked down at me and smiled when I opened my eyes.

"Suze," he said, "glad to see you. We weren't sure for a while."

The drowsiness wouldn't leave me. I remembered. As if I were dreaming. "Give me some water," I said. "God, I'm thirsty." I drank. A nurse came in.

"Your monitors showed some activity," she said, as she walked up to me. "How are you feeling?"

"Rotten," I told her. "Somebody beat the hell out of me. I hurt all over."

"That's not surprising," she said. "You've got a lot of stitches, and you lost blood. You need rest. Here, take this." She put a tiny paper cup to my mouth and held a glass of water with a plastic tube in it.

"Wait a minute, will you? I just woke up. I want to talk to this man."

She looked at me, then at Rafael. Her face was set, showed no emotion. She said to him, "I'll give you five minutes, then you must leave. The doctor gave orders for complete rest for at least two days."

"I'll take the five minutes. Privately, please. Police business," he said. The nurse walked out the room, closing a door with a little window in it behind her. The entire wall was glass. Doctors and nurses were watching me.

"Where were you? He almost killed me," I said, my speech slurred. My tongue was thick. The water didn't help much.

"You got him, Suze. And we got to you in time. You are going to live. Thanks be to God," said Rafael.

"I thank God," I said. "I prayed. I wanted to live, and I prayed."

"You had the courage and wit to bamboozle that sucker. You got him. That was Dwight Arnold. And you outfoxed him."

The nurse opened the door. "The doctor has given orders for Detective Cannon to rest."

"Right," he said, but he looked at me as he spoke. She closed the door.

"Suze," he whispered to me. "You persisted. It was your idea to check med school files. You arranged for me to go to Boston. If we had not gone we would not have his photo. We would not have known you were in trouble." I kept my eyes closed. I knew all those things. I also knew that I had been one of his victims. I had chosen a man who would kill me.

Rafael talked and talked. He brought me back from that dark night of sadness and death and hate and fear. I listened with my eyes closed.

"We took an earlier flight than we expected to, and when we arrived in Miami we took a cab from the airport. We did not wait for you guys to pick us up. It is a good thing we did not wait. Al went directly to the paper after he dropped me off at the station. While I was waiting for the team to show up, I looked through the package of photos you left on my desk. Do you remember those photos? They were the ones you took that day you went canoeing in the Everglades. The last shot was of the birds, in the background. But in the foreground, there was a shot of a man. He was all out of focus. I looked at it and looked at it. Even though it was out of focus, I could tell it was somebody I'd seen before. Then I said to myself, I know where I have seen this guy before. This is Dwight Arnold. The man." I felt Rafael's fingers touch my cheek. I didn't move. He must have thought I'd fallen asleep. He talked some more anyway.

"Raja called the unit. She was looking for you. When she got me on the phone, she told me she was worried about you. I asked why. She told me about the dog—and I had not heard about the dog, since you did not tell me about it—and how the dog had been punctured in the jugular. Like the women."

He talked to fill up the space, the void, the emptiness I felt inside. "Elton came in while I was on the phone with Raja. He heard some of the conversation. When I hung up the phone, I showed him the photo I'd brought back from Trenton and the one you'd left on my desk. We started to run toward the door. We both had the same thought. You weren't back. Raja could not get in touch with you. When I called your house, you didn't answer either your cell phone or your phone. Something wasn't right. Something could be very wrong. Craig came in, and he turned around and ran with us. We were panting and talking all the way to the car in the parking garage. I drove like a crazy man, slapped a light on the roof. Elton called SWAT from the car and told them your life was in danger. He notified Commander and she called SWAT to tell them to get their asses in gear. Their van pulled up right behind us. I do not know who got to you first. Armed men and women all ran in different directions. We were afraid we were too late." He stopped talking for a moment. "It turned out you did not need SWAT. You needed a doctor." I kept my eyes closed, remembering.

"Your neighbor in back called 911 at the same time. She told them a cop was in trouble, bad trouble. Your front yard was crawling with cops."

I hadn't opened my eyes, but lay still and felt safe and felt I could sleep peacefully.

Rafael spoke softly then. I don't think he knew I'd hear him. *"Coño, Suzita. Gracias a Dios estas viva."* Shit, Suze. Thank God you are alive. And then he said so quietly I almost missed it, *"Mi amor."* My love. He tiptoed out of the room. I heard the door close faintly.

Was he the figure I saw walking toward me as I lay losing blood in my bedroom? I tried to bring the dream into focus. I could not.

Tina said, "I guess Mom's like that dog of yours. Anxious. Skittish. When I went to take her away from your pool, she told me she saw a man holding a knife to Tina's neck." She laughed. "I looked and saw what she was talking about, except it was you," she said. "I got Mom back to the house as fast as I could and called 911."

"Didn't you hear a gunshot coming from my bathroom?" I asked. That was when I needed someone to call 911.

"You know you can't hear a thing when the doors are all shut and the air-conditioning is running. On top of that, I had Mom sitting in front of the TV. It was turned up because she doesn't hear well anymore," she said. "I didn't hear a gun go off. And I don't think anyone else heard it either."

"Have you seen Gilda?" I asked. "Does she look terrible?"

"She looks skinny," she said. "You'll fatten her up, I'm sure. Have you talked with the vet?"

SWAT members had checked the house and found Gilda. Raja had administered first aid to my pet. The shot had gone through her shoulder and chest. It was a small caliber shot fired at close range. Luckily for her, it had exited her body. If she had been unlucky, it would have torn up her insides.

Al's story ran on the front page. The background material he and Rafael had collected in Boston and Trenton filled two inner pages. He came to interview me at the hospital.

"I don't want to be interviewed," I told him. "If you talk to me, you've got to talk to the entire team. You've got to talk to Commander. There were many people involved in this."

He said, "PIO says I should interview you. I've already talked to the others. Please talk to me once. That's all I ask."

I answered his questions as briefly as I could. I was tired of thinking about these sordid murders and the women who'd been Dwight Arnold's victims. And while we talked in low tones, Al leaning close to hear me, I thought about the times he had mown our grass, and I had watched him push the mower up and down the yard. I had watched his strong strides, his bent head, how he noticed nothing around him. And I remembered the days before he left for Notre Dame University. That was such a long time ago. I loved him then. I loved him as he questioned me for his article, but in a different way. See, Dwight, I thought. There *is* love.

And there were victims. Why hadn't I seen? What had he seen in me? Where was the connection between what I searched for and what made me one of his victims? Dwight, I said to myself, you aren't dead yet.

"I'm sorry," I said to Peter, who visited the hospital one day. "I wrongly accused you. You must have thought I was crazy."

"You are," he said. "But that's part of the appeal."

"I think you misunderstand," I said. "I'm sorry I was unjustly mean to you. That doesn't mean I'm sorry we have separated."

He said, "Do we have to go through that again?" He shifted the roses he'd brought to his other hand.

"No," I said. "This time it's final. Dwight Arnold taught me something about myself. I don't fully understand it, but I'm not interested in what you offer me anymore."

"Dwight Arnold?" he said incredulously. "You must be joking."

"I'm very, very serious," I said. "It's not your fault. I looked for love where there was none."

Peter didn't answer me at first. Then he said, "Love. You don't know the first thing about love." Then he added, "What meds are you on? You don't sound normal."

"This isn't medication. It's me. There's nothing left in me for you." I was different. I felt calm. I felt clear. I felt free. He must have heard it in my voice.

"You'll get back to the same old Suze in a few days. Here." He placed the vase of roses on my bedside table.

The nurse rushed in, my monitors apparently tattling on me.

I guess Peter expected me to call him, as I had in the past. The abuser and the abused get together. Fat chance. I'd learned a hard, hard lesson.

I went to my parents' home for rest and recovery. A nurse's aide, provided by my insurance, stayed with me during the day while my parents worked. Because of my wounds I slept most of the time sitting up in a recliner my parents had bought for me. Gilda slept beside me on a rug on the floor.

In the evenings, my parents and I were together.

"Bill," I said from my wheelchair, "this bird book is the best I've seen. The photographs astound me. I can't take my eyes from them."

"How about taking them away long enough for a cocktail on the patio? Fran has cooked up something that smells mighty good," he said. He parked me on the patio and went inside for our drinks. Water for me since I was still on pain medications.

"The avocado crop is ready to pick," I said. "Have you called the avocado men to come by?"

"Not yet. Who knows?" he said. "You may have lots of avocados for dinner this fall."

Fran called from the kitchen, and Bill pushed my chair inside. Every night Fran cooked or ordered food she knew I loved. Fish, seafood, vegetables, salads, fruit, cookies, cakes, good bread.

Yet.

I hated being dependent. I couldn't wait to get the use of my arm and push the chair myself. I couldn't wait to regain my strength and walk on my own. I wasn't the least bit hungry, but I ate all I could to build up my body. I was extremely uncomfortable receiving what I perceived to be their unnatural attention. Only much later have I understood how deeply they loved me and how urgently they wanted to take care of me. At that time, though, I was ungrateful. I could not tell that they had given me a costly gift.

My house was spotless by the time I returned. But the images, the reminders, had not been cleaned from my home. The figure in the bathroom, the shot, the blood, the yellow cord, the liquor bottles, the odd little knife, the towel soaked with my blood, the floor washed in blood, Gilda. The pain. His words. Mostly, his words. They were still there.

Commander came to visit at my house. "You did it, Suze. You cracked the case. But remember, there's always another one waiting for you. Don't get complacent."

"I doubt you'll allow that to happen," I said to her. "How about I come back for some light duty."

"We need whole bodies in Homicide," she answered. "Whole live bodies, that is."

"I'm alive," I said. "Will that do?" I didn't want to stay inactive and think—of blood and the knife and my stupidity and my loneliness.

"You're itching to get back." She examined my expression for a full minute, then said, "You don't want all the pictures of blood and pain and death. And you don't want thoughts of 'what if,' do you?" I didn't answer. "I know all about it. As soon as you can sit for a while, come back for desk duty."

Whenever Rafael visited, he always had someone with him. I was glad because I felt vulnerable and weak. I didn't want to risk making a mistake. The words he'd spoken to me in Spanish while I was still in the hospital had touched me deeply. But I didn't want to feel.

One afternoon, though, shortly before I went back to work, Rafael came alone. I had stopped taking the strong pain relievers, and I asked him to have a glass of wine with me. He carried our wine and glasses from the kitchen to the patio. I walked slowly, steadying myself on furniture as I went along. Gilda stayed close to my side. We sat beside the pool. I wanted to talk about the case, wrap it up, and put it away.

"In a sense," I said, after we were settled, "the case is closed. Simonton is off the hook, Dwight Arnold admitted he murdered the women. Numerous other murders have been linked to him both on the East Coast and in the Bahamas."

I looked over at Rafael and saw he was listening closely. "And I'm coming to terms with what the experience has meant to me," I said.

"And what has it meant to you?" said Rafael.

"I haven't finished thinking this through. This is how my thoughts are going—I almost died. I know that. And I keep asking, 'What for?' And my answer: I wanted to be the best. I wanted to be strong enough. I wanted, ultimately, to be worthy of something I imagined was love. And I thought if I tried hard enough, put up with anything that came my way long enough, I'd find this thing I named love."

Rafael didn't laugh. He said, "Many people are like you. How do you see this behavior made you vulnerable?"

"It blinded me," I said. "Rafael, I was a woman I don't much like."

"Did you like her before this happened, Suze?" Rafael asked.

I smiled at his implication and didn't directly answer. "I'm too much like Carla or Jan or Conchita or Valerie. And they were needy, weak, vulnerable. Little girls." I stopped a minute. Rafael didn't speak. "That's what Martin, or Roy or Dwight or whatever his name is, targeted. That's why he could manipulate them and kill them."

We drank our wine.

"The only reason I survived is because I blocked out my pain and fear. I kept control. Do you understand?"

"I understand that blocking out feeling works sometimes. At other times it gets in the way of living." Rafael stood up. "And loving." He took our glasses to the kitchen. I heard him place them in the dishwasher. I remained seated, and when he came back, he said, "I will go now."

"Drive me down to the Everglades on your day off. Early. Will you?" I wanted—no, I needed—to reclaim the Everglades from the memories it evoked of Dwight Arnold.

Rafael picked me up at seven in the morning on his day off, the day before I went into the station for the first time since the attack. We talked about the case and some office gossip on the way down to the Everglades. As we drove past the park's entrance, I stopped talking and looked for the sights I'd known most of my life—the saw grass bending, supple in the wind, yet stubborn, unyielding, and harsh when you got close to it. I saw ghostlike battalions of dwarf cypress. We passed a hammock and I saw knots of bromeliads on the branches of mahoganies. Blue herons, egrets, and ibis floated skyward as we passed and startled them from their space. The water flowed silently beneath it all, and cumulus clouds built higher and higher above the flat expanse before us.

Rafael pulled onto a side road leading to a hammock and stopped on the road's shoulder. We got out of the car and in the distance, we saw a white-tailed deer step out of the small hammock.

We leaned against the fender for a while. And the breeze came like waves. I looked up when a flock of herons flew across the vista.

He turned to face me and reached over to brush my hair away from my cheek. And he said, "You must learn not to block all feeling. You have the will to live, and that is why you are here. But the will to live has to include the will to love. *Comprendes?*"

"*Comprendo.*"